CHASING DAD

CHASING DAD

by
Candace Flynt

The Dial Press
New York

F

F

Published by
The Dial Press
1 Dag Hammarskjold Plaza
New York, New York 10017

Manufactured in the United States of America

First printing

Library of Congress Cataloging in Publication Data
Flynt, Candace, 1947–
Chasing dad.
I. Title.
PZ4.F65Ch [PS3556.L95] 813'.5'4 79–28214
ISBN: 0–8037–1392–4

F

To Chuck

and to the memory of my mother

CHASING DAD

1

JAY

I see her dimly as I enter our front door, waiting for me on the far side of the room in a chair I've never seen. She has not turned on any lights or drawn any curtains or opened any windows because the day is so hot that she is willing to endure the stuffiness for a few less degrees Fahrenheit. Her pimiento hair, frizzy as Spanish moss, is the brightest spot in the room. It curls around her neck like a fur stole. Her legs are crossed so that her skirt lies high across her thighs as if it were just a napkin. I admit that the sight still tempts me. There are three more chairs like the one she is sitting in around a cheap new table. Our child sits beside her in a baby seat which she will say was a necessary purchase too . . . obviously, she will say. But obviousness is something I no longer believe in. I catch myself. It is obvious what she has bought. It is obvious that she is trying to drive me crazy. It will soon be obvious that she has succeeded.

Seven dollars a month for one year, she says, kicking her leg and making the skirt move sensuously. She smiles but her green eyes glint darts in my direction. With minimal effort I turn them around and send them flying back. She thinks that men and women are natural adversaries. From the first I couldn't convince her otherwise. She is pleased with my anger. She asks: Do you want us sitting on the floor? How can you let your family eat off where the feet are? She puts a sour twist on the word *family* as if it doesn't include her.

I ask through clenched teeth why can't she stand up to

eat? Why can't she wait until we have the money before she spends it? I understand her need to sit down. I am sympathetic about the weight her new pregnancy puts on her varicose veins. To a point. I can count. I know when I stopped . . . being able to. That truth is like sandpaper on my limp skin. If you go shopping one more time, I shout, I'll kill you, I swear I will. She doesn't even flinch.

I tell her that her new dinette set in this substantial space looks like a cracker on a dinner plate. She pouts, the wide pink bottom lip sticking out like a handle. I refuse to eat at it, I say. She says, Then you won't eat. I kindly remind her that she doesn't ever cook.

We cannot draw ourselves back. Do you know it's ugly? I ask. She answers, It's as pretty as we can afford. The fact is, the table looks like her: its beige top the color of her fat belly; its legs, pencils of metal like her mean brittle fingers. She likes to break the skin of your shoulders when you make love to her, which I guess whatshisname has noticed. I realize that the table was designed to be afforded, someone's picture of cheap grace, but its ugliness offends me. It is an inanimate Melissa with her hands on her hips and her chin jutted forth. Or am I seeing things? Is my wife a table? Is she an ill-fitting pair of purple slacks? Is she a blender on sale because the paint's chipped off? Or a lamp with a base like a rooster—"so cute." So cute? I see her shape in each of these things that she's had to have.

You're going to take this furniture back, goddamn it. Right this minute.

Belk's delivered it, she says. She starts picking the nail polish off her thumb.

I have never advanced on her before, but I am advancing now. Her eyes open wide as if she were seeing me for the first time, and I wonder if this is how I should have always behaved. When she breathes, she exhales fear, backing out of her chair to the wall where she presses herself like a trapped animal. Her whoring body is so hot that when I raise the chair against her, its metal bracing burns my hands. She throws her arms up to ward me off, like Eve seeing God after she ate that apple. I see specks of red fingernail polish in the air around her.

I turn away. My intention is not to smash her empty head but to destroy whatever ugly exists in this world. I heave the chair into the air and bring it crashing to the center of the table. The chair breaks apart, but the table stands firm. Only a long scratch in its Formica top shows what I have done.

Baby Jenny, whom I'd forgotten, screams. Melissa predicts that I will burn in hell. She runs, not to our child, but to the bedroom. The table stands resiliently, not even trembling . . . which I am. Not even changed by this act of violence . . . which I am. If I had gone after her, she would be dead, but I'm not yet to that point. Thank God, I will never reach it. Melissa has left Baby Jenny to the monster that is me, and I see once more that I was not wrong in wanting to steal her away.

In the bedroom, drawers slide open; the closet door squeaks; a suitcase slithers out from under the bed. She bought this furniture so that I would make her leave. She wants to go to him again. I had not expected it so soon, but I'm ready, for this was my plan too.

Jay, laughing at himself for falling so quickly to the enemy, sat down in one of the three remaining chairs, listening to its cheapness creak under just an ordinary weight. Tonight with her gone, he would probably eat in this very spot. One of his arms ached where he had wrenched a muscle in his anger. He rubbed it; then he rubbed both arms briskly. He felt cold even though he was sweating. His arms were weak, not from the excitement, but from some unidentifiable thing that had been making his whole body feel weak for some time. It had occurred to him that he was being poisoned, but *he* did what cooking was done. He ate lunch at the Army base on the days he worked, but it was usually from one big pot which not even Sergeant Jester, his commanding officer, could control.

He had decided today that his body was deteriorating at the direction of his mind. Not only did he feel weak, he felt smaller. He sensed that the meat of his body was pulling away from his bones, shriveling, until if someone shook him he might rattle. His shoulders had started hunching forward like an old bird's, no matter what he did to try to force them back. He did not feel sick, only as if he were losing himself. He thought it was the work of some pocket of his mind that had decided to help make leaving this world easier. Logically—if he felt bad, it would be easier to end his life; if he felt healthy, it would be harder to go.

Jenny whimpered and he handed her the cracker that she'd dropped. She dimpled; he worried he might have frightened her. But there was a time in early childhood and in old age—he felt very old now—that one did not feel fear.

He heard Melissa latching her suitcase and thought of how the bedroom would look when she left—drawers and doors open as if her escape had to be so quick that she had not had time to close them. As if she were running from fire. When she left, he would close each opening with a thump, getting the emptiness out of his mind, trying to forget not only that she had gone but that she had ever been here. He delighted that she would never come back, a fact that was not in her possession. He delighted that whatever she was throwing in her suitcase now was all that she would ever take from this place. She was such a superstitious woman that ever hereafter she would regard this home as haunted. He hoped she would leave something important behind.

He decided to have a beer to lubricate his insides. As he stood, he felt his shoulders curve forward, and he opened the curtain to catch his reflection in the window. He looked like a ghost—already he looked like a ghost. He was afraid to try a real mirror because he might see the same thing. He opened a beer in the kitchen. Then, so he wouldn't have to get up again for a while, he reached into the refrigerator for two more, found the opener again in the drawer, and carried the whole load to the dinette. He liked this dinette set, but then he hated it too.

He surveyed the scratched table, a sure indication of his damaged health, and let his eyes wander out into the living room. The living and dining spaces were combined because it was cheaper these days not to have to build an extra wall. He wondered why contractors bothered having walls at all anymore. Without them he could read the paper and watch Melissa taking a bath. But then she could be washing dishes (a rarity) and observe him masturbating over the john. He could hear himself crying out his defense, "It's the only thing I know to do." She would hate him for what he did without her as he hated himself. His only cover would be darkness, and that could be thwarted with a lamp.

In a calmer moment of their argument, she had asked him what *he* would have suggested for a dining-room table. She didn't think anything was tacky, she said, as long as it was all you could afford. Had he forgotten that he was the one who didn't make much money? He didn't say so, but he would have liked to tell her that his favorite kind of table was of the style called Queen Anne, like in the administration building at Duke. And that the only reason they were poor was that he'd married her because she was pregnant to try to teach himself something, but that all he'd learned was that you can't make a lady out of a whore. At a cocktail party for honors students, a whore might try to make a good impression on the man who gave you all that scholarship money. She might call him honey and run her fingers under the lapel of his jacket. She would certainly claim that she was only trying to help.

Melissa slipped out of the bedroom, her suitcase in one

hand, the eternal make-up kit in the other. A large red welt crossed her cheek, making him gasp. A piece of the chair had flown up and hit her. He had made a point not to hurt her and it had happened anyway, which must be some kind of sign. A sign that he was finally doing all the things he vowed he would never do. He had thrown the chair *away* from her; a leg of it had broken off and hit her face. So, actually, if you wanted to look at it another way, he had hit her. He had never hit her, but he had. He was finally like his father—like Merle—in every way, and he had tried not to be at all. But here it was, the message which he couldn't fail to recognize and which he might have seen immediately if there weren't all these walls everywhere.

He saw fear in her eyes, unwarranted, he thought. Anybody could see that the chair leg had hit her accidentally. She had changed into her traveling clothes, a pair of tight-fitting black slacks and a white blouse that with her red hair produced the effect of a flag. She'd worn that outfit before when she was *going somewhere*—God knows why—which meant putting four or five hundred miles on the odometer of a car that should have fallen apart four years ago. He'd tried to figure out where she was going, stabbing the needle of his geometry compass where the map read Columbus, Georgia, and drawing a circumference in red pencil at two hundred miles. He discovered that she could be going a wealth of places. One day on the bus over to Fort Benning, where he had the job of cleaning the latrines for a week (compliments of Sergeant Jester), he decided that her most likely destination was Atlanta.

A flag or . . . now that he watched her taking long deliberate side steps, her trail close to the wall as if it would protect her . . . a spider, a black widow complete with her red swirl of poison. The wall was only something to smash her against if he wanted, but he didn't want to. He smiled.

"You're crazy," she hissed. She liked to call him crazy because it made her feel less that way.

He deepened his smile, giving her the generous open-mouthed look that she always complained of as imbecilic, so if later they asked, she could honestly say that the last time she saw him he was acting nuts. He hated to give her the opportunity to make up a lie about him.

Out of his immediate reach, she moved away from the wall. He leaned back in the new chair, wondering if the legs would collapse. Jenny held out her fat baby hands and called "Mommy," but Melissa didn't even look at her. He thought it perfect justice that she would have this child forever.

"Have fun in Atlanta," he called.

"Who says I'm going to Atlanta?" The words struggled out of her mouth as if she were exhausted. If she weren't going there, she would never have said a word. She crossed from one side of the room to the other, darting to the coffee table to pick up her stuffed rabbit.

She claimed she had bought the rabbit for the coming baby, but she fondled it constantly. It had appeared two months ago, shortly after he realized she was pregnant, an obvious gift from her lover, the man he couldn't identify, the man he wasn't even sure existed. He had tried to extract his identity from Gurney, explaining one afternoon after a couple of beers—his treat—that Melissa had gotten pregnant and he couldn't understand how because he'd been punishing her by not sleeping together (he couldn't tell the whole truth). He mumbled something about trying to convince her the hard way (ha, ha) to cut back on her spending. Being the next-door neighbors, had Gurney and Rosie observed any funny stuff? The phrase *funny stuff* had almost made him gag. He felt like a character in Rosie's favorite soap opera.

Gurney reminded him of one night in April when the five of them were still friends and Marty still had the right idea about being his kid sister. Jay, Gurney said, had had too much to drink and was ready to unzip his pants and screw

Melissa on Gurney and Rosie's sofa. Gurney carried him home instead. Jay nodded, even though he had no recollection of the evening. When he questioned Melissa about it, she said maybe he'd screwed her and maybe he hadn't, but if he had, she hadn't been very impressed. Gurney insisted it must have happened then. It counted up right, but still he doubted.

There was a man in Jay's mind, a tall featureless man with curly blond hair, who, when he was least expecting it, would dart across one corner of his bedroom or step out from behind a door and point his finger and laugh. Who could tell, it might even be himself as he used to be, the man of whom he was now only a shadow. The figure in his imagination was looking for Melissa, looking everywhere—even in the closets, which wasn't as ridiculous as it seemed since that was where she often hid. The man had a huge erection—he was not much more than penis—and Jay surmised that he was looking for her with one thing in mind. Disgusted, watching him sneak around like an amateur thief, he had found himself wanting to shout, "In the closet. Look in the closet, fool." Because that was where Jay had discovered her so many times: sitting in the wicker laundry basket, snuggling in the soft smelly clothes, getting away from him, as she told it. And she thought *he* was crazy. It *was* a soft warm place to hide: he had tried it once when she was away, letting the clay smell suffuse him. When he got up, feeling foolish, the wicker basket creaked as if it would tell on him. Once he had seen the man disappear inside the linen closet and not come out.

Melissa whisked out of the apartment, not bothering to look back. In all these times he had never followed, never thought of following. He had nothing to follow in. When she'd telephone three or four days later, asking if he had made up his mind yet, he would not answer *that* question, but he would say she could come back if she wanted. He had never once begged. The only thing he *did* do was let her have whatever it was she had walked out over. His life was filled with those things. They hung on the walls, sat on the tables, filled the drawers and shelves. She never left him because he couldn't make love to her anymore, and what kind of woman was that?

He should feed Jenny, he supposed, although she had not started crying for her supper. She ate regular foods now, but Gerber's was easier so he opened a couple of jars. Would she notice if it were warm or not? He had this regret: he would not see her when she grew up. He would never know if she became the soft, elegant woman he imagined his mother to have been. He would not have the opportunity to introduce her to the mysteries of this world. But who had been interested anyway? Not his own little brother, not even his little friend Marty. He would never dance with her. He had not danced before anyway, but he thought dancing with one's daughter might be one of the glories of life. It was enough to make him change his mind, but not quite. She might turn into the despicable bitch that was her mother, and he would have endured all that time. Jenny ate the cold food willingly, like the little lady she was.

He wished they could have gotten to Alaska; he just wished they could have. He'd been on the verge of telling Gurney his idea—a small settlement on the edge of the wilderness where they could do things with their hands and not have so much time to dream up problems—when Rosie read Marty's diary. The idea was ruined. Marty had gotten it into her head that he was going to marry her, which perhaps in ten years he would have, but now she was only fourteen years old—Craig's age. The trip had nothing to do with her; she was just one of the people he wanted to take.

He put Jenny in her crib but she started crying, so he brought her back to the living room and set her between some throw pillows on the sofa. There was a timid knock at the door. In baby talk Jenny said, "Come in." He clapped a hand over her mouth. She began crying. He took her back to her bedroom and shut the door, swaying and crooning in the darkness.

He didn't feel like seeing Marty. Their last view of one another, with Gurney holding her by the shoulder as if she were property, had been a humiliating experience. Without warning, Gurney had opened the screen door and marched into Jay's apartment. Jay had never seen him wearing anything but an undershirt, but now he had on a white dress-shirt buttoned to the neck. He held several pages of paper, ripped out of some pad. He rowed Marty back and forth so that her long straight hair swung around her shoulders. Her face was vacant as if she had been crying a long time. She would not look him in the eyes.

"I know everything," Gurney said, tightening his fist around the papers. "You pervert."

A sustained silence had followed in which he could see Gurney talking and Marty crying and clawing at the starched shirt but could hear only a shrill whistling noise deep in his own head. His insides had started shriveling then and never stopped. He didn't offer a word in his defense. At the end his hearing suddenly came back to him as if he'd just found a station on the radio. Gurney said, "Why don't you say something? *Say* something."

He started toward Gurney, his arms slack by his side. He was going to hug him, tell him that he'd misunderstood, that he wanted Gurney to go with them too. Gurney, Marty, and Baby Jenny, and his half brother Craig and stepmother Audrey from Durham. But Gurney didn't give him a chance. He turned and pushed Marty out the door, tripping over her in his rush. He'd thought Jay was going to hit him.

From outside the screen door his only friend accused him of fornicating with a fourteen-year-old because he couldn't get it up for his own wife. So then he knew that *they* knew, that Melissa had spilled her guts to everybody that he wasn't a man anymore. So how could he dare go off with anybody? Gurney had called him a half-wit, a pervert, a miserable nothing. He had made a zero sign with his hand. Gurney was his best friend. It had ruined everything.

The knock came again, louder, along with his name hoarsely whispered. He felt a need to explain to Jenny even if she could understand only the slightest bit. "Daddy's angry at Marty and doesn't want to see her," he said. Just then he could hear the door of Gurney's apartment open and Gurney roar at Marty to get back inside. A smack followed by Marty's yell of injury came muffled through the sheetrock. He could hear her feet pounding back to her bedroom that was adjacent to his and Melissa's. Through the living-room walls came her torn sobs. Then the sobs stopped and Marty began knocking on the wall, a steady tattoo that pretended to be faithful and never ending. She just didn't understand what she'd done, did she?

For his own supper, Jay heated canned spaghetti and got out four slices of bread. He stood over his plate before he remembered the dinette set. He poured himself a cup of grape juice because there was no more beer or Coke and went to sit down, strapping Jenny in the baby seat. He took a bite of spaghetti and then he did something he'd always wanted to do: he folded up a whole piece of bread and stuffed it in his mouth. He could hardly chew there was so much of it, and he took a little juice to wash it down. He felt like a python swallowing the whole soggy lump.

He thought he might pamper himself a little more after he put Jenny down: read some of his favorite poems, have a huge bowl of ice cream, jack off. Nah, he wouldn't do that. It was *too* vulgar, too Mitchellian, or however you would describe his family proclivity. First though, he had to write his goodbye letters. To Dad, to Gurney. To Craig and Audrey. To his precious mother. No, not her. What was he thinking of? It would be like losing him twice if she ever found out. He would include in his letter to Dad not to ever let Jenny—the *real* Jenny, he thought, watching his baby yawn—know what happened. Tell her that he died in an automobile accident when he was five, if he had to say anything. But don't let her know that he got so old and lived so long and still couldn't make it. He guessed Dad could tell her the good things: that he went to Duke University on a full academic scholarship, that he was kind and decent and he loved people, that he had been a good son and a good stepson, that he had missed knowing her. . . . And that, tragically, he had drowned one night under a new moon at the Durham reservoir where he and some fraternity friends were horsing around. Say "fraternity" so she'd know he was liked. Or if that was too outlandish, say he was electrocuted when the radio fell into the bathtub. Let her think he had been a credit to her, no matter what.

Jenny began fussing. He rested his hand on the silky red curls at the nape of her neck. The color of her eyes wasn't defined yet, but he thought they were going to green like her mother's. She was going to be beautiful, he was sure. So that Melissa would not know he had eaten at the dinette, he took Comet from under the sink and cleaned it carefully. He put Jenny to bed with a bottle of juice.

After he washed dishes he gathered the food he was going to leave. He thought he would be found within a few hours, but who could tell for sure? People around here sometimes stayed cooped up in their apartments for days. And now that Gurney wasn't speaking to him and he'd turned Marty away . . . it was possible nobody would see him for a day or two.

He made peanut-butter-and-jelly crackers which he broke into bite-size pieces, and then he chopped several stalks of celery. He rummaged through the cabinets for more and found two cans of Vienna sausages, which he rinsed and spread in a bowl. There were two blackening bananas which maybe she would choose to eat before they totally spoiled. He peeled each one. He put water in four baby bottles and set them in the refrigerator, marking them in his mind so he wouldn't forget to lay them out. He would put the food on a tray in her crib before he left. For as long as three days, it was sure to be enough. *He* could live on it for that long.

The first writing paper he found was some Blue Horse looseleaf paper which he rejected because it made him think of being back in college. He rummaged through several drawers and discovered a tablet of wrinkled typing paper with dirty edges, not unblemished as he liked his stationery to be, but it had to do. He took a record album to bear down on and sat on the sofa. He thought how much more comfortable writing at the dinette table would be. He loved to sit at a desk with clean paper, a good fountain pen, a solid surface. All his life he had thought that he would eventually become a college professor for no other reason than he loved sitting at a desk so much. But no, he would not give Melissa the pleasure.

He thought he'd write his father first, the letter which would be longest and most difficult. If time ran out and he didn't get to everyone, at least the most important letter would be written. He dated the sheet of paper with tomorrow's date and noticed how difficult it was to write well with his elbow flopping around in midair. Hell, what if she *did* sense he'd used her table? What if he did give her this last little triumph at the end? Let her win one. In a small not totally acknowledged part of his mind, he wondered if she had won them all.

He moved swiftly, grinning a little as he pushed the table over to the window and sat facing the woods. The September sun was beginning to cast the trees into skinny fingers of shadow. He did not pay any particular attention to the large pine tree just opposite the window, even though it was the one he had already selected. Near the edge of the trees, so he would be sure to be found soon. He let his eyes scan the view, not concentrate. Now was too soon. He settled into the chair, enjoying how it felt to pull up so close that his stomach touched the table, to sit straight, to stretch his arms forward, to poise pen over paper. Perhaps being a professor wouldn't have been enough. They had to leave their desks to teach classes. Perhaps he should have thought about being a writer.

He balled up his first sheet because the handwriting looked so funny and dated a new piece of paper. "Dear Father," he wrote, and then crossed out "Father" because he wanted to say "Dad." Instead of starting over now, he would write the whole letter through and then copy it after he'd made his changes.

At the outset he had not been sure what he wanted to say, but words came easily. He stood up once to turn on the overhead light when he began to have to strain to see. Not that it mattered anymore whether he took care of his eyes. When dark came, he opened the window because finally it would be cooler outside than in here. The tree frogs began singing and waves of fresh air rolled through the screen. When he finished the letter, there was nothing he wanted to change except the salutation. That, he decided to leave as it was, crossed through: Dad would like to see the change of heart. He wrote:

September 2, 1961

Dear ~~Father~~, Dad,

When you read this, I will be dead. I know how unhappy this is going to make you, and I want to say how sorry I am . . . for this and for other pains I have added to your life. But I saw no other way.

It is important to me that you not blame anyone—yourself included—for my death. From the psychology that I briefly studied at Duke, I know that this can be a real tendency. Nor should you blame Melissa and Jenny; they did their best. The fault lies with me and me only. Anyone who kills himself could either not adjust to his life or could not figure out an alternative way to live. I had one alternative, but it didn't work out. I was going to Alaska.

You will find this ironic, but up until this week, I thought I knew what I was doing. To be honest—and now there's no reason not to be—I thought I could handle the setbacks in my life. Getting married, leaving Duke, being drafted . . . all were what I regarded as my personal trial by fire. I was going to be one of those men in the Bible (I won't take time to look up who they are now) who walked through fire to prove themselves. (Daniel in the lion's den—same thing?) Ever since I was a child and you left me with Aunt Florence while you went off to war, I thought that facing things—facing them successfully, I might add—was how to be a man. I _wasn't_ miserable as a kid when you refused to take me to the library or you made me go hunting or fishing. I _wasn't_ afraid when Melissa got pregnant twice in four months or when I decided I would educate myself out in the real world. (You were right about what kind of education _that_ is.) I almost looked forward to things being rough so that my character would have plenty of opportunities to grow stronger. Can you understand what I mean?

I guess what I'm trying to say is this: in the last few weeks, I have found that I haven't been building my character, I've been wrecking it. I've grown impotent, not literally of course, but little by little I've seen the person that was me dry up. I never read anymore, and though you never had much patience with that, you probably realize what that shows about my life now. I hate the Army too. I'm afraid that will hurt you, since you loved it so much, but I despise being here.

And this is peacetime! I also hate knowing that I'll never be what I wanted to be. You warned me: you told me what marriage meant. I just made a wrong choice. The real world didn't make me great like I thought it would; it consumed me. (Or something like that—I feel a little melodramatic.)

I guess that I could leave Melissa and Jenny and the little one approaching, but that's running away. So, I guess killing myself is running away too, but I can't help it. The Army's got me for another year and a half. I can't walk away unless I plain desert. And then I'd be a criminal the rest of my life. Duke wouldn't exactly want me back, do you think? And then there's the problem of not being able to go back to college anyway. Not because of money or my family. I'm different now—I don't think I'm capable of being a student again.

I'm sure the question comes to your mind, "Why can't he last a little longer?" I wish I knew the answer to that. I only know that there's something so stultifying, so suffocating, so oppressive in my life right now that in a year and a half. . . . There's no reason to finish that sentence. I don't have that long to wait.

I worry that you may blame yourself from the point of reference of money. Please don't. We had enough. I had a scholarship and two part-time jobs. (You didn't know I had two, did you? Besides the lab job with Professor Van Pelt, I ran the box office at the Centre Theatre downtown. Man, was I glad you and Audrey never came to a movie. You thought I should spend my spare time studying.) It wasn't money. I just didn't fit in with the Duke guys anymore. Dean Frazier told me I should come back when I got better organized. He said he'd save the money for me. (He might still have it.)

I've been thinking about my mother lately.

I guess you've been telling me the truth all these years when you said you don't know where she is. I've wondered what she was like, why you left her, what she did all the years I was growing up. I think she's dead. The feeling came to me right after Christmas last year when Melissa and Jenny and I were driving back to Columbus. I felt an incredible pull to travel by way of Charleston, S.C. Do you realize how far out of our way that was? About eight hours minimum. Melissa was furious with me. When we arrived, the feeling vanished. I figure she probably died that night. What else would account for that strange pull? Anyway, when you're getting ready to die, like I am, you're not positive about anything, so I do want to tell you one thing regarding Mother. If she is alive and you ever do meet her, I would like for you to tell her that I died accidentally. You make up the accident, I don't care. Just don't ever let her know that I killed myself. She might even try to blame herself.

Dad, there's one other thing I want to tell you. I lived with you most of my life and you'll have to admit that I never gave you much advice. (You may laugh that I think I'm even qualified.) But I guess I know you better than anybody, and I know you're not what you pretend to be. You're decent and honest and pretty smart, I have to say, but you're always trying to hide those qualities as if they aren't proper for a man like you. I don't know exactly what makes you tick—I don't think anybody knows that about anybody. But I see you treating Audrey and Craig like strangers. They're not bad, Dad. I love them both and I think you should too. (Craig would love to go hunting with you.) I mean, what do you have if you don't have them? Your job? Your booze? The whores you hang around with? (I know about them too.) It's your decision, of course, but I wanted to tell you how I felt whether you wanted to hear it or not. You're only in your forties now, but in the not-so-distant future you'll be fifty. Time can walk out on you if you don't watch out.

Now that this is all over, I want you to know one more thing: killing squirrels absolutely repulses me. I always wanted to tell you and never could. Maybe you are thinking how phony that sounds. Here I am saying that killing is repugnant to me and shortly after this letter is done, I'm going to kill myself. Well, they are two different things that I don't much want to go into right now. (Or ever. I guess this joking will sound horrible tomorrow, but at least you'll know I wasn't insane.)

You know, I feel as if I could keep writing this letter forever. If I did, it would keep me from the future. But writing letters, even your last, would eventually be stifling too. I want you to know that I love you. There, I've said it. It was the whole reason for this letter anyway. It just took a while to say. Please remember me like I used to be.

Love,
Jay

He folded the letter, rubbing the folds flat with the side of his pen. Temptation crept over him to open it again, see if he'd said anything hurtful. He went looking for envelopes, stretching as he arose from the stiff chair. On the crowded hat shelf in the bedroom closet where Melissa made him store his books, he found a packet of thin envelopes. If he didn't seal Dad's letter soon, he envisioned rewriting it again and again—clarifying phrases, soft-pedaling criticism, camouflaging feelings—until what was really the letter would disappear in mumbled blandness. Or worse, until the bleached September sun surprised him at his work and took away his plan. As he sealed the letter, the mucilage on the cheap envelope soured and thickened his saliva. He pulled out his handkerchief and spat into it.

He wrote Craig that all this would be easier to understand when he grew up. That instead of crying over him, he should buckle down to junior high school and try to be the credit to the family that Jay himself hadn't been. He said that failure could come from taking on too much responsibility, but that it could also come by taking on too little, and that Craig should remember both ends of most sticks. He reminded him once more about the importance of getting an education. He asked Craig not to forget him and joked that he'd be keeping an eye on him from wherever he landed.

He wrote Audrey about how decent she had been to love him as her own son. He said that she was the most attractive woman he'd known in his adult life and that he wished he had been Merle and had the chance to marry her. He suggested—with "ha! ha!" in parentheses—that she not show this letter to Dad. He said that, of everybody, he thought she would come closest to understanding.

He told Gurney that Marty had misunderstood, that he had not dreamed of marrying her, that his relationship with her was like his relationship with his kid brother, only Marty happened to be a girl. He explained that the trip to Alaska had been for anybody who wanted to go. He said that Melissa had lied about his being impotent: Otherwise how had she gotten pregnant? He explained how sometimes she didn't deserve love.

Sometime while he was writing, he began to feel part of an inevitable flow of events as if this were a birth and he were in labor. He sensed being in an unchangeable pattern —a barrel tumbling toward Niagara—whereas before he had wondered if he would hesitate, put this off until the next time Melissa walked out. The letters seemed to be building up like chapters in a novel whose end was not quite in sight but soon would be. There was still the possibility—when he said goodbye to his baby or even climbed the tree—that he would balk, but the possibility seemed more and more remote.

He had additional paper but he decided not to write Baby Jenny or his unborn child. He did not much want to look at anybody's future, especially theirs. His life was concerned with what had happened up to now and the next few hours. What good would looking at fifteen years later do? Only take the chance of making him forget the truth.

He checked his wrist to see what time it was before remembering he had pawned his watch so that there would be something to leave Melissa besides this month's pay. The clock in the kitchen read three-thirty. His stomach growled and he wished that there was another can of Viennas in the cabinet. Maybe he could eat the ones he'd left for Jenny and put something else out for her. He found a can of pork brains in the top cabinet. She couldn't eat these. Four eggs were in the refrigerator and he decided on a last meal of brains and eggs. He cooked the soupy mess and stood at the stove eating out of the frying pan. He burned his tongue and realized that it didn't really matter.

What other "last" things would he do? Give Jenny a kiss, go to the bathroom one final time, look at himself in the mirror, brush his teeth. Why shouldn't he masturbate? That was his way of life these last six months. He should drink a few beers to make it easier, except beer would just weaken him. Sink into his collar bones, slide through his legs, numb his fingers until he couldn't climb the tree. He remembered that all the beer was gone. His heart, which had raced at the worry of being undone by some alcohol, relaxed. He should stick to a few meaningful actions that nobody would know about.

He leaned back on the spindly hind legs of the chair,

closed his eyes, and contemplated the possibilities. He thought of leaving directional messages with rocks like he had taught Craig when Craig was growing up. He thought of rearranging things in the apartment so that only a sharp eye would notice a difference. He thought of writing a message—a cryptic one—in the dust on top of the refrigerator. He thought of hollowing out the pages in his favorite book, *Of Human Bondage*, and secreting some treasure inside, perhaps the pocket knife Dad had brought him from the war.

He thought of a few more things and then fell asleep. Suddenly for a conscious instant, he believed that he was already hanging himself, that he was falling through the air waiting for the rope to jerk him back. The front legs of his chair hit the floor. Before him sat the dinette table. He was not relieved. He examined the dark morning carefully, his eyes stretched to detect even the faintest touch of light. He'd been asleep only seconds, he imagined. The sky was still as black as his father's soul. He shook his head angrily. What had brought something like that to his mind? Foul. No fair. He'd wanted to leave this world feeling generous.

He had to tear up Dad's letter now. Thinking this, he couldn't let the letter stand. But then he'd have to tear them all up because Dad would never forgive him if Audrey and Craig each received one and he didn't. He'd never forgive *them*. Jay let the four envelopes drop through his fingers to the dinette table. They clicked like Melissa's high heels. He would hide them where someday someone might find them, not necessarily anyone he'd ever known.

He spread the letters in front of him and lay his head on his arms as at naptime in first grade. He felt that the flesh he was made of was vanishing at a rate he could feel. Very soon he would be empty. His chest hurt, as if inside some vacuum was sucking at his bones trying to collapse them. He raised his head and felt giddy and wondered if his brain were burning. He breathed rapidly, trying to pump life into himself, but he could accept air only in shallow gasps. His lungs were giving out too. He saw no hope for any of them. He hid the letters and set Jenny's food in the corners of her crib. He did not kiss her goodbye because he was afraid to. In the coat closet beside the front door he found his rope.

2

MERLE

The waiting room struck him like a checkers game with its black carpeting and stylish red Naugahyde chairs perched like crowned kings around the perimeter of the board. Merle stood at the edge of the room thinking how he didn't have furniture this good in his own house. It was the low-slung modern kind with fat cushions and chrome bracing. Ugly, but worth a pretty penny. Paid for with fat fees that laid fancified magazines like *Gourmet* and *Holiday* and *National Geographic* around on coffee tables for people who had trouble buying eggs. People like doctors had it made; people like him got the red licked off their candy. The magazines lay untouched, all the fancy artwork on the walls went unnoticed although there was an elephant herd of people in here, which went to show you.

You'd think paying twenty-five dollars to get his damn hand sewn up would cover having the stitches picked out, wouldn't you. But he'd called and this was going to be eight dollars more and the nurse on the telephone said that unless he had cash they couldn't do the work. He shouldn't have to pay this bill. He deserved not to. He bet he could explain for ten seconds and whoever was listening, trying to collect, would just hang up.

Merle walked to one corner of the room, leaned against the wall, and pulled out a cigarette. There was a no-smoking sign—in Durham, North Carolina, a no-smoking sign. Who'd believe it? But, hell, he was over in a corner where he wouldn't bother anybody. Out of view of the nurses' station too, so unlikely one of those sweet bitches would slap Little Merle's hand and make him put it out. He stuck his cigarette under his upper lip like a walrus tooth and struck a match right under his nose in order to sniff the scaring phosphorus. Put hair on his chest or else burn it out of his nose.

He shifted his weight and behind him something moved. Goddamn. He'd almost knocked a picture off the wall. A couple of other customers watched as he pushed at the frame with one finger. More crooked. He had lots of attention now and decided while there was nothing else to do, he'd give these people a little show.

Wiggling the cigarette between his front teeth as if he were going to use it to measure, he turned his back to his audience. Carefully he eyed the width and height of the painting, an oil of an Arabian horse named Spade, according to a brass nameplate screwed into the frame. The horse's head reared back haughtily like it thought—*he*, Merle noticed—like he thought he was more important than anybody here. With elaborate movement, he straightened the picture, stood back, straightened it again, stood back, straightened it again. Somewhere in the room, a girl child giggled. Got to them every time. The little girl began laughing out loud. Merle threw his head back in imitation of Mr. Pedigree, and his heavy wheat-colored hair swung through the air like a mane. Then he turned and looked straight over everybody's head as if nothing had happened. It took the idiots a long time to realize he was finished performing. The long ash of his cigarette fell on the carpet; he ground it in with his boot.

One thin man with an Adam's apple like a peach pit kept eyeing him curiously. Merle stuck his nose in the air and swung his glance around the room. Everybody was busy except this one. He pulled his wallet from his hip pocket, opened it, and thumbed through the bills. It took a long time because there were so many. Then he thumbed through them again. On his way here he had stopped by Otto's office to collect his compensation check for the fourth week in a row. At Audrey's window at the bank, even though she wasn't there, he'd asked for all ones in old bills, not new ones. He liked their feel, he told the substitute teller, a narrow-shouldered woman who looked at him like he was a royal pain in her ass.

Looking up quickly, he caught Peach Pit's eyes on the wallet and glared while the man's face turned as red as a checker. Merle leaned forward, resting his ass firmly against the wall. He let his hand with the fifty-three stitches show. Pit sat straighter, as if somebody'd jammed a corncob up him.

They announced Merle's name and cut off his intentions. Through a swinging door he followed a slender girl with a limp pony tail hanging down her back. The skirt of her uniform was stiff with starch and he knew that her ass was wiggling underneath, he just couldn't see it. That was, if she had an ass; she didn't have much else, he noticed, as she offered him a chair in a small cool room with light green walls. She sat at the opposite side of a table with scissors and tweezers. He wasn't even going to get to see the doc for his eight bucks.

"You going to do this?" he asked.

The girl nodded and began deftly clipping off the knots and picking out his stitches. She didn't say a word. Where was her natural curiosity? He did not look at his hand for the first few minutes, waiting to see if it would hurt. The little black threads wiggled out of his skin easier than splinters. Nothing to it.

"Ain't you curious what happened?" he asked.

"Certainly," she said. Trained well. After a pause, she continued. "Was it an accident?" But her voice sounded as if it were coming from Timbuktu. Maybe she was having boyfriend troubles. Maybe she'd *like* to have some.

"Nope," Merle said. "I did it on purpose."

"Oh." Her tone was dull.

He pulled his hand away and she looked up darkly. "Oh?" he repeated.

"Give me your hand, Mr. Mitchell."

He dropped it before her.

"What happened?" she asked, and her voice was husky, nearer now that he'd forced his way into her life. Maybe she'd go out and have a couple of beers with him after she went off duty. These shy ones you had to shoulder your way up to fast.

"I got mad at a door," he bragged.

"Lucky it wasn't your wife," she murmured.

How'd she know he was married? No rings.

"Oh, maybe so, maybe not," he said. He made a little purring noise to get her attention and when she looked up, he stared deep into her green eyes that he thought could become fierce if the occasion presented itself. Her eyes grew gray against him and she turned back to her work. He'd gotten to her.

In a few minutes she said, "That's all, Mr. Mitchell. You were lucky this time. But I wouldn't do it again." She stood and walked to the door. "See the cashier," she said without even looking back. At the nurses' station he asked nicely where he could take a leak. When he finished and thought they had forgotten him, he walked out without paying.

The air had been cool all day, but now it was mellow, even warm, as if the late September sun had finally made its point. Merle crossed the parking lot in the swaggering gait he used when he thought someone—maybe Peach Pit—might be looking. In the windshield of his Chevrolet were reflected huge clouds like cotton wadding, almost like a painting. He stopped to light a cigarette, watching the windshield change. Although Miss Little Tits had pronounced his hand well, he still preferred his new trick—striking a match with one hand. He thought he could have been ambidextrous if he'd worked at it.

The clock on top of the bank building read 5:15 P.M. Audrey was on her way home or else he'd go try to make a withdrawal out of her account. It was early yet to go to Chunny's since he never opened the bar until his grill customers moved along. But maybe he'd eat a hamburger and hang around back until Chunny arrived. He wanted to get to him early, talk before Chunny grew steamy-eyed and pitiful watching the evening hours limp along.

He drove out of downtown proper, running the yellow lights and creeping forward into intersections while he waited for red ones to change. He passed the cigarette factory, belching clouds of black smoke as if all they did in there was take samples. He guessed if he ever had to have another job, he could smoke cigarettes for the American Tobacco Company. If Chunny would listen to him, it wouldn't be necessary to have a job. Neither one of them would have to do much of anything ever again. They would be goddamn wealthy men. He felt his hands tighten on the steering wheel. Filthy rich.

He picked up speed as he drove out of the city limits and into sheriff territory. At least Chunny had been moving in the right direction. Ten years ago he had started with a filling station, but five years later the gas wars were killing him. Harder to fight, Chunny said, than World War Two. He called the Texaco Company and told them to come get their pumps. He had a wooden sign painted saying GRAND OPENING OF CHUNNY'S GRILL and posted it beside the highway. The sign was still there although the words had been obliterated by cars coming around the curve slinging mud. The grill had made a little money, but nothing compared to the illegal bar he'd opened two years ago in the storage room behind the grill. Merle was his first customer. He christened the bar one day while he was laying off work. He'd had to miss an occasional day of remodeling Otto's house just to keep his sanity.

Chunny slipped a hundred bucks to a deputy sheriff once

a year and had no trouble. None until six months ago when he began pouring out his liquor for free near closing time. His best stuff, not the rotgut he kept behind the counter. Saying hoarsely through tears that his customers were his only real friends in this world and he intended to treat them as priceless possessions. They drank, the damn assholes drank. Merle would change that. If Chunny would dry his tears and do what he said, Merle could change his life.

The grill always surprised him when he came upon it, lying barely beyond a long sweeping curve in Highway 62. On both sides were large vacant lots, but one held a wooden sign announcing that McDonald's would soon erect a hamburger stand next door. All the more reason for Chunny to make a move and make it fast. Merle pulled into the graveled parking lot. A Pall Mall CLOSED sign hung lopsided on the door, but around the building he could see the back ends of several cars. He squinted through his windshield into the restaurant. The narrow room was dark except for a lighted clock on the back wall over the men's room and Budweiser's lighted merry-go-round advertisement showing a bunch of Clydesdales chasing each other's tails. Across one side of the room was a counter with eight stools; across the other, a row of tables with their chairs turned upside down. Merle thought that the chairs looked something like four-legged women stretching their legs. A metal door on the far side of the room led to the bar. He thought that they might have to end up closing the grill if his idea worked out.

He swung out of his car, dropped his cigarette, and ground it out with his brogan. He peered through one of the thick panes of the garage's sliding overhead door. He could have torn his hand all to hell with glass like this. The room was big enough. Take all those tires out; put the four best ones on his car. Paint the glass panes in the door to block the outside view. Set up a few tables. Have all sorts of games: blackjack, craps, gin rummy, poker, maybe even a little checkers. He loved checkers. Large circles of oil spotted the floor where cars had been berthed. Hell, they might even carpet this place.

He walked to the grill door, pushing it just wide enough to slide in, easing it closed with the fingers of his good hand spread on the glass. He probably should have used the back entrance; Chunny might get p.o.'d and not listen to his idea. Although the grill and counters had been wiped up, an odor of old grease and french fries hung in the air. Merle's stomach woke up, but it didn't look like he was going to get anything to eat. He pulled two bags of potato chips from their display rack. Walking toward the back, he held out his hand palm down above the spread chair legs. They didn't do a thing for him.

The metal door banged loudly against the wall behind. Except for rising smoke, he seemed to have stopped life. Four men sat motionless at a makeshift bar. The bartender, not Chunny, stood with the cash register open against his stained apron. This man usually worked up front as the cook.

"He's legal," the bartender said, shutting the drawer. A man with an upraised glass drained it with relief. Hands that had risen around glasses to hide them relaxed.

"How'd you get in that way?" Chunny's substitute asked.

"Unlocked," Merle said. The bartender headed up front.

Its unpainted cinderblock walls gave the room a grim, lonely feeling. Two tables sat in the middle of the floor, but hardly anyone ever used them even when all the barstools were occupied. Merle took the only empty stool. He noticed that the calendar girl taped on the wall behind the bar looked deformed, her tits pressed to her neck by a counter she leaned across.

Propping his elbows on an ancient wide board that served as Chunny's counter, he waited for the bartender to return. The board had come from an old shed behind the station, and Chunny hadn't done anything but sweep it off. If they opened this new business together, Merle might refinish it for him.

Beside him sat a fellow hunched forward like a turkey, his neck buried in his jacket so that the fur of the collar rose above his ears. Smoke issued from the neck of the jacket where the man puffed a cigarette incessantly. He cleared his throat with a raw painful sound, and Merle averted his eyes.

On the floor behind the bar sat gallon cider jugs that held whiskey. You could get two-hundred percent, home-brewed if you wanted, but Chunny also served tax-paid liquor. In a bucket on the floor sat a block of ice which the bartender had to chip at every time someone wanted a drink. Chunny thought crushed ice melted too fast. He was going to have to upgrade his thinking.

The bartender—Merle thought his name was Fred—returned, and Merle ordered bourbon and water. "Where's Chunny?" he asked. The turkey beside him glanced his way for a brief second. Fred said that Chunny had been sneezing in the drinks—a bad cold—and had gone home. Else the grill would still be open.

Fred lifted his two bags of potato chips an inch off the counter. "All right if I put these on your bill?" he drawled. He hadn't even fixed his drink yet.

"Sure," Merle said. His tone was bland, but his eyes were dark with resentment. Fred leaned to chip ice, not noticing.

What a crying shame. Besides not getting to tell Chunny his idea, this was going to be an expensive evening. Maybe Fred didn't keep close count either. Fat chance: He slapped the drink on the counter with one hand while the other made a notation on his pad. The drink sloshed over the sides of the glass.

"How about a napkin, Freddie?" he asked, even though the holder was within his reach. Fred jerked one out, released it in midair, and let it float down beside the spilled drink. He picked up the black holder and set it at Merle's elbow. The turkey on the next stool shifted slightly in his seat as if Merle had farted.

Merle finished the drink and dropped his glass on Fred's side of the counter. "Put a little liquor in there this time," he said. The man beside him exhaled smoke his way. Merle stuffed too many potato chips in his mouth, but they dissolved like ice cream. Fred was quick with number two—finally doing his job—and Merle used it to wash down the potato mush. "Another," he said, tapping the empty glass on the counter.

The idiot next door swiveled his head out of his collar like a snake and stared. His face was lumpy and mean as if he'd been in a few fights. Merle held his breath, squared his jaw, and broke the turkey's gaze. He held his arms and shoulders tense for something new to concentrate on. Then he stared at the napkin holder, memorizing its shape. Like a loud noise roaring toward him from a distance, visions of Jay were breaking through from his subconscious. He wasn't ready yet. Not until he was less edgy, less alert. He gazed at his enlarged forefinger through the thick base of his glass and drummed his fingers on the bar. It was as if he were drumming in midair. He should be losing control, but his mind still felt clear. He wanted to feel fuzzy, numb, like his body wasn't his. He ordered a fourth drink and told Fred to stop cheating him. He usually studied Chunny's framed Army discharge certificate on a nail over the cash register to see if he were far enough along, but this evening the black words lay sharp on the parchment. He took the next drink in two long gulps.

"Jay," he heard. Her voice whined in his memory. Pregnant bitch. She might as well be calling him. He was who she'd rather have had, wasn't he? From the first moment she saw his fine powerful hands. He concentrated on the black face of the napkin holder until he had it fixed in his mind. There was only one napkin left.

His hand lay limply on the counter, finally free, no

longer caught by the tiny black stitches that looked like track from the German model train that Jay had mounted around his bedroom years ago. A goddamned German toy that Audrey hadn't had sense enough not to buy. And Jay hadn't noticed like Merle had expected him to. Even after all he'd told him about the war.

He closed his hand and then opened it, spreading the fingers tight away from each other. He had not been particularly careful of the stitches so he was surprised the hand had healed so soon. There had been five deep cuts and now five thin scars like red thread imbedded in his skin. Little branches of a sea of blood. He hated German blood. The nurse said the scars were supposed to turn white and disappear. She had had tiny tits, not even big enough to fill up the palm of his hand.

He turned the hand over, thinking of the night he broke the glass in the door, thinking proudly of the slashed skin and the spurting blood. He had not been injured in the war although he hadn't been particularly careful about that either. With his wife gone and nothing to go home to but a mewling baby. Every night he and Chunny would go to sleep with far-off explosions ringing in their ears. Bullets had whistled around him and once in Italy an Arab with a curved dagger had stuck the point in his belly and demanded all his money. A bullet had never grazed his arm; he'd never had a single scratch. The dagger had not pierced the white skin of his stomach. So how could Jay, stationed at Fort Benning in Columbus, Georgia, in the United States of America, 1961—peacetime—be dead?

Smashing the window pane was his first injury ever and he had cupped his hand for a minute and watched the blood fill it up. When he opened his hand, the blood spattered in a jagged circle on the kitchen floor.

He felt the pocket of his shirt for a cigarette and found an empty pack. Both his hands lay together on the bar so he could look at them. Waves of drunkenness came upon him and left. His back itched; he hunched his shoulders to stop it rather than move one of his hands. He spread his fingers. With them he could do anything. Tomorrow he could be back at work, the heavy calluses unsoftened by this month vacation. Huge competent hands that built the best houses in Durham, North Carolina. But always for other people, people who had enough money to send their children to college without scholarships or get them abortions if they needed them. And here he had to build their goddamn houses. When really he was the smart one. Smarter than Otto who was too dumb—like a fox—to hammer a nail straight so got to be president instead. Let somebody take care of *him* for a while. Let Otto. His hand still hurt; his hand would always hurt. Nobody could say it didn't.

Fred set a fresh drink before him.

He could squeeze this glass right now until it broke and reopened all his wounds or even made new ones. The hand might be permanently ruined this time and then he could collect compensation from Otto until the well dried up. And then Otto would give more out of his own pocket because Merle would squeeze it out of him with Audrey and Craig. What Otto wouldn't do to have Audrey. For that matter, what he wouldn't do. A surge of desire disturbed his genitals, making him feel proud. He was still as potent at forty as he had been at eighteen. He smiled at the face of his watch. He'd had a woman less than five hours ago and was raring to go again. Did anyone in this *world* have that kind of body? He thought of leaving now, going home to make love to Audrey, but he was having too much fun. A long night lay before him: he had time to do it all. No need to rush here.

The next drink he did not gulp. He had no more thirst, only the desire to maintain this plateau. Jay was creeping into his mind. He did not feel so wild anymore as if he were about to burst out of tight pants or healed skin. He felt soothed. Even though drinking brought that one violent vision to his mind—Jay's body hanging from the limb of the tree—he didn't mind. Because when he was drunk it didn't matter; he didn't give one good goddamn. He might shake his head, tears might come to his eyes, but they would be tears of shame for not caring, not of caring too much. He might cluck his tongue as if Jay were Otto's son and not his. The drinking made it all easier.

"Goddamn Army," he muttered.

"Huh?" his no-neck neighbor said.

"Got a cigarette I can bum?"

"Don't smoke."

"What's that in your hand?"

"My last one. What's it to you?"

Merle turned back to his drink, clenching his hand tighter around the glass. His scars seemed to throb. The man rose and moved to the other end of the bar where a stool had just been vacated.

"Shit ass," Merle whispered to his back, not quite loud enough. This couldn't be a friend of Chunny's. He took his last swallow and slapped the glass on the board. Fred cut his eyes at him but said nothing. He did not move to give him a refill.

Out loud to everybody Merle said: "How about a Scotch and soda for old times' sake?" Jay had drunk Scotch and soda here the night of his eighteenth birthday. Chunny had helped them celebrate. "Come on, I'll buy everybody's. Yours too," he nodded at Fred. No one said anything. Jovial group. The man on the far end lit a new cigarette. "Yours too," Merle said, pointing at him with his hand in the shape of a pistol. Under his breath he said, "You shit ass."

The bartender made four marks on his pad.

"Who's not drinking?" Merle turned angrily on his stool.

"I'm not," Fred said.

"Not for old times' sake?"

Fred shook his head. "You're sure you want Scotch?"

"I'm sure," he said. The hole where his brain was felt blank. "Don't you remember?" he asked. "Sure you do. That time me and my boy came in here just a while back. Couldn't have been a year. Or maybe two. Come in for his first drink. You were up front. Then you came back and had a drink with us. Remember?"

Chunny had served drinks on the house all night long, when, on top of it being Jay's birthday, he found out Jay was going to Duke University on a full scholarship. Merle twisted crazily from customer to customer, grabbing their elbows so that sometimes they spilled their drinks, telling them that Duke was *paying* Jay to come there, they wanted him so much. Paying him because he was so smart. Merle hadn't even known you could go to college that way. For sporting abilities, sure, but for good grades? Hell, none of his family had been to college or even wanted to go. No talent in anything. Otto had taken a one-year business course but that amounted to nothing, just like Otto did.

Merle said: "He was a smart boy, yes he was. He was a brain."

The man who had moved to the end of the bar slipped his stool back to speak. "What happened to him?"

"Got killed in the Army." Merle wiped his mouth heavily against his shirt sleeve.

"What war?"

"No war. An accident."

"What kind of accident?"

"What's it to you?" Merle was glad he'd remembered those precise words.

The man jumped his stool back close to the bar.

Nosy shit ass, he thought. Bastards like that got on his nerves. Them and the goddamn Army. Knocked the stool right out from under Jay. As if they put him up there . . . tied one end of a clothesline around his neck and the other around the tree branch. Then had some weasel come along and boot Jay's stool out from under him. There wasn't even blood. That's the least you can get, blood. Who's dead without it?

Merle asked Fred for a cigarette and he obliged.

Only a few lousy dollars. Less than most men spend on whores. He would have been glad to pay, but his fool of a son refused to let him. Couldn't abandon Melissa; couldn't do away with his first child. So where was he now? And Melissa? Pregnant with his "last" baby. Bullshit. That one was laid in her by somebody else if God is King above. And it could have even been him. That was the shame. Merle could have screwed her and she wouldn't have batted an eye. Jay didn't even suspect. The Army ought to have taught him something. But what do you expect with that crap they pass off as discipline these days?

He inhaled deeply. There he and Chunny were, jumping out on those beaches at Casablanca, a hot dry country cloudy with flies. All the men were carrying something in their shirt pocket or under their heel—a picture, a pair of panties, a gift lighter that by now had run out of fuel—something to remind them that home was somewhere at their backs, that it hadn't been plucked off the earth by some fickle god as soon as they went to sea, that there were loved ones waiting who wouldn't forget. A cruel joke. And Chunny the very worst. Smoking a cigarette—although he didn't smoke—so that in the dark tent the glow of the fire would light up the picture he carried of Priscilla, his new wife. And now, fifteen years later, Priscilla was married to Chunny's brother. Merle should have warned him. But, hell, how could he talk about it? Jenny had only been gone five months when he was called to war.

He'd thought he could forget Jay while he was there. Just leave him for his sister to raise when the war ended. He didn't have a picture, he didn't have anything to put under his pillow at night. But something happened. Nothing sudden: a bullet never even came near him; he never really got scared. But one night in bed with an Arab woman, he knew he was going back. It was like his whole soul turned around and faced backward toward the past instead of toward the shapeless future. He was going to take care of the baby Jenny had left him. No sister was going to do the job. He was going home if he had to kill every motherfucking German there was. So tell him, Jay, why wasn't there any goddamn *war*?

Someone tapped his arm. He looked up startled. He'd had his head down on the bar and hadn't realized.

"You gonna sleep, go home," Fred said.

"It's the damn slow service."

Fred pressed his fingers on the counter until his knuckles grew white.

"No sense of humor, huh? Give me a bourbon and water."

"What about that?" Fred pointed at a drink Merle hadn't noticed.

"I'll drink it while you fix the next one."

The telephone beside the cash register rang. Fred turned his back and whispered into the receiver. "How you feeling, Chunny?" From the back he looked like Otto. Thickset, a short fleshy neck with skin lined like an elephant's. Merle wished he had his pistol.

"Leave him alone, huh?" Fred repeated out loud, glancing at Merle. His apron from cooking all afternoon looked like a butcher's. He had a goddamn Army haircut.

Let him drink, drink, drink, until he got drunk, drunk, drunk. What was Fred doing serving him Scotch instead of bourbon? He felt too lazy to ask. He heard the telephone ring again. Fred was leaning against the cash register waiting for orders, his face a blank.

"Ain't you gonna answer it?" Merle asked. It seemed that Fred was growing larger.

"Are you crazy?"

Merle, a drink in each hand, took a swallow of Scotch and then one of bourbon. *This is Sergeant Jester at Fort*

Benning. Are you the father of Jay Mitchell. I'm afraid I have some disastrous news to tell you. Your son has committed suicide.

Lying bastard. Audrey?!? He slammed down the receiver. Audrey, he screamed. He could hear his voice bounding off the walls of the kitchen. The overhead lamp trembled. Audrey-y-y. He had to get out. A pane of glass in the kitchen door taunted him, held him here in this room that was suffocating him. He drove his fist through it. With his arm hanging through the ragged glass, he banged his head against the doorframe. Then the phone ringing again and Audrey there answering it, talking to that bastard. He yelled again, lunging toward her to take away the receiver, but she held him back easily with one arm. His hand burned. He fell into the chair at the kitchen table and cried, curling his hand into the front flap of his shirt.

Liquor dribbled out of the corners of his mouth and down his chin as if his mouth had accepted all it could hold. He crowded both glasses to his mouth and threw back his head, trying to finish them off. He felt weightless as if he were in a helicopter. He tried to reach for the counter to catch himself but couldn't get his arms to respond. Then he was too far away like the ground after take-off. Somewhere below him he heard a thudding crash. He expected to see smoke rising and scattered bodies but there were none.

When he awoke he was sitting slumped in his car. His whole body shivered. He thought that they must have thrown water on him because his collar was wet. He found the car key, stuck the tip into the ignition, and then, with the flat of his palm, jammed it into the steering column. Just like he was going to jam it into Audrey. He held his wrist to the window to look at his watch but there was no moon. It had to be after twelve. How much after, he couldn't tell. Audrey would be in bed. But he had seen the bedroom light click off too many times to believe she ever slept before he came home.

As the engine swelled, he fully awakened. Easing carefully out on the road—the same way he got out of bed with a hangover—he strained to drive well enough not to be stopped, concentrating on the white painted lines and on the tricky swing of the speedometer. There were no other cars. His lights swung around the edges of curves and into thick woods, and they illuminated sleeping houses. Why did everybody in this punk town go to bed so early? He began driving down the middle of the asphalt, straddling the dotted center line. Then he weaved back and forth over the two lanes as he might doodle on a piece of paper. Great fun. He felt sober enough to trust himself. A mile more and he would be home. He ought to go to sleep when he got there.

He lived in a development on the outskirts of Durham where all the houses sat like draughts on a checkers board, evenly spaced and identical except for the position of the screened porches and the color of the paint. The houses were single-story frame ones, only a cut above the mill houses built in the twenties. Their yards were spacious. Merle's porch was on the side of the house that they never used, off the living room. He had done one thing. All the houses on the street were painted the same pastel shade—pink, green, or yellow—that had first touched them. It was cheaper to keep the same color, and you didn't need to feel in such a hurry when you repainted. But when Merle had painted his house, the first time six years ago, he chose maroon. The rich color seemed to weigh his house down, and then it began to seem to him that his house sat as an anchor giving the whole neighborhood something to hang on to, as if those little pastel houses might go floating off into the sky like bubbles out of a blowpipe. Rain and wind had dulled his house from its original deep luster to something not so shiny, but something more settled.

As he turned down his street, he switched off his headlights and for a moment could see nothing. Then the pastels appeared evenly along the road. At night he could barely make out the shape of his own house. He cracked the window; the car rumbled like far-off shelling, but there was nothing he could do about it unless he wanted to stop and walk the rest of the way. He didn't. He waited for a view of the road, but it wouldn't come. With his parking lights he could see a few feet ahead. He imagined that his car looked like a giant firefly.

Every house on the street was dark. He turned into his driveway, dropping his right wheel into the side ditch. A light from his and Audrey's bedroom shone faintly in the yard. He killed the motor and left the car where it slanted, careful to press the door closed quietly. Now that he stood outside the car, he could see much better. He walked past the side door that led to the kitchen. A piece of white cardboard, where the pane of glass was still missing, shone like sand. He walked on to the back of the house, stepping on patches of grass that had grown up in the graveled driveway. A car suddenly turned down his street, its lights stretching ahead like antennae. Merle shrank to a squat. The car turned into Clayton's driveway next door, flashing an arc of light through Merle's yard, and then backed out again.

"Son-of-a-bitch," he grunted. The light from the bedroom evaporated from the grass. He had wanted to spy on Audrey.

In the kitchen he methodically opened cabinets until he found where she had hidden the bourbon. He took a long swig from the bottle. Then he dragged his blue toolbox from under the kitchen table where it had languished since Jay's death. The box was a mess; Craig must have been fooling in it. He'd get a whipping for this.

He pulled out the hammer, its oak handle worn to fit his hand, and held it cocked for action. He'd torn up some hammer heads before, but never this handle, which he'd used for sixteen years. He slipped it back and forth in the curl of his hand and watched his scars flex with the motion. He could be hammering tomorrow if he ever wanted to hammer again. Knocking bloody hell out of some cheap nails to build an oversized house for some rich bastard with an oversized bank account. He lay the hammer on the kitchen table beside the bottle of bourbon, closed the toolbox, and shoved it with his foot against the wall.

Here he was, the best carpenter in the whole town of Durham, maybe in all of North Carolina, maybe in the southeast. Hell, maybe in the fucking world. He had the hands. They were huge, more huge than he'd ever noticed them being, like they'd grown just by his bragging on them. And strong like a wrestler's who could break your neck with the flick of his thumb. He had the hands. He could build like nobody in the business but he was never going to build again. It was like Bing Crosby developing throat cancer or something. Except that he was *choosing* never to drive another nail for Otto who couldn't even drive one straight. Who lived in a hundred-thousand-dollar house built by his own brother's sweat for a lousy four bucks an hour. He could be hammering tomorrow, the muscles in his giant hand straining against the scars. He might even hope the wounds would reopen, letting his blood gush forth once more. But he was healed. Healed, the nurse said, but he felt wounded as ever. Why should he ever work again?

The bourbon, warm as pee, made him feel better, like nighttime milk when he was a child. Slowly, he raised the hammer, still deciding. Then with quick thudding blows that made his eyes widen and his nostrils dilate, he hit the scarred hand. Again and again. Again and again. The hand, tight with tension as he began, grew limp. He'd worked quickly so that he was almost through before he felt anything. Now his hand caught fire, burning as if he'd sunk it into hot ashes, aching like a poisoned limb that should be amputated at once. He thought that perhaps some bones were crushed, fingers broken. He put his good hand tight against his mouth to fight off the pain. For several minutes he could see only black. Then shooting stars of light crossed the black like comets. He was not going to pass out. Finally, his beaten hand came into focus, double its size. He moved it off the table to get it out of sight. Better already. For some time he lay immobile with his head across the good hand on the table and the broken one hanging limply toward the floor.

When he awakened, he felt as if he were not alone in the bed, that something or someone—but not a woman—was there with him. He was aware of what he had done to his hand, the terrible wreck he had made of it, the way it burned and ached with the pains of last night and further back too. But he was not yet aware that it was the presence he felt. He stole a quick glance at the expanse of bed beside him, careful not to look on the pillows. Empty. He closed his eyes and then he opened them again. He had to look. *Some*thing was in the room with him, if not in his bed, perhaps standing in a corner watching him, ready to strike. Rising on his elbow, he surveyed the room. The animal brown of one of his brogans stopped his heart although he was used to never taking them off. Nothing. He relaxed. Then, even though he had expected the worst, he looked at his hand and lost his breath. He shrank inside at his stupidity.

The hand, a pillow of bruised flesh, was ugly to behold. He held up his good hand, comparing them. The injured one was twice as large and like a flame in its range of color. Only his little finger, which had escaped the blows, seemed untouched. He wiggled it cautiously without experiencing pain. Then faster. Oof. When he wiggled too quickly, he couldn't keep his third finger from moving too.

Except for small dark threads outlining his fingernails like grime where the blood must have jumped out of his skin, he had not bled outwardly. Under the skin though, he was sure that there was a bloody mess. He had crushed veins, tendons, and nerves, probably irreparably. Not even if he had the money could he get them fixed. The scars from his earlier injury had swollen outward, turning white as they stretched. They looked like cold lips. He could not see the bones which controlled his fingers at all.

He probed with his healthy forefinger. The area around his thumb had no feeling. For the first time he looked at his palm, hoping that it might be unharmed, but the bruising seemed to have sunk through, crisscrossing in faint color like lifelines. He found that it was numb too.

All at once he decided he liked this pain. He wiggled his middle finger slightly and his wrist jerked like he'd put his finger into a socket. But it was bearable. He found that if he held very still, he could feel no pain, only the steady throbbing of his heart. He wiggled all five fingers at once, but it was too much to take. He bit his bottom lip, drawing blood. God.

He went to take a leak, feeling more sober than he hoped. In the kitchen he opened a beer and found some saltines. The cat clock, whose tail wagged the seconds, read ten. Audrey was at work and Craig at school. Little wind-up toys doing their jobs. He wondered if she had even noticed his hand, even come to the bedroom this morning to check on him. He hoped to God she'd seen it, so that she would send Craig to Mrs. Rice's this afternoon instead of home to pester him. She had to know that he was in pain last night, that she had hurt him when she slung her pillow and hit his hand. Her way though was to sneak away and return only when things were all right. He imagined her sliding out from under him after he'd fallen asleep, gathering her clothes for the next day, tiptoeing out and not looking back. Then sleeping in the same room with her "baby," trying to ruin the brat even more. Maybe they had something going. Who could tell these days?

Merle looked for the stinky wool shirt he had on last

night so that he could wear it to see Otto, but Audrey must have hidden it somewhere. She never let him wear his clothes as long as he liked. He decided to have one more beer since the first had made him feel so chipper: his hand scarcely hurt. He carried the beer to the bedroom. With this injury it would probably take him a while to dress. Could he even get his arm through a shirt sleeve? He chugged the beer and rummaged one-handed through his bottom drawer. Then he had an idea that would burn Otto's hide. He found his camouflage suit, stained with squirrel blood from the last time he went hunting. Otto would love him in this: he would just love him.

He felt like a cripple trying to dress, but finally he got on his shirt. He backed against the bed for help in holding up one side of his pants while he pulled at the other. He was lucky that Audrey hadn't taken his boots all the way off last night. He would never have been able to put them back on. He might have had to go in socks to Otto's office, which would have been kind of funny. He had trouble tying the laces now, only being able to pull each string tight and tuck it into the top of each boot. He vaguely wondered why Audrey had tried to take his boots off when she knew he planned to wear them forever. On the floor of the closet he found a camouflage hat wadded up under a pair of shoes. He whipped it through the air to straighten it out and pulled it down around his thick hair, the bill backward. He walked into the bathroom to look at himself in the mirror. The stubble on his chin he decided to let grow into a beard.

In the anteroom to Otto's office, a secretary who had worked for Otto for ten years but never acknowledged that Merle was his brother, motioned him to sit down. He'd hoped to arrive on her coffee break, walk into Otto's office unannounced, and scare his pants off. While finishing a telephone conversation, she twiddled a pencil with long skinny fingers. Her hair was teased into a ball of fuzz that squatted on top of her head. What was her name? He couldn't remember. Maybe he'd try Mrs. Pissant, or more likely *Miss*.

"That was Mr. Mitchell," she said, hanging up. "He's been delayed but will be here to see you in about ten minutes. He asked that you please wait. If you like, you may have a seat in his office where you should be more comfortable." She stared pointedly at his bad hand which he held like an offering in his good one. It helped to lay it somewhere instead of just letting it hang. He thought she would have noticed his clothes first. He felt his hat slipping and reached up to secure it, holding his injured hand carefully at his stomach. The simple effort of keeping it in midair brought perspiration to his upper lip.

The "Mr. Mitchell" was a new thing. Otto had always let everyone call him by his first name. To promote camaraderie, he'd told Merle. He would probably move his office next, now that the *Herald* had reported how he'd kept it on the ground floor for twenty years in the very place he'd started as the company's bookkeeper. The newspaper article had called him one of Durham's few honest success stories. A man who had yanked himself up from the poverty of southern Georgia by traveling north in search of work, finding a job as a carpenter with the Arch Martin Construction Company, working his way up the ladder of success to the presidency. Otto had supplied the paper with a photograph of the family taken by a traveling photographer when he was sixteen and Merle fifteen. In the picture Mother had had on her waitress uniform; she'd been on her way to work. They had stood on either side of her, encircled by her arms. It had always made Merle happy that her broad, worn face, her whole body in fact, was inclined toward him. Success, hell. If failure was what success was all about, Otto would surely win first prize because he had to be the worst carpenter in forty-eight states. In the article he'd joked about getting where he was because he couldn't hammer a nail straight. He'd said his brother Merle was good at that, meaning the dumb stuff.

In Otto's office the desk was cleared of everything but a telephone, a green blotter, a letter opener, and a foot-tall jar of lemon drops half-full which gave the room a candy-case smell. Merle had seen Otto eat those things by the handful and then lick the sugar off his fingers with his fat red tongue. When he talked he would stop to suck between sentences.

Against the left wall a bookcase held a photograph of Otto sitting behind his desk, trying to look pleasant yet solemn enough for the position he held. That picture had also appeared with the article. On another shelf sat a plaque from the City Beautiful Committee for Otto's landscaping efforts. The only books in the case were a collection of Stoddard's lectures, whoever he was, that Otto displayed to pretend he was smart. A long, narrow table against the right wall held cardboard models of several houses the company had built, including Otto's, a two-story Colonial with four Otto-like columns spaced across a flagstone veranda. Among other things, Merle had installed the dentil molding all around the roof line. He hadn't quite been able to bring himself to do a lousy job, but he'd managed to use twice the amount of material he'd actually needed. It had cost Otto a wad.

He started to take one of three chairs in the semicircle in front of Otto's desk but changed his mind. He threw his camouflage hat in the direction of an antique coatrack beside the door to Otto's private john, missed, and sat down in Otto's chair. He leaned back and began rocking. The chair springs squeaked horribly but he kept on. He saw a button on the telephone marked with a six, probably Miss Pissant's number. He punched the button, lifted the receiver, heard the buzz in the outer office.

"Yes," she said, cold amazement in her voice.

"Coffee. Cream and three sugars." He hung up. On his next rock forward, he reached into the jar for a handful of lemon drops. He sucked on them for several seconds and then spat them into a trash can under Otto's desk.

In a few minutes Miss Pissant walked in with his coffee. She looked at the three chairs and the bathroom door before she realized he was sitting in Otto's place. "My heavenly days," she said, her mouth wide.

"Over here," Merle said, pointing at the corner of the blotter. He gazed intently at his hands, ignoring her; the right one looked as if it belonged to a man twice his size. She set down the coffee. When her quick steps reached the door, he spoke sharply: "Miss."

"Yes sir," she answered shakily, as if she were about to cry.

"See that I'm not disturbed."

"Yes sir."

Merle discovered that Otto's chair turned circles too. He swiveled himself around, careful not to spill the coffee. She had sugared it perfectly. When he faced the wall behind Otto's desk, he saw a new nondescript painting, an oil of a lifebuoy during a storm at sea. Stupid. Most people would have had a ship.

Merle remembered when Otto used to have pin-ups all over these walls. Not one or two, but something like fifteen. None of the secretaries would look in here. All you ever had to do for a giant hard-on—depending, of course, on your capabilities—was visit this office. It used to be the damnedest funniest thing in this world to see a guy walking out the door straightening himself. The Marilyn Monroe pin-up had been Otto's prize, purchased about ten years ago before anybody knew who she was. (They got to know quick.) But then Otto started being promoted. Anybody past a bookkeeper had to set examples. He'd traded his pin-ups in for wallpaper and seascapes. Not exactly: he'd wallpapered over them. Did it himself the weekend between the

Friday he was promoted and the Monday Merle was sent in to make a door for his office where before there had been just an opening. In dress befitting his new position—black bow tie and white cufflinked shirt—Otto'd jerked a thumb over his shoulder. "They're all still there," he said, arching his eyebrows and smiling lewdly. "They're just under the covers." It was a lousy papering job. He put one finger to his lips. "Don't tell." You wouldn't have caught Merle doing something pussy like that or talking about it.

But . . . he hadn't had a chance to have an office. He was too good a carpenter. People had forgotten that the only reason Otto was where he was today was because of Merle. World War Two was beginning and Arch Martin had decided he didn't want to have to take Otto back when it was over. No one had expected Merle to protest—the quality of Otto's work infuriated him—but his life was so perfect. He had become Mr. Martin's golden boy, the foreman of every major job Arch undertook. Jenny had just had their baby, a beautiful pink-cheeked boy that they named Jay. Otto had married too, but a whiny blonde named Theresa, who announced after the wedding that she couldn't have children. It was easy to give Otto a helping hand. Merle told Arch that if he fired his brother, he'd have to leave too. Arch put Otto in the office. Within six months Jenny had vanished, war was declared, he was sent overseas, and Otto went to Washington.

Merle spoke in a low mean voice: "You grateful to me? Are you?" He stared hard at the chair opposite, conjuring the image of his fat nervous brother.

He looked at the door, still hanging perfectly. What had Otto done to Marilyn Monroe anyway? He stood close to her, didn't he, and jacked off. And then he rolled on that last crooked piece of wallpaper. . . .

The telephone rang. "Yes," he answered, a little breathless.

"Mr. Mitchell has arrived and will be in the office momentarily if . . . if you want to . . . adjust yourself," the secretary said.

"Adjust myself?" Merle hooted. Through the connection he heard the outer door open and close.

"Thank you, sir," she said and hung up.

When Otto talked, he tried to bowl you over with how smart he was. "To what do I owe the honor of this visit?" he would probably say. Like some dressed-up nigger. Merle heard him in the anteroom telling the secretary not to disturb them. He sounded as if he were in a hurry, not taking time to listen to her feeble attempts to warn him of what was going on. Merle guessed she didn't really know. He leaned back, and watched the door open.

Astonishment flashed across Otto's face. "Welcome back," he said. He walked forward, his hand outstretched, short and congenial like a new neighbor you would rather not know. He wore a flat-top that looked comical with the smooth flow of his mustache. He had a large mouth and an unusually red tongue which should probably be yellow from eating all those lemon drops. Nobody would ever guess that they were brothers. Maybe they weren't and their mother had never told them.

Otto had still not noticed his hand, so Merle drew it into his lap like a special belonging. A frown puckered Otto's bottom lip. He moved around the desk to claim the seat, but Merle stayed where he was. He held out both hands, knuckle-side-up.

"I thought your hand was well," Otto said. He laid his briefcase on the desk and waited for Merle to move.

"Relapse," Merle answered. He rocked in Otto's chair, making it squeak. He rolled his eyes to the disbelieving face floating above him. Otto seemed unsure of where he should go. He walked around to the far side of the desk. Suddenly he took a chair.

"Why are you dressed like that?" he asked.

"You wouldn't believe it if I told you."

Otto leaned to the jar of lemon drops and took a handful. "Probably not. But if you can't work, why are you here?"

"Need money."

"You're getting as much as you normally make," he said, his voice garbled by the candies. He began breaking into them with his teeth.

"Need more. Behind on car payment." Merle watched a point several inches above Otto's head.

"Are you drunk?" Otto asked.

"Nope."

"What happened to your goddamn hand?"

Merle lit another cigarette, one-handed.

"Why are you talking like this?"

"Like?"

"Goddamn it, you know what I mean."

He held up his injured hand like a sign. "I came to tell you something, so listen. I don't think this hand's ever going to be any good again."

"Oh yeah? How're you going to support yourself?"

"You tell me."

An ugly sneer that Merle remembered from their childhood warped Otto's face for an instant. "What do you mean?" he asked calmly, but Merle could hear the rage on the outskirts of his voice.

"I mean that you're going to take care of me and Audrey and Craig. No cheap stuff. Understand?"

Otto got more lemon drops, slowly. "How do you propose to force me into this?" he asked before throwing them into the wide hole of his mouth.

Back to the old shit, Merle thought, making what he says sound bigger than it is. "I'm not," he said. "You're going to offer me money because I'm your brother and I've worked for this company as many years as you have and you're where you are because of me. If you don't take care of me, where will your damn image be?"

"I sure as hell don't need you for my image."

"That's right," Merle growled. "You need me *gone*. But, buddy, I ain't going nowhere. You can count on that." His hand had begun burning without the numbing effect of beer.

"When are you coming back to work?" Otto asked.

"I'm not."

"Never?" His eyes opened into white circles.

"Not in the foreseeable future."

"Too many pressing duties, huh?" Otto's voice grew high-pitched like when he used to tattle. "You expect me to support you for the rest of your life." Veins in his temples stood out like his head might explode.

Merle took a long draw on his cigarette and looked over his shoulder at the lifebuoy. "Why not?" he asked the picture. "I put you where you are now."

"Bullshit. You've been saying that for fifteen years. Do you think anybody believes you?"

Merle faced him again. He thought of Otto as a fat toy. "You know the truth and I know the truth and that's all that matters. If it hadn't been for me you would have been out of this company on your ass twenty years ago."

Otto took another helping of lemon drops. He sucked on them for a few minutes, looking at the floor. When he next spoke, his voice was disarming. "You still think you're the best carpenter in this town, don't you?" He curled his lip so that his mustache looked as if it were growing crooked. "Not that you weren't good in your day," he added. "I won't take that away from you. But think back. When's the last time you did good work on a house?"

He should ignore Otto. "What about the Ragan house?" he said, sure of himself.

"No dice. Some molding you put up had to be redone. Maybe your eyes are getting bad, I don't know. But it's been . . . well, five years since you've been worth what you're paid. We haven't put you on any finishing jobs since the mess you made at my house. And you haven't even noticed."

"You bullshitter," Merle laughed angrily. "You bullshitting son-of-a-bitch."

"It's true; think back." Otto leaned over to pick up his letter opener from the blotter. He tossed it from one fleshy hand to the other, crunching his lemon drops. "And now look at you," he continued. "You'll probably never get to use your hand again. Hold it out. How did you hurt it, and don't tell me a relapse."

So goddamn smart. . . . Merle lunged out of his chair, both hands reaching for Otto before he could stop himself. He bumped his body against the desk hard, once and then again, trying to shake himself out of his fury. His hand hurt so bad he thought he might pass out. Otto flinched but did not move.

"Get out of here," he said. His voice seemed to come from great depths. "Get out of here," again.

"Not yet," Merle said, breathing hard. "I want you to know one thing. You ain't any smarter than I am. You just couldn't do anything else. Hell, I went to *Germany* and you sat on your ass in Washington. You've always sat on your ass and I've always worked. And *I'm* not good anymore. Shit. If I'm not, it's because the nails are shit cheap. They curl up like worms when you hit them. The wood splits like kindling. But you bought the materials, you fat son-of-a-bitch." He sank back in Otto's chair. This hand was using a lot of his energy.

Otto said, "You know, Merle, I'd like to think all of this was because of Jay."

"Wrong, Otto." He stood up angrily although he thought he might like to rest in Otto's chair all day.

"No, listen to me. Did you know Jay was going to die?"

"Shut up."

"Is that why you gave up? I mean, I saw this coming when Jay was in high school. *High* school, Merle." Merle looked at him suspiciously. "*Your* problems, not his. You say I haven't treated you like a brother. How many other men are on my payroll doing sloppy work? None. Just you. *Because* you're my brother. I'll tell you why more than that. Because you *used* to do good work. Not just good. Great. I'm paying you for what you used to do and what you might do again."

Merle's hand felt like it was frying. "How about that," he muttered, attempting an amused expression. "Since you have all the answers, I want one more. How much?"

"How much what?"

"Money, fool."

Otto flushed. "I'm not going to support your habits, Merle, but if you and Audrey need money to live, I'll help you along for a while." He paused. "Not forever, though." He fondled the letter opener with one large thumb. "And only as long as you give Audrey enough to pay the bills."

"She'll get some of it."

"She'd better." Otto drew the letter opener across his throat. "Or I'll cut you off so quick. . . . I'd suggest you catch the house payments up first. You're behind three months."

Merle stiffened. "Audrey tell you that?"

"As a matter of fact, she didn't."

"Who did?"

"The bank, little brother."

The crap you had to put up with to get what you wanted. "I *said* she'll get some."

"Just make sure it's enough."

Otto walked to his side of the desk. "Now get out of here," he said sternly. "I've got some work to do."

"I guess *so*," Merle grinned. He moved away from Otto's chair. "You need to make us some money."

"You're pushing your luck, Merle." Otto settled behind his desk as if it were his private tank. Not that he'd even known what a tank was, sitting in Washington and telegramming the families of America about their casualties. Merle had blown up two German tanks with hand grenades. Otto took papers from a drawer and pulled up so close to the desk that he looked like he wore it. He ignored Merle even when at the door Merle turned and said "So long."

Faye was new to town. From Dallas, she purred, as she swiveled to face him on the stool at Muzzie's bar. She looked like she was from some big city, dressed up in a straight black skirt and white cardigan sweater buttoned all the way up that smelled strongly of her own personal perfume. He'd hardly gotten through the door before she turned to give him a blazing look that sent chills through his neck. One of his regular honeys must have been bragging on him. She was not so bad looking although he could do without the blue eye shadow that looked for all the world like her last date had slugged her.

He ordered two beers, one for him and one for "this beautiful creature beside me." They liked being called creatures, he had noticed. She put her hands behind her head, running long fingernails through a head of moppy black hair and exposing the front of her sweater which covered a substantial pair of jugs.

"Dallas?" he asked, looking straight ahead and taking a long draw on his beer so she would have plenty of time to look him over. "Cowboy town."

She didn't respond.

"You rode one lately?"

She turned to him, her eyebrows raised as if it were an idea she'd never considered. "Maybe." She leaned close and giggled once. "I can't remember." He ordered two more beers so that when she was ready for her second one, she wouldn't have to wait.

"Were you looking for me or something? I mean, I don't

remember seeing you around before. And I *would* have." He flashed her his sexiest smile.

"Sure I was," she said.

He had his injured hand resting on the bar, and she caressed it once with small gentle fingers like it was a regular hand with nothing wrong. She acted as if wearing a camouflage suit was no big deal. He asked what she was doing in Durham, and she said a man here had promised her a job, sent her bus money, but she hadn't been able to find him since she arrived. And the telephone operators in this part of the country weren't one damn bit of help.

He ordered two beers in paper bags and asked her to go to ride in his car. She wiggled off her stool like a mermaid slipping into the sea. He kept forgetting what her name was, but finally fixed it in his mind by thinking about taking a tumble in some *hay*.

After the beers, he took an old leather flask from his glove compartment and weighed it in his hand. Full. How in the hell did it get full? This was his goddamn lucky day. He turned it up and guzzled deeply. He took another long swig before he offered the flask to her. After she drank twice herself, she drew away from him and turned on the seat, one leg hiked on the cushion so he could see what she had. It was dark between her legs. He steered with his left knee and grabbed at her underneath her skirt. The hurting in his hand had subsided. She was woolly and warm and wet without any underpants. The car ran onto the shoulder, jolting them, and then returned to the asphalt. He held up his wrist trying to read the time, feel her, and steer all at once. Only two o'clock. He had time to take her home, lay her, and get rid of her before Craig arrived home from school. Even if he came in, so what? Time he was learning how this world worked. Or how certain lucky people didn't.

Faye was one of these women who liked her work. She undressed him—God, nobody undressed him anymore—

taking care of the swollen hand. Didn't even blink when he said to leave the boots on. She brought her nipples right to his mouth and massaged his genitals with two hands. What had he stumbled on? When he entered her, she moaned with pleasure, and when she came she dug those long fingernails into his trembling ass.

He gave her eight dollars—three more than he normally gave—and the keys to his car and instructed her to drive herself back to Muzzie's. She wanted to go to sleep instead. Which would have been a great idea, only the brat would be home soon. He kicked her out of bed, only not too roughly because he wanted her back again tomorrow. "Get up or I'll call the cops," he said. "The cops?" She reared back on her knees and showed her body to him. She grinned, knowing how good he felt. "And what do you think I'll say when they get here?" "Get going, bitch. I'll take you for a turn tomorrow if you get going now." He sat in bed smoking, the sheet up to his hips. He turned it back and grabbed his penis to waggle before her. "I get it," he said. "You want me again, don't you?" "Tomorrow," she suggested, moving into her tight skirt and saving the sweater for last. When she did put it on, she fastened only one button in the middle. He reminded her that in case she got any wise ideas about the car, he knew where to find her. Then she kissed him goodbye.

He felt warm inside like after a big meal. Millie had come home with him yesterday and he'd hardly been able to concentrate long enough to finish. Millie, the carp, who gave up just as soon as you caught her. No fight, no fun, lying on his bed like something from another world that he really had no idea what to do with—except the usual. There was some advantage to that, but he preferred this Faye, who, he suddenly realized, reminded him of Jenny. That was why he felt so good. Jenny had been in bed with him, or almost. She hadn't had the figure of this girl, but she'd loved him in the same way. The sex ended but never really did. She would keep hugging and kissing him, loving his body long after they had both had their fill.

The window facing the backyard was up. A small breeze wafted through the screen and touched him gently. He threw back the covers, spread his legs, and let the gentle air caress his body. He wondered if she knew Jay was dead. He had not known where she was to tell her, but she had magic about things like that. When they were married, she had known when he was with another woman although he always cleaned himself up before he saw her. She probably sensed that Jay was dead the instant it happened, and he hadn't known until a telephone call came that night.

Was she married again? Had she had more children? He imagined her as a nurse in some famous hospital, perhaps even Duke, although he doubted it. He would have sensed her being that near. She had always wanted to be a nurse. He was almost sure she had never gotten married again. Hell, she wasn't even pretty, no body at all . . . but as delicate as a blossom, the way Jay had been. She'd run away from him one night, leaving Jay, her clothes, the single bottle of White Shoulders that she used on special occasions. Put on her navy blazer, left the apartment to buy cigarettes, and never came back. He didn't even call the police, he had been so sure within an hour that she had left him on purpose. They had never been divorced, but no one knew that.

He had silently blamed Jay. If a child hadn't come along, she would still be there. Nothing else had changed, had it? He'd made one phone call—to Otto telling him to make up some excuse, any excuse why he wouldn't be back at work for a while. The next week he learned how to take care of a six-month-old, bathing, feeding, playing, cuddling. When Jay napped, Merle lay down on the cold wooden floor beside his bed. They did not leave the house, but she did not come back. Every day he expected her. Every day he got Jay up, dressed, held and loved him. He wanted her to see he wouldn't let her down. At the end of a month he hired an old colored woman to take care of his baby and went back to work.

Four months passed before he was called to war, during which he paid only scant attention to his job. He hardly tried, but it seemed that his tools managed to find an inner precision that helped them hit their mark perfectly. He didn't talk to anybody. At lunch he ate cheese and crackers instead of the thick sandwiches that he'd used to bring. He did not squat with the other workmen. When he arrived home at night, he often paid Marybelle without a word before sitting and listening to the radio with the volume turned down. The only other sound those many nights was Jay screaming for his bottle. Sometimes, but not often, Merle did not feed him, wanting instead to listen to him scream out all the anger that he himself felt.

Before Craig's bus arrived, he walked to the kitchen naked for one quick drink. There he examined the door-pane carefully, thinking he ought to fix it. He tapped the fragile cardboard with one knuckle, while he looked through the door across the yard to the next house. He would bet a dollar that Paulette was at her breakfast-room window looking at him. He wagged his hips slightly so his penis would dance. Then he looked up quickly. It seemed that the edge of her curtains had moved. He wanted to walk outside and show himself off. If he were going to hang himself, he'd sure as hell do it naked. Something for people to feast their eyes on. The school bus appeared over the top of the hill. Merle took a full bottle of bourbon from his liquor cache. Audrey didn't pour out his booze like she used to; he'd made it not worth her while. He grabbed a glass from the drainboard and opened the refrigerator for ice. All the trays were empty. Damn lazy woman. Hell, he'd drink it hot. The bus whined to a stop outside and he walked back to his bedroom.

Merle leaned back on the hind legs of an old slat chair in the "sitting room" at Buck's Texaco. The chair squawked, but then settled down like an old horse to accept his weight. Wrapped in a napkin in his good hand was a huge dill pickle that he bit and chewed thoughtfully. Around him floated a conversation about the rumored layoffs at the cigarette factory next week. He was not particularly interested.

He'd awakened this morning thinking of Jenny and had not been able to get her out of his mind all day. Where *was* she? Jay had always wanted to know, had pestered him constantly up until the week before he killed himself. Merle wished he knew. Jay had also asked why Merle had left her.

She'd been a small woman, gentle as a little mouse. He could have drowned in her eyes, liquid warm gray eyes that showed the sex her girlish body did not. He'd never expected what she gave him in bed because she looked just like a teen-ager. But that wasn't what had been important between them anyway. He'd loved her. She left him five months before he was called up for World War Two. Maybe it was his whoring, but she'd known that and seemed not to care before they were married. Or perhaps it was Jay needing her so obviously. She was afraid of need, always telling him not to count on her being around forever. She would say it only after they had made love—he propped on their pillows, she nestled in the crook of his arm—and he had never believed her. In those moments, he always felt such a hold on her. He thought she liked him being with other women because, somehow, that made him less dependent on her. Only it hadn't. The full weight of their past together sank into him again, and he took a crunching bite of the pickle to put something in its way. He had not answered Jay's letter because he had not known what to say.

The fellows were talking about some kind of raid last night. If he didn't say something soon, they would start nosing into his personal life. Could those questions about Jenny have had something to do with Jay's death?

Buck came into the station to ring up a sale. "Haven't seen you around in a while," he said to Merle. Buck looked as if he were here working his way through college, but he was over thirty. Had moved to Durham during high school and taken an afternoon job with Elmo Jones, who'd run the station for years. Then business had slowed down: Elmo's was just a gravel-lot station and the traffic became mostly dollar's-worth buyers. When Elmo retired, he sold the station to Buck for peanuts. Buck deserved it, he told his friends, for all those years of cleaning windshields for cheapskates who ran their lives on fumes. In Merle's opinion, Buck had been no dummy.

"Been recouping," he said.

"How's the hand?"

"Not so good." He raised it to show. It was not hurting badly at all today. "Had a relapse."

"That so." Buck stood with the door open on his way to serve another customer.

"Seen Chunny lately?" Merle asked. Buck and Chunny had gotten to be friends when they were both running Texaco stations.

Buck inched through the door looking like he didn't believe the question. "Don't you know?"

"Know what?" Merle asked, biting his pickle.

"Chunny got raided last night," Buck said, telling the best part himself. "Somebody else tell him the rest." He let the door go.

Merle tilted his chair farther back and let his legs hang slack, surveying the group before him. One guy he didn't know, but Joe Davis and Curt Rainer were there. Joe was a runty guy, not like him, but thin through his body. His hands were smaller than a woman's. Curt wore thick glasses and an intense expression. He worked a night shift and had a bitching wife which were the reasons he hung around Buck's all day. Merle said: "Wednesday night Chunny was sick, and then last night I went by about nine and he was closed."

"Happened earlier," Rainer said. "Fred never showed up and somebody who wanted a drink real bad called Chunny at home. He still had a cold, but he opened up anyway." Rainer pulled out his pocket knife and began cleaning his fingernails. Joe cocked his head as if he were listening to music. The man Merle didn't know stared dully over the top of his head.

"Well, what *happened?*" Merle asked, irritated.

Matter-of-factly, Joe said one of the members of Chunny's club had gotten angry at Fred and wanted him fired. The guy called up this deputy friend of his, who didn't know that Chunny and the law had an arrangement.

"Yeah?"

Joe plopped his own slanted chair back upright. "Yeah, Merle. Chunny thinks maybe it was you."

"Me? I never even talked to Chunny about that lunkhead. Don't even know his name."

"Sure knows yours." Joe leaned the chair back to the wall again. His eyelids drooped as if he didn't care.

Merle knew he should say nothing, but it was so damn hard to let silence defend you. "You believe that?"

"I don't believe anything. Only told you what I heard. You ought to thank me."

"Yeah. Thanks for nothing."

No one spoke for a few minutes, not even when Buck came in to ring up his sale. He looked at them strangely but said nothing. Merle felt uncomfortable, but not because of Chunny. Chunny knew he wouldn't do a shit-ass thing like that. He thought Buck was watching him again, but was it because of the quiet or the pickles? Last time he'd hung around here for an afternoon, he'd gotten into an argument with Buck about how many pickles he'd eaten. Buck said he couldn't have eaten only two because every time he'd come in, Merle had another one in his hand. This wasn't a charity stop, he'd continued, and Merle, who'd been nudging Joe about somebody who gets p.o.'d about a couple of sour cucumbers, finally got angry. He lifted the top of the barrel and threw what was left of his sixth pickle back. Buck really yelled then, sputtering that he was going to call the police unless Merle got his filthy ass out of there.

Two days later, Jay killed himself. Buck must have read about it in the newspaper because the morning before Audrey returned with the body, he drove up in his truck, hot-wired Merle's car, and took it to be washed. Merle watched him out the kitchen window, but he was drunk and naked and had decided not to try to do anything about it. It had been Buck's way of making up for the pickles.

Audrey had thought *he'd* washed the car. She'd burst into the house after her taxi ride from the station, thinking that because the car was clean, he must be all right. When she opened the door though, the odor of Southern Comfort had told her different. Lying on the sofa in the living room, naked except for the brogans Jay had given him the Christmas before, he heard her gasp. He pointed at her, laughing as she came through the living room, his finger following her path, his head lolling against the arm of the sofa. "Where's Melissa?" he had yelled. "Where is that little sweetheart?" She hadn't even come for the funeral.

"Your boy's out here, Merle," Buck said from the doorway.

For a moment Merle didn't catch the words, but then he blanched, bringing his chair down loudly on all fours. "Shit," he said.

The four men looked at him.

"Tell him to get his ass out of here."

Buck looked at Merle, pulled a dime from the cash register, and got himself some coffee from the machine.

"I'll kick his ass," he said rising.

Joe interrupted: "Just because Chunny's pissed off . . ."

"Shut up," Merle said. He swung through the door with his good hand, throwing the bad one behind him in a gesture that couldn't quite take shape because of the pain. He wished they would all go to hell.

Outside Craig walked toward him, scuffing his shoes on the gravel, grinning that dumb-ass grin of his. "Hi," he said.

"What are you doing here?" he asked brusquely. Spend an hour with this kid and he becomes a permanent leech. Because the men inside were watching, he squeezed the back of Craig's neck playfully.

"Ouch," Craig yelled, pulling away. He stood rubbing his neck, his blue eyes wounded.

"Don't follow me around, do you understand?" Merle moved quickly toward his car, parked in the far corner of the lot. A lady in a brown station wagon pulling in for gas stirred up a thick cloud of dust. She began honking her horn for Buck. Craig ran around the back of the car to get in the other side. Fortunately, it was locked.

Merle swung into his seat, stuck the key in the ignition, and started the engine. The woman in the station wagon kept honking. Craig knocked on the window until finally Merle looked. He was crying, the stupid kid was crying. He jammed the gears into reverse and glared at Craig while the car rocked back. Craig jumped out of the way. He slung the shift to forward and put his foot to the gas. Glancing around, he saw Craig grab the locked handle. The car yanked him off his feet. Merle hit the brakes, sliding through the gravel to a stop. In his side mirror he saw Craig on the ground.

The woman had gotten out of her car and was screaming

and waving one fist. Goddamn bitch. Buck came running out of the station. Craig pulled himself to his feet by the door handle. When he'd regained his balance, Merle lifted his foot from the brake, locked the door on his own side, and drove slowly off the crunching gravel onto the highway. He pushed his rearview mirror up so that it faced the roof.

3

AUDREY

Audrey had been sitting in the bedroom buffing her nails with a wad of cotton when she heard the telephone pull Merle away from the Jack Paar show. The travel alarm clock on his side of the bed had run down but she knew it was late. One of his girl friends? They usually weren't the type to bother him at home. The sticky summer air crowded her body like a towel as she stood up and sat back down again, changing positions. For a moment the creak of the old bedsprings confused her. Then she realized that she had heard something: Merle was talking loudly and then he screamed her name. She was afraid to go to him to find out what it was, but her legs did not seem to know it. Audrey-y-y. AUDREY-Y-Y. Like someone plummeting to his death. Her legs kept moving even though her arms grabbed at the doorjamb. The telephone hit the floor, ringing short bells. She turned the corner and saw him pull back his fist and smash it through one of the glass panes of the door. She shrieked for him to stop. His arm hung through the hole; he beat his head against the frame as steady as a hammer. She grabbed his free flailing arm, but he flung her back toward the dining room. She hit the doorway with one shoulder, slipped, and fell. Beside her lay the receiver. She picked it up and listened. "Who is this?" She registered the unfinished underside of the dining table and how the ceiling looked like a floor. No one answered. Behind her Merle sobbed, less violent. The phone rang again.

"Hello." At the sound of her voice Merle turned and

stared. "Hello," she said again, although someone on the other end was already talking. The connection grew better. Merle wrenched away from the door, sliding his arm over the rough edges of the glass, ripping his sleeve, opening more wounds. She was finally able to hear. The man was Sergeant Jester from Fort Benning, Georgia, where Jay was stationed. He said Jay was dead. Merle lunged, the injured arm leading, grabbing for the receiver. She swallowed a scream before it hit the air, putting out an arm to protect herself. He fell back easily, docile again, watching blood drip off his fingertips to the floor. His thick blondish hair stuck out wildly around his head. Across his jaw was a smear of blood. Audrey heard Craig's door open. She told the sergeant she would have to call him back for details. He said there was one other thing she should know now: Jay had killed himself. She knew that. He offered more: Jay died by hanging. She felt herself nodding. While he offered condolences that sounded memorized, she quietly hung up.

For a moment she couldn't turn around. Gone. The best part of Merle was gone. She could not feel disbelief, but confirmation of her worst secret fear. She felt her shocked body adjusting to a new lesser world. She had a tight hold on the telephone receiver. Grief lay heavy in her arms. Finally she heard Merle's moans.

Merle had moved obediently to the breakfast table. She went to Craig's room. He opened his door, but she pulled it to a crack again, between them. She did not want to touch or be touched. She whispered that everything was all right, that his father had lost his temper and cut his hand, that she was driving him to the hospital to get it sewn up. Practically all she could see of him was his agreeable blue eyes, not pushing her for any answers. He probably thought they'd been fighting. Her heart ached for him.

"Can I go?" he asked, too eagerly.

"No, but if you need anything, call Clayton." She closed the door firmly and turned toward the kitchen, but there was a slowness to her steps that she didn't understand. She made herself hurry.

In the kitchen Merle lay half-conscious across the breakfast table. She telephoned Clayton to tell him what had happened, but Paulette answered. Audrey fought off the urge to ask for him. "Sorry to be bothering you so late, Paulette. Merle's injured his hand and I've got to take him to the hospital. I'm going to leave Craig here." Silence. She imagined Paulette in her flat cap of pincurls. "I wanted you to know in case there's any emergency." What else could happen?

"Is there something wrong, honey?" Paulette asked.

Audrey glanced at Merle. The drip of blood from his fingertips had slowed. Red droplets speckled the kitchen floor. He emitted low moans. "I'll have to talk to you later," she said. In the background she heard Clayton's sleepy voice asking who it was, but she hung up anyway.

She got some dish towels from a drawer, but when she tried to wrap one around Merle's arm, he said, "Get away." His words were slurred as if he were drunk. She began to feel less sorry for him. She realized that she might need help getting him to the car. Clayton's help. Merle was surprisingly pliant. She guided him toward the door. He mumbled something about hunting. Blood dripped faster from his hand as he walked. One whole sleeve was wet. On the stoop he lost his balance; she pushed him against the house for support. The bloody sleeve blended with the maroon paint. Next door the porch light came on and Clayton hurried down his steps and across the stretch of grass between their two yards.

"What happened?" he asked. They locked arms, helping Merle toward the car. Tears jumped from Audrey's eyes.

"Jay's dead," she said. Her throat was sore with the dread of knowing. Clayton stopped. Merle's head hung between them. He looked first disbelieving and then angry. "He killed himself," she explained quickly. "He was miserable."

Merle went unconscious and they struggled under his weight.

When they shut him inside the car, Clayton took her elbows. "I'd like to go with you, but I'd better not." Why did he do this to her? He could go to the hospital with them out of simple neighborliness. She felt her sense of control slipping away.

"What if he tries to grab the wheel?" The possibility suddenly seemed very real. She moved away from his touch, feeling guilty for wasting so much time. Merle could bleed to death.

He bent to look through the window at the head slumped low on the seat. Merle's mouth had dropped open. "He won't," he said, but his voice lacked conviction. "I'll go check on Craig," he said, trying to make it up to her. She told him he need not bother.

She drove to the hospital without Merle regaining consciousness. Somehow she had hoped that he would wake up for one harmless swipe at her. At the emergency entrance a policeman lifted him from the car and she felt less alone again, watching the starched blue uniform work. He had kind eyes and didn't wipe at his hand when Merle's blood smeared it. He talked in a slow, soothing voice, not saying anything that required a response. She noticed for the first time that blood spattered her blouse like paint.

The policeman set Merle in one of the thin-cushioned seats that were attached to white walls dirty with handprints and smears from oily heads. He motioned her to the reception desk, indicating that he would sit with Merle while she registered. Exactly what she wished Clayton were doing. The nurse, a small, stuffed-looking woman with neat-cropped hair, told her there would be a short wait while the doctor finished with a man wounded in a knifing. Her face had lots of color as if she were very healthy. She looked sorry for Audrey as if Merle's hand had been cut in some wild lunge at her throat.

Audrey gave her a small polite smile. The word *knifing* sounded ominous. There were other people here, but Audrey guessed priority went to people like Merle.

"I'll check on him in a second," the nurse said, in case there was worry in that face she couldn't see. "Has he lost much blood?"

How much is much? "No," Audrey said. "I don't know." She made an apologetic motion with her stained hands and asked directions to the bathroom. She soaped her arms up to her elbows and then rinsed them carefully. After drying them she sniffed the sterile Ivory fragrance on her skin and felt better.

In the waiting room the stink of dirty bodies and liquor, matted blood, burned flesh, and ether bombarded her again. Her hands felt like bright ornaments. Her policeman sat with Merle in a deserted corner of the room. Merle's eyes were closed; he jerked like someone having a bad dream. She produced a grateful smile, and the policeman offered to stay if she felt she needed help. With a slight bow of her head, she said he'd done too much already. He stood up and his tallness took away her breath. How stupid she was, but he seemed so much what she wanted. His last name, Crowder, was printed on a silver bar pinned to his chest, and she printed it in her mind in case she ever saw him again.

"I'm sorry about your uniform," she said. He looked at it for the first time.

"It doesn't matter," he said. Then he turned and walked out of her life.

Merle seemed to have passed out again. Earlier in the evening he'd been drinking heavily, slumped in a chair talking to the girls on television, so it could be liquor or loss of blood. He was still bleeding. She thought of notifying the nurse, but then decided to let things happen naturally. Her father had died in a natural way. He'd begun coughing after a cigarette and couldn't stop. She'd run to the telephone but he waved her away. She tried to pound the passage to his lungs clear, but he used his last strength to knock her against the couch. She'd not tried to do anything else, and a few minutes later he was dead. Back in this corner they were out of sight of the nurses' station. If they forgot him, she would say she had thought they were too busy with a patient more important. She didn't know how much blood he had lost. How much was too much? They were the experts.

In time they cut off his shirt, bandaged the superficial wounds on his arm, and stitched up the gullies in his hand. They dressed him in a hospital gown to wear home over his khakis. With sedation he grew sober and melancholy. Grief flattened his eyebrows close over his eyes. He surprised her, looking to her for comfort, planting his good hand on her shoulder and squeezing like it was an exercise ball. His eyes glistened with a constant supply of fresh tears. She had never seen him cry. He leaned on her as he thanked the nurse, and she braced her feet so that she could take his weight. She could not look at that healthy efficient woman who watched first Merle and then her with the curiosity of a bird. The nurse wanted to know what had *really* happened. Where Audrey's bruises were. Beneath her clothes, of course. The woman must have been marveling that Audrey's eyes were not black or her nose broken. In fact her shoulder ached badly where Merle had thrown her against the dining-room doorway. But in fact he had not beaten her. Not guilty for once, she wanted to say.

An orderly helped her get him to the car. Outside the moon was pushing its way through holes in the clouds. A cool wind blew the stench of the waiting room out of their hair and clothes. She looked around for her policeman, but he was gone.

At home she could not wake Merle or get him out of the car. Clayton's lights were out. She would have liked to get him to bed. She brought a blanket and a pillow to the car and arranged them around him. He was breathing quietly. She cracked the windows to give him enough air.

Craig was asleep the wrong way on the bed where he had been waiting up to talk to her. She looked at his face, pink in the heat of sleep. She tried to think how she was going to tell him about Jay, but ideas escaped her. He would never understand, she knew that. She guessed that no one would. She covered his feet, picked up a scribbled note that said "Call Clayton," and turned out his light.

She knew that she should get some rest, should take care of herself tonight for the exhausting days ahead, should, should, should. . . . But it seemed so wrong. Merle seemed wrong lying out there in the car—injured, it was true, but still managing to get his rest. Not having to make the choice to think about Jay because sedation had put him to sleep. Had he hurt his hand on purpose? She hoped his rest was rotten.

In the living room she opened a window so she could hear him if he got out of the car. The night air was alive with sound: crickets, tree frogs, the wind scraping the house with unpruned tree branches. To sit in, she chose the most formal chair they owned, a carved wooden one with a tight narrow seat and carved back whose acorn design struck the mid-bones of one's spine. It had belonged to her parents. Her father had sat in it for years, forcing first her mother and then her to suggest daily that he take another more comfortable seat. "This will do," he always answered. There was no self-denial in her house, so the chair was not used. She took it now, knowing that it would not let her rest, that she would not be lulled into any halfway state of sleep. She wanted time to give Jay's memory its due. Tomorrow things would move too quickly and ever afterward she would be trying to forget, or if not trying, simply forgetting.

She guessed it was because of Melissa. Melissa and the

baby and the Army. And having Merle for a father. Never knowing his mother. It hurt her to think it, but it was true. He loved her but never in the way he loved Jenny. She leaned back and the carved acorns dug into her back. Jay had not looked well at Christmas, the last time they'd been together, but he'd been working two shifts every day for a week to accumulate time off. He was tired, but he seemed giddy too. When he looked about, his eyes were piercing, but then she would catch him in a gaze so vulnerable that she wanted to cradle him in her arms. Sometimes when someone called his name, he flinched.

They had arrived Christmas Eve and that night Jay reopened those long, crazy conversations about him and Merle going into business together. She wasn't sure if they ever went to bed. The opening of presents the next morning was punctuated by the jacking sound of the church key on beer cans. Jay told her that this was his vacation and he intended to enjoy it. For the first time she wondered which of them was the worse influence.

He didn't talk to her, although she had thought he might if she made herself available. Twice she invited him to go to the grocery with her, but he declined; once she took a day off from work, hoping to see him alone. But no one left the house. Melissa lounged in the kitchen drinking coffee and reading the Sears catalogue, although Audrey told her the car was hers. Merle missed work, mostly, she thought, because Jay was inflaming the old hopes. Craig was off school for the week, and the baby fretted all day from colic. Audrey cleaned up behind them all.

The chatter of the night insects grew quiet now as if they had gone to sleep or been disturbed. She listened for Merle. The house, which had been the listener, seemed to be stirring itself. Nothing obvious, just a rising creak here and there, the louder tick of the cat clock in the kitchen. Noises present all along but drowned out. Still, they seemed like the second half of a conversation.

She thought of Clayton, something she'd been putting off because of a strangeness she'd felt tonight in the driveway. A gulf had opened between them, wider than the grass between their cement steps. She felt that Jay's death had snatched her back in time, brought her to that moment in her life before Clayton had existed. Oh, he'd always been here: they'd been neighbors for nine years. But she'd noticed him only a year ago. Before, he was only a butt for Merle's jokes. When Paulette said jump, Merle kidded, Clayton asked how high. Behind his back he called Clayton Chicken Little, but to his face, he called him Mr. Prince. Clayton always grinned; he didn't like the name King either, he said.

Then one day he helped her change a tire in her own driveway. He looked at her with soft brown eyes that said nothing but were waiting to be said *to*. She saw the gaze twice more before she was sure. And then she said, "You have beautiful eyes." Which was almost true. His eyebrows could have been thicker. For a long time, while they were still only friends, she fought against comparing him with Merle. Now that she knew him well, she found they both had their faults. One thing was true: Clayton got his way with her, and he never even raised his voice.

Her body began to soften, thinking of loving him. If someone with a crane could just roll up to their house, open its jaws, and pick up the Chevrolet with Merle in it. Carry it off to a junk pile. Why was Jay dead and not Merle? Why couldn't he have killed himself and taken his burden off her? Maybe now he would.

She heard the refrigerator start up. If only Merle had cut himself worse or grown delirious, so that they had kept him overnight at the hospital. Then she might have been able to signal Clayton to visit her. When they made love it was on Friday nights at his house after Craig had gone to bed and before Merle had come home. Paulette spent Fridays in Lexington with her sick mother.

It seemed as if Jay had been dead for a very long time. Merle should be simply sleeping while she waited for enough time to pass so that she could legitimately run away with Clayton. She looked at her watch, a silver one with tiny diamonds clouded by age. The largest diamond, still only a chip, was missing, had always been missing, was probably missing when her father gave the watch to her mother. Four o'clock. An hour would pass before the unkind sun revealed this littered landscape: Merle asleep in the backseat of the car, his hand a pattern of black stitches; the kitchen floor, a mess of glass and blood; Craig's face which today would lose its innocence forever. If the three of them could somehow hide in the dark and not have to show themselves. At least for a few days until their bodies had absorbed all this.

Of all the nutty things, Clayton was outside raking last year's leaves. Audrey stood at the bathroom window looking out on their backyards. She powdered her neck in the morning sun and down her throat to where the fragile collar bones protruded. Her skin softened with the pale coloring. She used pencil to define the slight lines of her eyebrows.

When she tugged at her blouse, hanging on the shower rod, the hanger accidentally fell into the tub. Just what she hadn't wanted to happen. She reached for it, but then left it there to avoid another accident. She'd been paying too much attention to how nice she looked and probably awakened Merle. She listened for a moment, and then put on the brown cotton blouse that nicely complemented her dark hair. She picked up her canvas shoes. The cotton-batting rug in the back hall and the braided one in the living room helped her. Her bare toes squeaked on the dining-room floor but she was too far away from him for it to matter now. In the kitchen she drank from the bottle of juice so she wouldn't have to open the cabinet for a glass.

Audrey guessed that yard work to Clayton meant raking

leaves. She had not thought to specify when he called her Friday at work to ask when they could see each other this weekend. She'd been cashing a check for a man with rubbery lips and wavy black hair. Neither he nor Clayton had liked sharing her attention. She had hoped that today they could sit down at the wire fence that divided their backyards, pull weeds, and talk, but he looked totally occupied. He looked silly too, raking 1960 leaves a month before 1961 leaves were due to fall. She slipped into her shoes; too cool for bare feet. The leaves on the trees were green and fresh-looking like nothing could make them fall off. Clayton threw up a hand at her. Every once in a while he would expose a patch of lingering Bermuda grass, white like untanned skin, but mostly the yard grew gray and bare.

Audrey sat down at the fence in a spot in the sun and began pulling weeds. If he didn't join her soon, she would go back to bed. She studied the windows of Clayton's bedroom where Paulette still slept and then the windows of her own where Merle was wearing off last night's drunk. He'd been too used up to bother her last night, and she was in need of someone bothering her.

Clayton raked like a machine. Dust flew ahead of him in the air. There had been no rain in two weeks, and even her house, normally the shiny maroon of an eggplant, looked dull. If he kept coming in this direction, she would have to go back to the house to get out of the way of his dust storm. Several blocks away a chain saw started up. A faint breeze stirred the trees.

"Clayton," she called, not gently in case anyone was listening. "Clayton?" again, with a hard question at the end of his name. He tilted his head in her direction so she knew that he had heard. He raked faster, pushing a group of leaves into a straight line with some others. He came to where she sat, carrying his rake.

"Why don't you help me weed along this fence?"

"Do you think it would be too obvious?"

What had he thought they were going to do? Make eyes at each other from twenty feet? "No, honey," she said, smiling sweetly. "I really don't. To tell you the truth, if anything's obvious, it's you out here raking last year's leaves."

He blushed, not thinking she was so funny. Then he shook it off.

Audrey heard a noise from the direction of his house. She turned and pointed toward the back corner of her lot as if she were asking him a question. He grinned at her and then glanced toward his house which he shouldn't have done. "Did you hear something?" he asked.

"I thought I did," she said, "but you're not supposed to look. If you act guilty, they're going to suspect something. Come look at this tree in my yard so we can get away from the houses a little." He walked dutifully to the end of the fence, propped his rake against it, and followed her to a large oak tree.

"I don't know anything about trees," he said when she stopped.

"Pretend like you do," she said. He was exasperating her.

"Paulette knows I don't know anything about trees."

She felt like going back to bed or at least reading the paper. "Relax, Clayton," she said, unable to keep the contempt out of her voice. He flinched. A few seconds later, she was able to say she was sorry. He shrugged her hand on his arm away.

"This is our own backyard," he said fiercely. "What do you expect?"

They were both as edgy as hell and finally she realized why. "You're about to explode, aren't you?"

"No," he said, still irritated. "What do you mean?"

"Don't you know?" she teased. She'd received a passionate letter from him yesterday at the bank.

"Yes," he said. He was still irritated. "Is there something we can do together that won't look so obvious?"

"We can weed the fence."

He walked ahead of her without the courtesy or casual chat that one would show a neighbor, but it was a hard thing to make him understand. Their friendship was better before they became lovers. She used to be able to talk to him about Merle, but now "Merle-talk," as he called it, made him angry. That would surely change when she went off with him. He seemed to think Merle was his rival.

Clayton sat down cross-legged, his work pants hiking up to show skinny white legs covered with long straight hairs. She was fond of those skinny legs. "What should I do here?" he asked. "Pull everything?"

"Everything." They silently pulled weeds. He didn't hesitate when their hands were near each other, and she wondered if she had been so abrasive lately that he was losing interest. "Hey," she said, low and purring. He looked up, pulled away from his thoughts, his eyes searching and serious with something more important.

"How long are you going to make me wait?" he asked.

"For what?"

"For you."

She felt relieved. The antagonism between them was only nerves. She snatched at some jimsonweed that was giving her a hard time. She dug for the roots, feeling dirt pack under her fingernails. "I'm not making you wait," she said. "I'm just waiting. It's so soon after Jay. . . ." She trailed off.

"What's different?" He held a clump of dandelion greenery in one hand. "You were ready to leave before he died, so why not now? Nothing's changed. He didn't even live here."

She told him what she always said: that she was waiting for Craig to adjust to this change before she put him through another one. That it was hard for anyone, including herself, to go through two traumatic events in such a short time. That Paulette was about to lose her mother, and she was thinking a little bit about her. That if they both left right now, everybody would guess, and she didn't want Merle coming after him.

"He's not going to come after me," he said.

She waited, but that was all he said. "I have to stay here a little longer, Clayton. A week. I want to make sure Merle's all right." His dark eyes narrowed suspiciously on her. "It's normal concern about another human being." Then she grew irritated. "You can take it or leave it."

He dragged his body to a spot farther along the fence. "A week then," he said. "You promise." It was not a question, but she nodded. Her hands trembled against the strain of too large a clump of weeds. She was afraid to say it might be longer.

Just then Merle walked out the side door and stood on the stoop about fifteen yards away. He wore khaki pants and the worn-out brogans Jay had given him one Christmas. He had put them on while she was in Columbus collecting Jay's body and hadn't taken them off since. Even in bed. A cigarette dangled like a straw from his lips. He tightened it in his mouth to light in his awkward one-handed motion and flung the match out into the yard.

"Whatcha know, Merle?" Clayton called. His wavy black hair glistened with sweat and Vitalis. He stood, as if Merle were a good excuse for him to get up.

Merle's eyes settled briefly on her. "Less and less all the time."

Clayton walked over to him, wiping his hands on his pants as if he were going to shake Merle's hand. He had forgotten about Merle's stitches, but then he remembered and slid his hands deep into his pockets. They began the toneless conversation of "man-to-man" which she pretended to ignore. Why did Clayton have to act buddy-buddy with him? Merle thought he was a shrimp. Clayton toed the black dirt at the bottom of the steps, drawing designs. Just so long as he didn't draw a heart with her name in it. Merle watched him, slightly amused, glancing over at Audrey every few minutes to make eyes like Clayton was half nuts.

Her cheeks began a slow burn. She felt awkward, unsettled. She smiled at Merle, and the betrayal shivered over her skin. What else could she do but accommodate him, the same way Clayton did even though he hated Merle's guts. *Did* he hate his guts? It was hard to believe that now. They were telling jokes and laughing, Clayton heartily at Merle's, Merle half-assedly at Clayton's. She felt wrong that she didn't hate Merle right now. She wanted to slap them both, knock some sense into them, walk over and lay all the cards on the table. Tell Merle she wanted to go off with Clayton . . . or tell Merle she was going off with Clayton if he didn't straighten up . . . or tell Clayton she was staying with Merle. Her stomach felt sick at herself. Suddenly she knew what it was to want to injure yourself. If she had the courage, she would stab this trowel into her wrist and then into the other one. Hit a major artery but not scream, not let them know. Jut lie here and die while they laughed with each other on the stoop. Make a deathbed confession to them both. What would she say? She didn't know.

This was all Merle's fault. She loved Clayton, but he could so easily be made a fool. He pampered Merle like Merle was his boss. If he would back off a little, she could back off too.

In a movie in her mind, Clayton walked over to her, grabbed her off her knees, and propelled her toward the stoop. Clouds of dust burst around his feet with each step and sparks flew from his taps as his shoes struck bits of gravel. His shoulders grew broader by a foot. "Audrey and I want to talk to you," he said to Merle, his voice solid like she had never heard it. The high pink of Merle's cheeks drained away as if Clayton were holding a gun. Audrey glanced down. Clayton was, in this movie, holding a gun. At least he looked like he had a gun pointed against the blue pocket of his work pants. She thought she could make out the cold lines of a barrel. "Audrey's tired of a runt like you," he said. "Her and me are going off and we're taking Craig with us. She don't ever want to see you again. Y'hear?" He pawed the ground like a young bull. "She don't love you anymore; she loves me." He put his arm around her and fondled the underside of her breast. She turned slightly to give more of it to him. "Ain't that right, honey?" Merle's eyes swung to hers for confirmation. Her body felt like sawdust that might collapse before his stare. Her throat clogged. Clayton squeezed her breast. "That's right, honey," she said. The "honey" floated foolishly in the air; she had never called him that. He turned her to him for one long adoring moment. Merle sprang through the air like a wildcat. But Clayton neatly sidestepped, pulling her with him, and Merle fell on the ground. He turned around to come at Clayton again, but this time the gun was flashing in the air like a fast squirrel, pointing out the path toward Merle's car. "Don't even come back until Monday," Clayton said. "We're slow packers." Merle vanished like the devil had got him.

Clayton walked on past her to where he had leaned his rake across the fence. Merle tripped down the concrete steps toward his car.

"Merle," Clayton called. "You got a dead oak tree back there."

"Oh, yeah?" Merle stopped to light one more cigarette.

"Might ought to get it taken down." Clayton fluffed a clump of Bermuda grass with his rake.

"Want to see about it for me?" Merle flipped his match in Clayton's direction and took a long staring draw of his cigarette.

Clayton's milky skin turned ashen. "N-naw," he said. Then quieter, "Just thought you might like to know." He turned his back and began raking again, but with slower, smaller strokes.

Merle sped out of the driveway, squealing his tires when he reached the asphalt. Then he roared down the street to show off for all the neighbors. Clayton was putting muscles into his useless job. She stood up, leaving the pulled weeds lying there like casualties of a battle, walked into the kitchen, and started bacon for Craig's breakfast.

Audrey extinguished her bedside lamp, but the car was already in the driveway. Too late. Normally she could hear Merle's motor knocking as he turned the corner at the top of the hill. It was just past midnight; he was home early. She felt along the edge of her bedside table for the bottle of nail polish she'd been using and closed it. She hadn't gotten to finish three toes. The lights of the car began walking up the trees as it backed out of the driveway. Not Merle. As the car drove back up the hill, she blew air faintly in the direction of her wet nails. Then she heard the back door open; he was home after all.

She wished she had thought sooner to move into the extra bed—Jay's old one—in Craig's room. Merle staggered around the kitchen, opening and slamming shut cabinets. She was afraid to pour out his liquor anymore, but she regularly changed where he kept it. By now her toenails were dry, so she slid under the covers, tucking her edge of the blanket under her so he couldn't hog the covers when he got in.

Why was he home so early? She dismissed the question even as she thought it. One possible answer insisted on itself anyway. He might be going to work tomorrow; he might think he needed some sleep.

A whiff of his odor floated to her, a combination of soiled clothes, cigarette smoke, and whiskey. It rode him like fleas, scattering about the house whenever he came home. Probably her imagination. But it was possible, in the quiet air of the house, that the smell of his body reinvaded each room. She imagined that there were pockets of his smell in corners of every room, under the bed, in his drawers, his closet, just waiting to drift by her nose. He had decided he didn't need to bathe anymore. Since he'd stopped working, why bother? He didn't sweat. Sometimes when he took off his clothes, he folded them and put them in a drawer as if they were clean, so she couldn't find them to wash. She refused to sniff them. She should probably burn sulfur in the house, the way her father had done after her mother died to kill the germs of her disease. A wretched, ugly action, she had thought then, but now she wondered.

He was spending a long time in the kitchen. Usually he took his nightcap to the bathroom and read magazines or brought it to the bedroom while he pestered her. She heard him drag his toolbox out from under the kitchen table where it had sat untouched since Jay died. He rummaged through the tools. She wondered—she tried not to, but she did—if he could possibly be straightening them for work tomorrow. She sat up in bed to listen, straining to hear exactly what was happening. She couldn't tell whether he was only fiddling with his tools or actually putting the box back in order. He had torn it apart while she was in Columbus; she had only taken time to stuff everything back inside.

The pressure in her chest grew lighter as if a huge bubble were rising through it. But who was she kidding? There was no chance things would change. One chance, maybe, but only slight. Maybe now that his stitches were out, he would take hold of himself, go back to work. Occupy his hands, so he wouldn't have so much time to think. There would be scars, but they would fade.

She turned on her stomach and snuggled against the bed, wide awake. If he were anywhere close to sober, she would let him make love to her. From the kitchen she heard movement and a muffled groan. What in God's name was he doing in there? She lay waiting for him. The mattress pressed against her like it was him. She thought of Clayton and how sad he would be. She thought how, this way, more people would be happy and less people hurt.

She was awakened by the sound of Merle's brogans clumping back to the bedroom. His steps were softer the closer he got because the rugs were thicker. She had no idea what time it was or how long she had slept. The moon was bathing the room in a cold white light. He stood at the doorway, his breathing heavy as if he had come a much greater distance. She pretended to be asleep. He did not flick on the overhead light so she couldn't turn from it as if disturbed.

"Audrey," he said. His voice was thick but with something more than drunkenness. He bumped into the chest of drawers, knocking off one of her framed pictures. She hoped Craig wouldn't wake up. She continued to breathe steadily. She heard her pounding heart echo in the bedsprings.

"Audrey," he said again. She recognized a straining lilt to his voice as if he were trying not to cry. The metal of his belt buckle clicked. He fumbled at the button of his trousers. The room darkened. He stumbled toward the bed, his pants tripping him. Suddenly moonlight whitewashed him and she saw him pushing his underwear down his hips with one hand. The other hand, the one he'd smashed through the door, he held curled at his chest.

"I know you're awake, I saw the light." He had lost track of time too. "*Audrey*." His voice pounded like a wound.

"Hush, Merle. You'll wake up Craig."

He scrambled onto the bed, crawling after her with more agility than he'd managed crossing the floor. She leaped from the bed, throwing covers toward his reaching arm. He groaned angrily.

"Leave me alone, you bastard," she said from the end of the bed. She kept her voice low, hoping to control him that way. The wooden floor was cold. For some reason she thought of her three unpainted toenails.

Then his tone changed. "Come on, Audrey. It's cold out there. Get back in bed."

She wondered if she could trust him. "Let me shut the door."

"I'll get it," he said, but she was faster.

She shut the door. He seemed harmless enough tonight. "Let me help you with your boots," she said, walking around the bed. He obeyed, and she knelt to untie the brittle laces. Usually he would take them off to get his pants off and then put them back on before he slept.

She was loosening the first lace when he grabbed her by her neck. Forcefully he drew her into his spread legs and smashed her face into his genitals. He stank. She cried out in surprise and then was silent, not wanting Craig knocking at the door. He leaned backward on the bed, pulling her on top of him. His boots made loud clumping noises on the floor. She struggled unsuccessfully. She could have clawed him with her fingernails or perhaps kneed him in the groin, but she didn't really want to hurt him.

He gnawed her breasts until she felt sure the skin must be broken. He chewed on her mouth and ran his tongue along the outside of her teeth. The taste of liquor and bile was unbearable. He kept one hand spread as far away from them as he could, but with the other he explored her body with sharp ungentle squeezes. Finally he put his mouth to her, trying to massage sobriety back into his penis with his own hand.

She tried not to let it happen, but she couldn't help herself. It felt so good. And it was really no different from masturbating, not really. As soon as she came, she took herself away from him. He groaned in protest, but not so loudly, and kept moving against her side, her back, her legs, her front. Weaker and weaker thrusts. After a while he fell asleep, and she crawled from under him, yanking her pillow hard from beneath his head. One of them had to work tomorrow, and she doubted it was going to be him. Her pleasurable feeling had subsided. She could have waited for Clayton.

His body stretched awkwardly on the bed, but she didn't straighten him up. This was his punishment: to awake tomorrow as sore and exhausted as she felt now. Let him survive the deathlike sleep of a drunk on his own—neck stretched awkwardly, legs turned wrong, arms twisted—so that even if he could shake the pain of the alcohol, the pain in his muscles would linger on and on. She watched the shadow that was him a moment more. There was no natural movement of his body to straighten itself. He was too numb; perhaps he was even a little bit dead.

She found her nightgown among the sheets and went to the bathroom to examine herself. In the mirror she saw a softness in her eyes that she did not expect, that she immediately tried to get rid of, turning down the corners of her mouth in disgust. The corners of her eyes corresponded. She brushed her teeth and looked angrily into the mirror. She chewed up two aspirin to help her sleep. In Craig's room she slid under the cool covers of the spare bed.

Through her teller's window she smiled at a woman and three small children whose mouths were ringed with chocolate ice cream. But when her mouth stretched and her eyes tightened, she thought she might cry again. She concentrated on the customer. The woman leaned forward on her steering wheel, locking her arms about it like a lover. She did not look at Audrey or at her children. She had acquired so much patience that she was boring herself to death. Audrey put the money and three suckers—all one color—in the metal pocket. The woman reached for her things and said thank you without looking up.

She guessed she was feeling better. All day long she had flinched every time she saw a hand reaching toward her. Thin hands, fat hands, dirty ones, ones manicured and smooth. All healthy, all well. But they seemed to be coming after her. This morning when she slipped into the bedroom to gather her clothes, she had seen what it was that made Merle cry out—a swollen, purple hunk of flesh at the end of his fine muscular arm. A rotten eggplant on a healthy stalk. He groaned painfully in his sleep, and she moved to Craig's room to dress, hurrying him along too so that they would be gone before Merle awakened. When she found the hammer lying at his place on the breakfast table, she pictured the whole scene. She wondered if he would kill himself before it was all over.

She scooted Craig off to his bus before she let herself cry, and then she laid her head down at the very place he had sat and tried to let go. She couldn't cry. She even blinked her eyes several times to start the tears flowing, but nothing happened. You could cry, she guessed, when you still had hope. So she had gone to work, the hardness caught in her throat like a big pill swallowed without enough water. She finished the morning paperwork, still fine. And then she had her first customer and tears began to seep out of her eyes like seeds popping from a grapefruit, just when she thought she would never cry again. Jean, her best friend, asked what was wrong, and she said she thought she was allergic to something—*Merle,* she thought silently—and then nobody had said anything to her all day.

She checked her mirror and saw no one coming. She thought she would have Jean relieve her while she called Clayton. She was ready to get away. Clayton had in mind living in a trailer park on the highway between Durham and Raleigh. Most of his customers lived in this area, he'd said, explaining to her why he didn't want to leave town. It didn't make sense: once you'd put aluminum siding on your house, you didn't really need to buy it again. He said he needed to be around if something ever went wrong. She wanted to go to Florida, but maybe they could compromise and simply leave town.

The telephone rang and her fingers fluttered to it. Just

when she was thinking of him. . . . She let it ring once more while she made up her mind unalterably that she was ready to leave. Of course, she was. She'd been ready for a long time, but Jay's death had gotten in the way. "Hello," she said, hearing a tremble in her voice. She tightened her hand on the receiver to keep it from shaking.

It was Otto. What the hell was going on, he wanted to know, but as soon as she started talking, his tone softened. She doodled her name and Craig's on a scratch pad in front of her. She wrote the *M* of Mitchell over and over, making the humps tall and the tails swirly. Oh Audrey, oh oh Audrey, he said, as she explained what had happened the night before. Tears filled her eyes and she turned her face so that the drops would fall on her lap and not streak whatever make-up she had left. She didn't know what she'd do if she had a customer.

She'd never been so open with Otto, but in the back of her mind something nagged that she'd said enough. Otto's sugary sympathy perhaps. Her words tumbled on out of control: Merle's entrance at midnight—early and, to her, hopeful. The sound of the toolbox scraping along the floor toward a new start. She began crying again, looked up, and saw a car. "Hold on a minute, Otto." She mouthed "Sorry" to the customer so the other girls wouldn't hear. Everybody had trouble and this broad-faced man with thousands of freckles the size of pinpricks looked as if he knew it. He smiled kindly at her, and she organized her face as best she could. He looked as if he might be willing to take her home, and right now she thought she might let him.

Back at the phone she said "Okay," but he had put her on hold. She cradled the receiver against her neck while she found a tissue to mop her eyes and nose. One more customer came and left and then Otto clicked back on the line. She felt that she had to tell him the worst, or it wouldn't seem bad enough. In a rush she said, "Merle hit his hand with his hammer. I heard it, but I didn't know what I was hearing. It was a dull thump, thump, thump. He was killing his hand." To her own ears she sounded hysterical. Deliberately, she dug her nails into her palm. "Afterward he came into the bedroom," she managed more calmly. "He took a long time to unbutton his shirt because he had only his right hand to use. I didn't know what was happening because the lights were out. But I knew something was wrong because . . ." She had told enough.

"Because what?"

"Nothing, nothing. Something you don't want to know."

His voice came thick and choked over the line: "I don't see how you live, honey," he said. "But it's no more than I expected."

A customer drove up, wanting to cash a check for ten dollars, and she made the transaction while talking. "Don't misunderstand," she said. "I only wanted you to know the truth."

"I'd give anything to get you out of this," he said. What did he mean? She had not seen him or Theresa since the funeral and before that, not in six months. Perhaps Otto did feel guilty at having so much when they had so little.

"You're kind," she said, "but it's not your problem."

"I care about you, Audrey." His voice was as soft as the hum of an electric typewriter.

She flushed, caught a glimpse of Jean looking at her, and, with a hand over the receiver, told her, "My brother-in-law."

"Can anyone hear you?" Otto asked, his voice in a higher register of worry.

"Of course not."

He was quiet. Then, "Did you hear me that I care about you?"

"Yes," she said, still uncertain of what he was getting at. "I appreciate it," she added.

"No, I mean it. If it weren't for Theresa . . ."

"Don't, Otto," she said gently. "That's not what I need."

He cleared his throat, the end of a page. The voice remained comforting, but his fever was gone. "I saw him today; that's why I called."

"At work?" she asked eagerly. He might still have shown up.

"Here at the office. Before lunch. I would have called earlier but I was tied up. He still thinks he can draw compensation pay." Otto's voice turned hateful. "He shouldn't have got it the first time, but I was trying to be nice." He paused to clear his throat. She heard him spit into his wastebasket. He resumed in a pleasanter tone: "If I went to court I could block paying him, of course, but, of course . . ."—he giggled at his repetition—". . . I wouldn't do that to you. I've told Merle that the only way I'll continue to give him money is if he gives you a larger share. I want to know if you don't get what you need."

"Thanks," she said, sniffling away from the receiver. "I feel better. Not because of that last, but you know . . ."

"Sure, babe." And then he had to go—someone was calling him from "cross-country," as he put it.

"Babe," "honey"—all new from Otto. Designed to make her feel better, she guessed. He reminded her of a submarine torpedo, looking around for something to explode against. The only thing he had was money, and she knew from Theresa's comments that it didn't flow without a lot of lubrication. Now if there was a man with Merle's looks and Otto's wherewithal, that would be a man. Not quite Clayton, but Clayton had other things, namely a good nature, and right now anyway, she thought that was worth the other two put together.

On her way home she decided to drive by Otto's office. She had not seen it in a year, since the newspaper had written its article about him. For the occasion of the interview, Otto had landscaped the entire grounds with boxwoods no bigger than croquet balls. He had also dug huge wavy beds in no particular sequence or shape—which later he bragged about—and planted them sparsely with pachysandra. Merle was dying for her to see it, so she'd gone.

Otto had happened to be outside inspecting his grounds. She congratulated him on the newspaper article which had appeared that morning. He said he thought he might be nominated for a City Beautiful Award next; the City Beautiful coordinator had driven by several times and once she stepped out of her car and came to the front door.

They had walked together around most of the beds. Graciously he offered her pachysandra for her own yard when it got thick enough here. She thought that might take about ten years. He explained seriously that the reason he'd done all this was that he felt a responsibility to the people of Durham not only to make the company a good employer, but also to make the physical plant an attractive place to ride by on Sunday afternoons. He had lifted his shoulders and turned up the palms of both hands, full of his own generosity. She had almost reminded him that the interview was over.

For a whole evening she and Merle had giggled. When one of them lapsed into silence, the other called out "pachysandra" or "the good of the com*moon*ity" or "I can't hammer a nail straight"—which to Merle's amazement Otto had admitted to the reporter. They had shared several beers. It had been one of their happiest evenings.

She turned into the employees' parking lot. Otto's baby-blue Cadillac sat with the top down. She wondered how Theresa felt when she rode around town with Otto. Pretty rich, she supposed, even though money was wasted on Theresa. She spent it, but on things like crystal goblets and copper pots, never on herself. She still wore her ten-year-old house dress shopping in Raleigh, and at the grocery store you could usually see a quarter-inch stubble of hair on her legs. She never bothered to wash her hair so it was always tied up in a scarf. Audrey wasn't sure she'd recognize her bareheaded.

If it were *she* riding around Durham, the convertible wouldn't mean a thing, only Otto's generosity. Well. . . . For a moment she commiserated with Mrs. Got Rocks, as Merle called her. After a while the money must not matter so much if every afternoon a torpedo smelling like a lemon drop comes home to you. Perhaps that was why Theresa let herself go like she did—to keep Otto out of her bed.

She thought about dropping in now and saying hello. The reason Otto had attracted the *Herald's* attention was because through all his promotions he'd kept the same basement office that he'd started in. Merle said that as soon as the article appeared, Otto had moved upstairs. She was mildly curious whether or not that were true. She would also like to see if Marilyn Monroe's bosoms had popped the wallpaper off Otto's office walls yet, as Merle had always predicted they would.

One of the side doors of the building, flanked by boxwoods not visibly larger than last year, opened, and a group of women came out. She shouldn't be seen cruising around Otto's parking lot. In the past Theresa had confided that she kept friends among the secretaries to watch Otto for her.

She speeded away from the building not sure now why she had come. Tonight instead of cooking, she would take Craig to the drive-in for some barbecue. Merle, she was sure, had been at some bar all afternoon trying to numb the pain of his hand. She needed to explain to Craig some things about his father. She also needed to make plans for him to start going to Mrs. Rice's again in the afternoon. She wondered if he'd gotten the message she'd sent to school today. He would hate not going home in the afternoon, but she couldn't let him be exposed to Merle day after day. He would have to go to Mrs. Rice's until she thought of something better.

Things might have been different if Merle and Otto had gotten along. If Merle had ever honestly thought that building houses was as important as figuring out what they would cost. The two of them might have left Mr. Martin and organized their own company. Heavens, there was enough work. Actually, Merle wouldn't have needed Otto if Jay had lived and meant what he said. That was another thing that had disappeared with Jay: Merle's future.

She tried to be realistic because maybe Jay hadn't meant a word of it. Maybe it had been something to talk about, to amuse Merle with when there was nothing particularly amusing around. But, a couple of months after Jay and Melissa were married, he began dropping by at midnight for a beer. One beer became two and so on. They sat at the kitchen table and in low tones talked "serious business." When Jay left, Merle would come to bed wanting to make love. He would never tell her what they said, but a new intensity filled his eyes and he'd speak of "giving old Otto a run for his money." It didn't take a genius to guess what he meant.

Jay had seemed less interested in college, but he was also changing in other ways, she noticed. The few times she ventured into the kitchen to try to hear what they were saying, *Jay* was giving *Merle* a run, matching him can for can of beer and building a pyramid with the empties. His eyes had a thin glaze, and it was then that he began hugging her flirtatiously and not filially as before. He did not seem to want to let her go. He acted less and less like a stepson. When she left, the low hum of conversation resumed. She'd lain in her bed dreaming of a name for the business. She dreamed of keeping its books. In the unambiguous light of day she knew nothing would come of it. Then Melissa miscarried—if she had ever been pregnant at all—and Jay was drafted.

4

CRAIG

"Squirrels are sitting ducks the way Dad hunts," Jay had said. "I mean, you're there in your nest minding your own business and suddenly a couple of bullets whiz through the floor. Think about it. What chance do you have?" He turned the corner and stopped in front of Bessie's Do Drop In to let Craig out. He gave his order quickly as if he had come up for a breath of air: "Three with chili, mustard, and slaw," as if Craig didn't know. He started talking again about the fairness of hunting even though Craig was getting out of the car. His animated face nodded at things he said that he particularly agreed with. He kept talking as he drove off; Craig could see his moving mouth.

The same two old women that Craig had known for years bustled about behind a long counter, their tempo increasing as he entered. Someone had told him they were deaf. They spoke rarely (he had never heard them, but Jay had), took orders without comment, gave change without saying they hoped you enjoyed their food. But they had always been particularly kind to Craig and his family. When Dad used to bring the family downtown on Saturday afternoons, one of them would always fix the Mitchells' order ahead of everyone else's. Mom used to kid Dad about being friendly with Bessie, whichever one she was.

They timed it well: Jay turned the corner to pick him up just as Craig walked out the door with lunch. "Ready," he said, and then felt foolish for saying anything. All their lives they had been together, but now that Jay had gone off to college they hardly saw each other. There wasn't time for casual talk. The smell of hot dogs filled the car too soon after breakfast. Jay decided to put the sack in the trunk. In the middle of the street he gave a hand signal, jumped out of the car, and hurried to the back. Four cars were stopped behind them. Jay waved amiably at them and the woman in the next car waved back. He had that effect on people.

Later, Jay had asked him how he liked the seventh grade. "Fine, except for the teachers," Craig said. Jay tried to laugh, but Craig could see it was hard for him. Teachers were people his brother loved. Jay ignored the comment, his face more clouded than Craig thought he deserved. Then he gave his standard lecture about taking advantage of your opportunities, working hard now because it will make a difference later, blah blah blah.

"A poor kid has to stay on the right track his whole life," he had said. "The only way you'll get anywhere is by not fucking up." Craig looked at him in astonishment; Jay didn't talk like that. He continued, not noticing: "Why, you can get messed up inside of . . . two weeks. . . ." His voice trailed off and he turned up the radio. With his high-school ring he drummed the steering wheel in time to the music. When he knew the words he sang along; he moved in his seat to the rhythm. Every once in a while, he offered Craig that open-mouthed smile of his that didn't look like a smile at all. Craig stretched, raising his arms above his head until they touched the roof. When the song ended, he turned the dial looking for a new one.

They had driven for twenty minutes to the rich unposted fields outside Durham. Dove season had just opened and the birds, not wise to it yet, lined the telephone wires. Conversation between them limped. Craig asked if he liked college and Jay said of course he did. Craig heard "stupid" on the end of the sentence. Jay was curious whether Craig had enjoyed *A Boy's Look at Jefferson.* He said yes: he hadn't had time to finish it, but what he'd read so far was pretty good. Luckily Jay didn't press him on how many pages he'd read, which was three. To make him feel better, Craig said that he'd listened to Sharon Fritts play her piano lesson last week, which wasn't true, and that he'd checked out another book the same day he'd gotten the one about Jefferson. Only he couldn't remember the name of it. "It's hard to think about all that stuff when you're not around," he blurted. What was the point anyway, when the only reason he did things like that was for Jay?

"You're going to have to learn to work on your own, Craig," Jay had lectured. "I'm off at college, Dad and Audrey are gone all day, you've got to depend on yourself."

At the field they had loaded their guns in silence, and then the anticipation of hunting seemed to warm them to each other again. Jay said: "Look, I'm sorry I haven't been home. I've been busy. The work is so hard. College is different from regular life."

Regular life. Craig thought of their rock collection in four boxes under Jay's bed. He thought of lying together in the hammock, reading Archie comic books, and how now, without Jay, the ropes weren't steady in the wind. He thought of the hidden clearing, half a mile from home, where once a year they mixed their blood. "No big deal," he said.

"Audrey said you'd really been lonely." Jay moved closer to him, trying to force out the truth.

"I haven't," Craig said. Well, he had, but not that much.

The fields were dark orange from all the rain they had been having. He followed Jay, stepping in the impressions of his heavy waterproof boots. He had only tennis shoes. Jay left him at a clump of rye grass and headed across the field to where the scraggly growth picked up again. He squatted behind some weeds so that only his barrel showed. Craig scanned the perfect gray sky and saw a single bird behind Jay, but it was the wrong kind. His nose dripped because of the dry field grass. He set the butt of the gun beside him on the ground and blew his nose into his hand. It was wet but not slimy. He rubbed his hand on a tuft of stiff grass and dust caked his fingers. He wiped his nose tenderly on his sleeve. To his right, not so high up, he saw a small flock which was going to cross directly over him. His hand slipped on the barrel from perspiration. When they were too close to veer away, he stood up. He crooked his finger around the trigger. There was a loud report. Short tufts of grass stuck into his back through his shirt. His left hand lay in a puddle, the gun beyond it. He hadn't expected to fall down.

"You got one," Jay yelled. He felt his sore shoulder where the gun had bumped him and hoped for a big bruise. He saw that his barrel had gotten muddy.

His brother dashed toward him across the field. "You okay?"

Craig nodded, feeling the last trace of awkwardness between them dissolve. He wiped the muddied barrel on the bottom of his pants leg. "Where is it?" he asked, the line of his chin stiff and manly. Jay held open his arms, and laughing sheepishly, Craig moved into them for a hug. He winced at the pressure on his sore shoulder. He felt too old for this kind of affection. He held the gun carefully pointed away.

"What were you doing shooting both barrels at the same time?"

So that's what had happened. "Just wanted to make sure I got one," he said, grinning. "Look at the strawberry I have coming." He rolled up his sleeve. The skin was bright pink on his upper arm and chest. After a few minutes of searching, they found the first bird Craig had ever shot dead on a stretch of red mud.

Not until midafternoon had they gone to the car for lunch. Mom's breakfast had lasted them both a long time. The hot dogs were cold and greasy, but anything would have tasted good. Jay asked if Dad were all right. He had visited him in the bedroom this morning, but Dad hadn't wanted to go hunting with them.

"I guess," Craig answered. He hadn't realized there was anything unusual.

"What's he working on now?"

"Remodeling Uncle Otto's house."

"You better believe he loves *that,*" Jay said.

Late in the afternoon when the sun was hurrying toward new places, Jay had taken him on a driving tour of the Duke University campus. The rose-colored light transformed the stone buildings into gingerbread houses. They drove past Jay's dorm, a red brick building with the plainness of feature of their own house until Dad had painted it maroon. Jay stopped the car. "Why don't I show you my room?" he asked, surprise in his voice for not thinking of it earlier. Since Mom's supper hour was upon them, they had to hurry.

Walking across the courtyard, Craig had seen young men coming from all directions, most of them serious-faced with dark hair and olive-to-paper-white complexions. None seemed to have the fair hair and the healthy good looks of his brother. Jay said they were on their way to the dining room for supper. Where did they all come from? Foreign countries? The North? They didn't look like people he knew. Everyone seemed in a hurry as if they hardly had time to eat.

Jay's blue and green plaid bedspread from home shocked him into a sense of familiarity. Maybe this was their room, transported. He sat on Jay's roommate's bed, crossing one leg over the other. He saw on Jay's desk his school picture from last year; he looked like a kid. Maybe Jay would let him come live here.

Jay explained that he was in one of the newer dormitories, and that nowadays, architects didn't believe students needed much room. At Duke you were supposed to study in the library anyway. Even after their small room at home, Craig thought that this space must be hard to get used to.

"I wanted you to see it," Jay had said, waiting for a response that Craig didn't know how to give.

"It's a nice room," he managed, but he felt rotting jealousy. Of Jay, of Jay's roommate, of Jay's own room. Of a room that Jay didn't share with him. "It's not as nice as ours," he added brusquely.

"Of course not," Jay'd said. He swallowed like his throat hurt. He sat down beside Craig, but before he spoke he had to choke back one thick sob. "I'm really sorry," he said. Craig looked solemnly at him, pretending to know what he meant. Maybe Jay didn't like college so much after all.

Jay draped his thin arm around Craig's shoulders. "I do miss you, buddy." He gave him a squeeze. With more enthusiasm he added, "I want to show you something. While we still have time."

They had gone back to the car, driven a quarter of a mile, and stopped in front of the famous chapel. The last piece of the sun lit the solemn steeples. The solid gray bird-hunting sky had broken into wispy clouds. "Makes you want to cry, doesn't it?" Jay said. The car crept more slowly than they would have walked. "I wanted to get married there." He looked guiltily at Craig as if he were sorry he had said that much. "Of course, not now," he'd added hastily, breaking into a trembling new kind of laugh.

The sun shone in behind her when she walked through the front door so that he could not really see her, only that she was mostly bright green like tended grass. She had worn a green wool dress with matching jacket. Her green high heels flashed at him. Tinted stockings made her legs look like lichen-covered trees. A real beauty, Jay had said. She had no ankles, her legs rising out of her shoes without an inward slant. He glanced at his mother's legs which were thin and ordinary.

The door closed and his eyes again grew accustomed to the dimmer living-room light. Her lips were pink, thick greasy pink, like pieces of cotton candy rolled into worms. Her eyes and eyelids were green too, not the color of the dress, but lighter like her legs. Her eyelashes were very long and when she blinked, it seemed as if they lagged sleepily behind her lids.

Wow, he thought, but everyone turned to him and laughed, so it seemed he had spoken instead. His neck grew as warm as a potholder.

"See?" Jay said, as if he had proved something.

"Oooh, what a darling child." She walked to him, her stockings whispering, and kissed his nose. She smelled like a department store.

Jay announced that this was Melissa as if they didn't know. She was not what Craig expected.

Dad smiled. He shook Melissa's hand not at her waist, but up close to her chest which stuck out a lot farther than Mom's did. It was as if they already knew each other. Melissa stood a fraction taller. He whispered to her and they turned their faces to Jay.

"Cut it out, Dad," Jay said kiddingly, but Craig thought he meant it.

"This your girl? I thought you brought her home to me."

Melissa pushed Dad's hand back from her, her cotton candy mouth forming a circle. She said what a pleasure it was to meet the family. Mom offered to take her jacket, but she said she would keep it on awhile, thank you. "Audrey?" she said, repeating Mom's name to be sure she had it. "And Merle," smiling again at Dad. Her hands were reddish with freckles and her fingernails had paint the color of her lips. Her eyebrows were pointed like arrowheads.

"Hiya, little brother," Jay said, cradling the back of

Craig's head in his palm. He looked tired, the same as last weekend when they went hunting.

Mom offered them a seat.

"You think this yellow velvet will come off on my suit?" Melissa asked, leaning down and brushing the couch. Mom said she doubted it. Melissa examined her hand and sat down, crossing her legs grandly so that Craig could see the suspenders holding up her hose. The foot of her crossed leg rested lightly on the coffee table.

"Would you be more comfortable in a chair?" Mom asked.

"Oh, no, besides, I can have Jay's little brother sit right here beside me." He wiggled up next to her, and she laid one hand on his knee and took Jay's hand with her other.

Later they made him go out of the room although the walls were so thin he could hear everything. Jay was getting married to Melissa. The wedding was going to be Monday afternoon at the justice of the peace's office after Jay's biology lab. They were all invited. The living room was as silent as pine woods. Jay continued his monotone. He would finish his freshman year. Then he would defer the remaining three years of his scholarship for one year more. He would lose nothing. In fact he thought he actually might gain. He needed some time out in the world so that he could discover exactly what he wanted to do. He was no longer sure he wanted to be a professor. "I think I'll probably discover what I *don't* want to do, but that will help too. Make me make a decision. Then when I go back . . ."

"You're quitting?" Dad bellowed, finally responding. Craig lurched on the end of his bed, startled. He guessed they all had grabbed hold of whatever was nearest. "Getting married to this *whore*?" It was like he had just woken up. "Have you lost your mind, Jay? Have you lost your *mind*?"

No one said a word, and then Craig heard the front door slam.

"*Merle,*" Mom chastised.

"I knew this would happen," Jay said. There was something lifeless in his voice.

Dad's tone suddenly changed. "Oh . . . I get it. You're in trouble. You've gotten this whore pregnant and you think that because I want you to go to college I'll bail you out. I'll tell you one goddamn thing. I'm not paying for no goddamn abortion."

"It will only be for a year, Dad." Jay's voice was agitated. "I've already figured it out. I'm going to work like crazy. Two, maybe three jobs, until I get enough money to pay for the baby and a place for us to live and food . . ."

"Has she been messing around with anybody else? Can she prove it was you?"

"I'm not going to do that to her."

"Not going to . . . shit. What do you think she's trying to do to you?"

"She wants a father for her baby."

"She has a choice? Not that I'm surprised. I could have laid her if I'd seen her first."

"Will you shut up?" Jay was crying. "Things will work out," he said.

Dad's voice grew softer. "Will you tell me what's wrong with an abortion?" Craig cracked his door so he wouldn't miss anything.

"She's Catholic."

"She don't look Catholic." Silence. "What will she do if you don't marry her?"

"Nothing. Sue me. I don't know."

"So she's forcing you into this."

"If she's going to have it, I feel like it's my duty to stick around."

"Listen, son, give this up. Maybe I can find the money for an abortion."

"That's out, Dad, just don't even consider it."

"Why not?"

"Because . . . she was an abortion that didn't take."

"What?"

"Her mother went to have an abortion, the woman was a quack and didn't get Melissa. Her mother was too scared to go back so she just had her."

"You believe that?" The living room was quiet for a long time. Craig began to wonder if they had all left. Finally, Dad began to speak: "When I was your age, I was going to try too, but it never quite worked out. You came along, and then the apartment got too crowded for your mother and we had to move to a larger one. There was always something else. She wanted some new furniture and she wanted to dress you up. There was nothing left to try *with*. Don't you see? Don't you *see*? When you spend every cent you make, you gotta keep working. You can't ever stop." The room was quiet again. Dad yelled, "I feel like I'm talking to a goddamn brick wall."

Jay's voice had calmed. "I need your help, Dad, not this."

"I can't pay your way."

"I didn't ask you to." But the conviction in his voice was weaker than before.

Someone stood up and walked across the room. "You're a goddamn fool," Dad said, his voice floating from a new position. There was a loud smack of flesh on flesh. The front door opened again. "You ask one hell of a fucking lot," he yelled at the top of his voice. The never-used front door slammed again.

When Craig came out into the hall, Jay was hugging Mom, his cheek pressing tight against her hair. His brimming eyes found Craig. Dad's car skidded out of the driveway and down the street. With his arms still holding Mom, Jay opened out his hands, large beautiful hands with slender fingers, for Craig to hold or touch. But Craig waited a moment too long, not going to Jay when he should have, not taking those hands when he could.

The front door clicked open. "That was nice," Melissa said. She reminded Craig of a snake. Mom and Jay broke their embrace. Mom told Melissa not to worry about Merle, he was just upset about Jay leaving college. A meaningless smile strained across Jay's face. His eyes—the tears gone—looked nowhere.

"There you are, you darling boy," Melissa said. She patted the sofa again. "Come sit with me."

Craig wanted to sock her. "I don't want to," he said.

"Be a little brat," she'd said, but nobody seemed to notice. She frowned at Craig, and he'd hated her like he hated this whole wide world.

He was halfway through a long drag on a Camel in the school bathroom when Miss Salmon's voice crackled over the loudspeaker. "Would Craig Mitchell—crackle crackle—for a message." Reflexively he got rid of his cigarette on the gray cement floor. At the sink he swished water through his teeth to weaken the tobacco odor. Outside the bathroom he hurried through the crowd of kids leaving school for the day. No one but him, he noticed, ever bothered to sneak a smoke after the dismissal bell although there were ten minutes before the buses left.

The school secretary, a small blond woman who always commented if you were much taller than she, leaned forward in her chair, making her small waist look smaller and her chest larger. She handed him a pink memo slip. He felt her eyes playing on his face as he read. The message was from Mom. He was to go to Mrs. Rice's house this afternoon after all. She would explain when he got home.

"Did I take it down right?" Miss Salmon interrupted.

He nodded, not wanting her to realize how angry he was, and slipped out the tall doorway. If he had left the building when the bell rang, he'd never have gotten this message. When was Mom going to realize that she didn't have to protect him from anything. What did she think he might do? He kicked at a loose stone which connected with a girl's ankle a couple of yards ahead on the crumbly sidewalk.

"Ouch," she said, looking over her shoulder. Her pony-tail bobbed in the air. Beyond her he could see buses pulling out of the parking lot.

"Sorry." He touched her arm as he ran by. It was firm and its warmth clung to his fingers like a cobweb. He surprised himself by winking at her, and she surprised him by smiling back. "I'll see you tomorrow," he called. He didn't even know who she was.

He had to knock on the door to get the attention of the driver, a middle-aged man who drove with his eyes half-closed. He worked three jobs, he'd told them, because he'd never gotten enough education to hold one decent one. Craig slid into the seat behind him. "Let me off at my house today," he said. He would pretend to Mom that he hadn't gotten her message. He knew she would never call school to check.

The noise of the kids behind him buoyed his spirits. He was not so friendly with any of them since the Monday after Jay's funeral when he'd gotten on the bus and not known exactly how to act. Some of the girls had cried which he himself hadn't done yet. Not because he wasn't sad but because at the time he didn't totally believe Jay was dead. Sometimes now he didn't believe it. The bus had been hushed except for the sniffles and hiccups of the crying girls. The knocking engine had reminded him of Dad's brogans clomping down the aisle at the funeral. He felt strangely back there for a moment. Then a voice that he recognized as his own said, "Look at that stupid wreath." On his front door was a black crepe wreath with ribbon streamers that lay lifeless in the muggy September air. It looked like an old lady's hat. Everyone had stared, but no one answered. They kept looking out the windows the rest of the way to school.

Later that week he had begun getting off at Mrs. Rice's house, and the other kids avoided looking at him even more. He couldn't explain to them. He hadn't been sent to

Mrs. Rice's house in four years. Mom said she didn't want him disturbing Dad while his hand healed. But Dad's hand had hardly bothered him after the first week. Dad had gone back to work today, so finally he was allowed to go home. At least before Mom's message.

He had used to like Mrs. Rice. When he was a little boy, Jay took him to visit her, pretending that she was their grandmother since they didn't have one alive. She always had ideas of things to do. Once she and Jay took him on a scavenger hunt around the neighborhood and collected a kitten (the list said catnip) from a new litter that Mom had actually let him keep. Sometimes, whether it was Christmas or not, they would string popcorn and cranberries on thread to drape on a tree outside his and Jay's window. Once the three of them had ridden downtown on the bus which Dad hadn't liked since they had a car and didn't need public transportation.

Now Mrs. Rice only sat and crocheted, looking at him as if he were somebody she didn't know or as if he should *be* someone else. Each day he would burst through her back door in a dead run from the school bus, hoping she would be the way she used to be, but she never was. An ancient radio blared gospel music from the kitchen. She looked at him, her thick hands working a crochet stitch as if she had not been asleep. Of course, she had. She blinked her blue eyes dry, trying to remember who he was. When she remembered him, she would offer a snack and remind him that he had to stay until five, his mother's orders. Inside or out, she didn't care. But the house was full of porcelain objects that he was afraid he might break, and the yard was clumps of dried-out grass that he could cross in one running broadjump. She never watered it because she didn't want it to grow because then she would have to pay someone to mow it. He wondered if watching him was how she got money. If she would just let him go home, he told her he would mow her grass for free.

"My dad needs me," he'd said yesterday, loudly so that she could hear him over the radio.

She raised a finger to her cheek until she remembered and when she did, she resumed crocheting. She answered in a small deliberate voice that discouraged questions. "No, he doesn't." She beckoned him to her, rubbing the back of his head with a hand as rough as a potato chip. He didn't understand why she said that. He waited for her to fall asleep from the rhythm of the music and her moving hands. Her head dropped by quarter inches, and then her eyes, and then all motion ceased as she leaned forward, the baby sweater half-fallen out of her hands, so far forward that she looked as if she were about to stand up. He tiptoed under the crackly details of a fair-skies report, held the door until it caught quietly, and ran.

His feet had flown for him, perfectly nimble as he ran through yards, jumped ditches and curves, picked up speed along cement. Mrs. Rice could bolt awake at any moment if some loud commercial came on the air. He just wanted a quick visit with his father who then might telephone Mrs. Rice and explain the situation. He turned the corner to his house in a slump in the lay of the land, a purple Tootsie Roll Pop among cream mints. His father's white Chevrolet, wheels at a jazzy angle, sat in front of an unknown junky Ford. He circled the house away from the Kings' side so that Paulette wouldn't see him. At the back corner he scanned the yard for anything unusual but saw only the expected: the rotting gray hammock deep in the yard where Jay used to read, his old sandbox with no sand, a weathered picnic table spattered polka dot by bird droppings. Wild rose bushes bloomed along the back fence.

For some reason the screen was off Mom and Dad's bedroom window. Out of it flapped faded blue curtains, their nickel weights knocking lightly against the sash. Craig crept on his knees. The grass close to the house was thick and cushiony. A smell of cigarettes floated to him. He crawled directly underneath the window. A lady giggled. Then she said, Ouch, what did you want to go and do that for? Who do you think you are anyway? Dad whooped like an Indian. Who do you think you are? Why was that funny? Craig slid away from the window while laughter still covered his movement. When he reached the opposite corner of the house, he could still hear the harsh noise. Long blocks away it had sounded in his ears like a jackhammer tearing up a street, and he'd had to shake his head to be rid of it.

The school bus trembled in neutral gear while the orphanage kids trudged out. Craig moved to the middle of the bus to get away from the driver's unwashed smell. Sometimes he thought that Jay had been dead forever. Other times, though, he forgot that it had even happened. Then the hope of a trip to visit him would enter his mind. Or he'd think about writing him a letter. Or he'd open his mouth—but remember in time—to ask Mom if they could call and see how he was. The worst had been today when a new girl at school, Janie Jackson, asked if he had any brothers and sisters. He'd answered one brother before he remembered. Why did he keep forgetting? He was ashamed to tell Janie none anymore, so he didn't talk to her again. Could Jay not be dead and that be the reason he kept having these feelings?

The stupid bus driver stopped for him to get off at Mrs. Rice's. He motioned for him to go on, but the old man didn't see, head ducked waiting for some feet to slide by. Craig had to announce in front of the five kids left that he was getting off at home from now on. The door slammed shut, the buzz of conversation halted. He wondered what they all thought. No one had asked him anything, not even Marcia Livengood, his neighbor across the street. A few minutes later he followed Marcia's red pigtails out of the bus. She didn't even turn around and speak.

No Mrs. Rice. No stale snacks. No remarks about his father. But the driveway was empty. He thought of Dad lying in bed recuperating all these weeks, and how he'd never been home to keep him company. Craig dragged his feet. Fuck, he said. Fuck, fuck, fuck. Someone had said it on the bus this afternoon, the first time he'd heard it spoken aloud by anyone but his father and Jay. He liked the way his teeth scraped his bottom lip when he said it. He swung his foot at a rock in the middle of the driveway. Now it was too late to keep Dad company. Trudging up the side steps, he wished he felt enough anger to put his fist through the pane beside the one that Dad broke. He wished he'd been here to do it at the same time. But he was always being shuffled into some closet by Mom so he couldn't see for himself what was happening.

He faced the door, his eyes level with the white cardboard. He wondered if Dad would get around to fixing the broken pane any time soon. Perhaps it should stay that way, even in winter, a reminder of the night Jay died. Who would fix it anyway? Mom? You don't hire a repairman for one pane, and Dad always refused to do jobs around the house, telling Mom she ought to hire a carpenter. He thought that was a great joke, and Craig did too, sort of.

What would it feel like, he wondered, hitting his fist into his palm. Mom had knocked out the remaining jagged pieces of glass still firm in the frame, until the hole was smooth and safe. Then she'd cut a piece of cardboard from one of Dad's shirts to fit. He guessed he could practice on the cardboard, drive his fist through it to see what the moment of contact felt like. Then, drive his fist through the pane next to Dad's. He rubbed his hand. Knowing his luck, he wouldn't even get cut. And then Dad would say he'd used a rock because he was too chicken to use his hand. He stood in front of the door for a long time.

When he decided he might bleed to death with nobody here, he reached for the key under the rubber mat. The key was gone, but then he noticed that the door was not completely closed. As he pushed into the kitchen, Dad called from the back: "Fix yourself a snack, son, and come on in here."

Barechested, Dad sat in bed propped against the cool plaster wall. The sheet stretched high over the rounded toes of his brogans and then lightly covered him to his waist. He was not looking at a magazine or drinking a beer or smoking a cigarette. Just waiting, it seemed. Craig could have kicked himself for wasting ten minutes outside. He walked around the bed to his mother's side, balancing a bottle of Tru-Ade, crackers, the peanut-butter jar, and a knife.

"I was wondering when you were going to get here," Dad said.

Did he mean today or the whole four weeks? Craig opened the jar of peanut butter. He'd forgotten a paper towel.

"If you're going to spill crumbs, keep them on your mother's side," Dad said, winking.

"Think I should get a towel?"

"Hell no. She don't care." His voice was gruff but intimate. "About nothing," he added.

Craig spread peanut butter. "How come you're home?" he asked. "Mom said you were going back to work today." He thought for a moment that someone else was talking. His voice sounded unfamiliar like on a tape recorder.

"Screw work."

Craig looked up, trying to fight off the giddiness he felt.

"Screw work. And screw Otto." Dad smiled as if they shared a secret. "You disagree?"

Craig liked Uncle Otto, but if Dad didn't, maybe there was something he didn't know. "Heck no," he blurted, and Dad nodded as if he'd said the right thing.

"How about spreading one of those for me."

Craig sat cross-legged. His tennis shoes were muddy but Dad didn't seem to mind. In fact he dipped his head once like the beginning of a nod. Craig prepared a cracker, working on the peanut butter until it perfectly covered the whole surface. He stuck the knife into the jar with the flourish of a chef. When he looked up, he saw a huge hand coming toward him, blue and ugly, open like a strangler's. He pushed to the edge of the bed before remembering that the hand was his father's.

"What happened?" he asked breathlessly. Only last night, or was it the night before, he'd noticed Dad's hand being almost well. Not last night. Dad hadn't come home until after he was asleep. Earlier though, his hand had been nearly well; only tiny stitches like the binding of a baseball showed that anything was wrong.

"It looks like a jellyfish," Craig said, but Dad didn't smile. "Does it hurt bad?" he asked quickly.

"Depends on whether you're a man or not." He held out the hand to receive his cracker, and Craig placed it there carefully. "No, not particularly. Not anymore."

Craig couldn't take his eyes off it. With his well hand Dad picked the cracker off the jellyfish. He held the jellyfish flat, turning it palm up and then palm down, letting it swim before Craig's eyes. "What happened?" he asked again.

"Relapse," Dad said.

"Relapse?"

Dad explained how early this morning he had been awakened by a terrible pain and when he became sure that this was not another dream about Jay, he opened his eyes. His hand lay before him on the pillow as if it were a creature separate from him. First it began itching under the surface but as he reached with his other hand to scratch it, it began trembling. The trembling grew violent. His skin turned the orange of a stove eye and the scars from the old injury lighted up the color of blood. An intense heat began issuing from his hand, but the hand itself wasn't hot. Suddenly it swelled like a bladder after five beers. He closed his eyes and waited for it to explode. He figured he must have passed out from the pain because when he woke up, it looked like this.

Craig didn't understand. "How?" he asked tentatively, afraid that "how" had already been answered.

"Don't you see? My hand wasn't ready to have the stitches out. It wasn't ready to work again, hammering for your rich uncle. It said no. . . . Just like Jay."

Craig took a long draught of Tru-Ade, looking at his father down the side of the bottle. He put a whole cracker in his mouth so he wouldn't be expected to talk right away. He didn't understand. Perhaps he would if Dad explained the connection with Jay. "What do you mean . . . like Jay?" Several crumbs of saltines dived from his mouth.

"You remember. When he had his nervous breakdown and the Army wouldn't discharge him."

Craig nodded, unsure.

"Jay's whole body had a relapse. Only my hand did. When they wouldn't let him go, his body rebelled and . . ."

"Hung itself?" Craig finished.

"Sort of. Anyway, I think somebody up there"—he pointed at the ceiling with his thumb—"means for me not to go back to work. And I wanted to explain it to you first. Your mother will have something else to say, I'm sure."

Craig began spreading another cracker.

"I'll never forget that horrible explosion in the middle of my hand." Dad looked out the window the way he did when he talked about the war.

Craig thought Dad had been unconscious when his hand exploded. But he decided just to nod. He offered Dad another cracker.

"Your mother's sorry this happened," he said, raising his hand slightly.

"Me too."

"Not for the same reason though. She wants me away from here. Working. So I can't talk to my boy."

Craig did not laugh out loud the way he wanted to. He did not cut a flip off the bed or jump in the air to shake the tension out of his bones. He started tightening his legs at his toes, working up past his calves and thighs, and then he relaxed the muscles in the reverse order. He did the same thing with his arms. It was a trick Jay had taught him to help bring sleep. He thought it might relax him as well.

"Dad," he said, waiting to see what reception he got. His voice sounded like his own now. "Is Jay really dead?"

Dad's jaw jerked like a soldier's. His blue eyes looked for a joke. Craig put his hand on the bed nearer him, but he didn't notice. "Well, I don't know, son." His thick lips pursed, considering. "I've thought he was, but I didn't actually see his body. Your mother probably knows better." So he would ask her next.

Craig no longer felt compelled to look at Dad's hand. They were both silent, but not uncomfortably. Dad was getting ready to say something. "I-I've been wondering," he began, "how you like school this year?" He mumbled Jay's name and then he said clearly: "Jay always kept track of you before." He cleared his throat several times. "He did." His voice trailed off.

"I like school fine," Craig said, and then again: "Fine." The word rose in the air like a wall. He frantically searched for more to say, but his mind was empty. He liked art. "I like art," he said.

"Art?"

"Not art really. I like my art teacher."

"Oh." Dad lit a cigarette. "Nice knockers, huh?" He riveted his gaze to Craig's face.

Craig nodded, his face a pincushion of red. Miss Robinson didn't have hardly any knockers at all.

"Would you get me a beer?"

He leaped from the bed. On the way to the kitchen, every step jarred his stomach, and his eyes burned from looking at things. He felt the coolness of the air racing into his lungs. The beer can fogged over when he touched it. As he walked back to the bedroom, he held it once to each cheek. He felt exuberant and terrified in the same moment. Terrified that things would change while he was gone or that Dad might not really be there at all.

For hours they talked. No one had ever told Craig anything about Dad's side of the family except that they lived in southern Georgia near where Jay had been stationed. Now he found out that his uncles, other than Uncle Otto, were half uncles because they were Dad's half brothers. Dad's father—Craig's grandfather—had abandoned the family for the warmer climate of Mexico. For five years Dad had eaten turnips until he thought he was going to turn into one. Then the wife of the blacksmith died in childbirth, and his mother had married him. "Momma started having babies all over again," Dad said. It was odd hearing his father talk about having a mother. "About that time, me and Otto decided we were old enough to make our own way. I was about your age and Otto was sixteen. We headed north for factory jobs and wound up here." Dad drained what was left of his fourth beer. Craig's stomach trembled, knowing he would have to get him another and fearing again that Dad would be different when he came back.

"You think *we're* poor," he said. "You ought to see how they live. Why Abner only added a commode last year. They'd been walking to an outhouse all their lives—those pretty little cousins of yours too." Craig had already formed a mental picture of his uncles and their wives—dark-skinned, wrinkled people, thin with gapes in their throats where the flesh had sunk in. He imagined his cousins wearing hats that had failed at protecting them from the sun and faded gray dresses that had begun to shrivel around the hem and sleeves.

"I used to try to get Abner and Stewart to come up here," Dad said. "Told them Otto would give them a job if they'd just show up one day. Whether he would have or not,

I can't guess. But they thought they knew him better than I did, so they stayed home."

Dad was quiet. The peanut-butter jar sat closed on the bed. Craig had been thirsty from the crackers a good hour, but he wouldn't take a chance on leaving. Let Dad end it. Craig would sit here dry-mouthed until he had no more to say.

"I'm not going to talk about your uncle," he said. "He's done well for himself. I'd call him a millionaire, as a matter of fact. At least one million. Sure he's stepped on people on the way up—including your patsy dad here—but he'd say that he had to.

"We're like Jacob and Esau. You know that story?"

Craig shook his head.

"Jacob stole Esau's birthright, meaning everything that was rightfully his. And Otto stole mine. Someday he'll pay, only it looks like it's not going to be on this earth."

Dad stared out the window where Craig had noticed the old hammock shifting in the October breeze. The bedroom was growing dim as the sun set over the front of the house. Dad snapped his fingers in a pretense of waking from a spell. "Well," he said.

An ache in Craig's throat moved like molasses toward his nervous stomach. (*Mole*-asses, Dad had said over and over again this afternoon after some joke he'd told that Craig didn't get.) What if this never happened again? It was okay if they stopped now though. Listening so closely for so long had made him tired. He at least wanted to get up and stretch. Now Dad's blue eyes, more solid and dark than his own, stared at him, looking like they wanted Craig to say something. A half smile lifted one side of Dad's mouth. Craig returned his smile at least, only dropping his eyelids every once in a while when his eyes got too dry. Dad must be trying to tell him something, but he had no idea what.

Finally Dad lifted himself off the bed with his good hand.

Craig had almost forgotten about the smashed one until Dad moved. Dad was naked except for his boots. All that time he had been naked. It was strange: Craig was never naked unless he was in the bathtub, but Dad sat around like that. Dad lit a cigarette, and then as Mom opened the back door and yoohooed, he pulled on his khakis and zipped them awkwardly, taking care not to catch his thick hair.

"Got groceries, Mom?" Craig called.

"No," she said in a strange tone. "Why are you here? You're supposed to be at Mrs. Rice's."

He reached the kitchen. "I am?" he said.

"Anyway, it doesn't matter." He could tell she thought Dad wasn't home. Pecking him on the cheek, she unwrapped the package of pork chops left thawing this morning on the counter. The bathroom door shut. "Who's here?" she asked, turning quickly.

"Dad." Craig had taken a seat at the breakfast table and was folding napkins from a wrought-iron holder on the wall.

The soft curves of her face squared in anger. "What's he doing here?"

"His hand," Craig stammered.

"That much I know." She dumped the pork chops onto the counter and threw the cardboard tray toward the trashcan. Drops of pork blood spattered the floor.

"He hurt his hand *again*, Mom," he said, trying to persuade her to be fair, but she was scraping the chops and wouldn't look at him. "He couldn't help it," he said. Each pork chop hit the counter with a dull sucking sound.

"You don't think so?" she asked fiercely.

"No, I don't." His voice was loud, rude. She always looked for the bad.

The bathroom door opened and Dad came toward them. There was something strange about his walk that Craig didn't recognize. He glanced quickly at Mom to see if she knew. She cocked her head toward the ceiling. Then she reached for a sack of flour in a cabinet. Just before the last step that brought Dad into the kitchen, Craig figured it out for himself. Not so much a new sound as the absence of an old one. Dad had taken off Jay's brogans. He came into the kitchen in loafers, looking expectantly at both of them.

"Did you tell your mother about Uncle Otto?" he said.

Craig stopped breathing. His heart pounded like a volcano in his ears. There was no recognition in Dad's eyes, only a transparent glaze of disinterest. Toward Mom, he directed a bullying smirk. She took carrots out of the refrigerator, walking around as if no one else were in the room. Her eyes were edges of razor blades that shut them out. She began skinning the carrots with short jerky motions, but she finally couldn't hold her tongue. "What about Otto?" she asked, her voice raging.

Burning needles pricked Craig's face. Did Dad want *him* to answer? Dad sat down at the table, crossing his legs so that one loafer dangled out in the room. This was like a slow game of checkers. Mom stood over the sink with a fresh carrot, waiting to see if there would be an answer. The instant she began peeling again, Dad told her she wasn't smart enough to understand. She flung the carrot at him, but he didn't flinch. He shook his head as if she were a spoiled child. Once, Craig remembered without wanting to, he would have slapped her for acting like that. She almost deserved slapping, he thought, and then his throat quivered inside as if he were close to vomiting. Jay had always stopped Dad from hurting Mom. Always. And she wasn't even his mother. Craig felt ashamed. She didn't deserve slapping, but someone needed to tell her the truth.

Dad walked casually to the counter where the telephone was stretched from its dining-room nook. His good hand snatched her car keys off the counter.

"You're not taking my car anywhere," she said weakly. She lunged to grab them, but he was faster, holding them above his head. "Go to your room, Craig," she said, pointing toward it. He didn't move, thinking he might have to pull them apart. Dad swung the key ring around and around his middle finger. Craig looked from one of them to the other. Mom stared accusingly. Dad's eyes bored into him, recognizing, knowing, touching.

"Want to go off, son?" Dad asked quietly as if no one else were there, as if there had been no screaming, as if there were really no question.

"Sure," he said. He did not look at his mother directly, but in his periphery saw her take her place at the table. "Be back soon, Mom," he said. He guessed they would be. His body floated down the steps and into her car. He felt for a moment like a thief.

Want to go off, son? was what Dad always said to Jay, as if there had been only one son in the room or one son worth inviting. It would be a Saturday morning and the three of them would be at the breakfast table, Mom having gone back to bed after cooking for them. Usually Jay would say, "Why don't we take Craig. He's getting old enough." As if old enough had anything to do with it. Dad would say: "We've only got two guns." Or, "I can't spend my time worrying about him." Or "He makes too much noise." Jay never gave up: "He doesn't need to be shooting yet anyway." And "I'll watch him." In their room getting dressed, Jay told him he was as quiet as an Indian. Of course he wasn't, but when they stepped out of the car onto the muddy orange road near Butner, he tried to be. He especially liked walking with them after a rain because it was so much easier to be stealthy. They would go after birds or squirrels. Dad would take one side of a field and Jay the other. Craig would follow Jay, trying to match the widespread footprints in the soft earth. He avoided sticks, and when he passed through dense branches, he would ease them carefully back in place so that they wouldn't snap. He would think he was doing well until they met again around the field and Dad told him he would have to be quieter.

Dad leaned slightly into the steering wheel, curving his back so that he looked smaller than he was. His right hand dangled over the seat nearly touching the floor; his left wrist lay on the crown of the wheel, steering perhaps with the pulse of his blood. He did not drive particularly fast, but he seemed not to be able to take the curves, swinging into them too wide so that he ran onto the shoulders. He did it again and again, until eventually Craig's stomach relaxed and began to absorb the strange swings as natural. Dad stayed draped over the wheel like a bat, not looking anywhere but straight ahead.

They stopped at an old filling station that Craig at first thought was out of business. There was a cement island for pumps but no pumps. The first three letters of Texaco in plastic were mounted on the front of the building. The inside was dark except for a pale lighted clock on a back wall. Dad drove around the building, his posture not changing except to extend his neck looking for signs of somebody. There were no cars. "Story of my goddamn life," he said.

Craig sat as inconspicuous as he could. Dad stepped on the gas, taking the last corner of the building very close and not slowing down at the blind curve where the parking lot met the road. He began mumbling the way he did when he was drunk. Sometimes the sounds seemed like a disguised moan, but then Dad would suck in and say something hard like "Shit."

They stopped at a Seven-Eleven store, so bright with fluorescent tubing that it hurt Craig's eyes. Dad told him to stay in the car. Craig watched him select two six-packs of beer, pay, and then smile at the cashier, a black-haired girl with two bouffant curls on top of her head. She leaned over the cash register, propping her chin on her hands. Dad took out a cigarette and offered her one, which she accepted. Craig thought that watching them was like watching T.V. They smoked one cigarette and then another, and he began to lose interest. It was okay with him if Dad just stayed there and talked to her. He turned on the ignition switch so he could listen to the radio. Another car with two young guys pulled up. Dad reached for the woman and came back with a pencil which had been stuck in her hair. He wrote something on the paper bag holding the beer and put the pencil back where he had found it. As the new customers walked in, he walked out.

In the car Dad tore off the part of the bag where he'd written her telephone number and offered it to Craig. "Interested?" he said. Craig smiled. "Huh?" Dad insisted. Yes, no, what was he *supposed* to say? He shrugged as if he could take her or leave her. "She's not bad," Dad said, throwing the scrap of paper on the dash . . . Mom's dash. If Dad left it there, Craig decided he would destroy it.

Dad had bought Blue Ribbon. He put the two six-packs on the floorboard under his feet and handed Craig two bottles. "You'll have to open these. Can't quite manage yet with this hand." Craig opened them and handed both back. "Keep one, dumb ass," Dad said. Craig didn't mind being called a dumb ass. He *was* one, thinking Dad could drink two beers at once. He turned up the bottle and tasted the sour ginger ale flavor.

They cruised the countryside, Dad holding his beer with the same hand that steered. Each time he took a swallow, he raised one knee slightly to guide the wheel. He didn't use his injured hand for anything. In the time it took Craig to drink two beers, he drank ten, but Craig had to spend a lot of time opening. The car zigzagged like Dad owned the road. Once they ran onto the shoulder on the opposite side. After a while, Craig stopped worrying. Nothing had happened. Nothing was going to happen. He did not much like the taste of beer or how it made his stomach feel heavy enough to fall out on the floorboard. He did like the way it played with the nerves in his shoulders and in his fingertips. He wanted another one, but Dad said there was none left. He tried to count the empties under his feet, but they kept rolling around and he lost track. Dad wouldn't lie to him anyway. They hadn't said a word to each other besides about the next beer, but he knew how Dad was now. They were buddies, actually. They could drive around all night—why not—and never speak a word and it wouldn't matter. You didn't have to talk when you were this close. He thought that perhaps he and Jay had always talked too much.

They were back on their street and Craig hadn't even realized. Dad pulled into the driveway, put the car in neutral, and revved the motor. Each time it swelled, he resumed the strange talking to himself that would change into a quiet moan if you listened for it. Only the moans were louder now, rising and falling with the sound of the motor. Dad leaned his head against the steering wheel like it was a pillow. His forehead was a sheet of sweat. He moaned, racing the engine as he got louder.

Craig walked around the car, balancing in case Mom was watching. He reached in and turned off the ignition catching Dad in the peak of a wail. Dad cut it off as quickly as he could. He grabbed at Craig with his healthy hand. "What the hell are you doing?" But he was ineffectual and weak and Craig wasn't afraid. He helped Dad out of the car where the cooler air roused him. "Keep your hands off me," he said, pushing Craig's arm vigorously away. Craig kept his distance, but near enough in case Dad fell. The autumn air sweeping through his thin cotton shirt roused him too, so that the stars, the house, the white cardboard in the door looked as bright and well-defined as the fluorescent Seven-Eleven store. He saw what Dad liked about drinking. He'd forgotten to tear up the phone number so he ran back to the car while Dad was managing the steps. Dad would forget he'd ever written it down; still he hesitated. He crushed the paper into his own pocket, planning to transfer it to Dad's wallet later.

"Open up, woman." Dad pounded on the bathroom door. Craig stood proudly behind him. "There're a couple of men out here who want to take a leak." Dad kicked the door. Craig heard water slogging in the bathtub.

"Just a minute," Mom said. The anger in her voice tore at Craig's elation. She came out with the tips of her hair wet and her bathrobe snuggled closer to her than buttoning. She seemed small and frail as she pushed between them, head down, barefoot.

"That was close, woman," Dad said, feeling her fanny as she passed by. "You almost had you a rug to clean." She slammed the bedroom door and locked it. Dad shuffled across the bathroom floor to the john. Craig stood at the door waiting his turn. "Something you want to see?" Dad asked. He reached over and flung the door closed.

As he turned to wait, Mom cracked open her door. "Bedtime, Craig."

"He don't have a bedtime," Dad yelled from the bathroom. He opened the door, holding his pants together with one hand.

"That's okay, Dad, I'm pretty tired."

"What are you . . . a pussy?"

Mom looked at him expectantly. Dad headed for the kitchen, not waiting for anything. He was not so loud without his brogans.

"Hell, no," Craig flung wildly after him. In a thick, punishing voice, Mom uttered his name. He hadn't even been talking to her. He closed the bathroom door firmly behind him, but not too firm, in case either of them would think he was slamming it. He barely got to the commode in time.

Dad's car was not there when Craig got home from school, but he hoped that, like yesterday, the car was just gone somewhere. He wasn't home, not even asleep in the hammock where Craig looked last since it was one of his favorite spots. He ate an apple from the bushel basket in the shed and picked a thorn off the hawthorne tree. He tested the tip against his thumb and found it to be sharper than he expected. Now that would have been a tree. Jay would have looked like Jesus by the time he'd climbed up far enough. Would have died of loss of blood instead of a noose. He thought of the scratches on their arms the last time they went hunting, the weekend before he brought Melissa home to meet the family.

He heard a car turning into the driveway, but when he ran to the front yard, it was only Paulette creeping along. Her hands clutched the steering wheel as if it might jump out of her hands. She hadn't seen him, so he slipped toward the back and lay down in the hammock. Before Mom started sending him to Mrs. Rice's, Paulette always used to corner him to help her bring in groceries. Then she went to knock on their door. He lay perfectly still, so that the only movement was the natural push of autumn. She knocked again. Through the weave of the hammock, he saw her tap the cardboard with one finger as if she were scolding it for being there. She looked behind her, and seeing no one, peered into their kitchen. He hoped he wouldn't be stuck out here for long. In times past he'd seen her pick through the grocery bags for the items that needed refrigeration and leave the rest for whatever male came along first. She was twice as big as him and a third bigger than her husband, so he never understood why. He settled back in the hammock in case his eyes might sparkle and give him away. He'd seen her sniff out Clayton from an even better spot than this.

As she began her toiling climb up their tall steps, he felt a quick throb of guilt. Jay had always helped her whenever he was around. But if her own husband avoided her, why shouldn't Craig? At the top step she put the bags down to rest before opening the door.

He lay back in the hammock, studying an old squirrel's nest in the dying oak tree. Dad had always wanted to tear into that nest with his shotgun, but because they lived inside the city limits, he couldn't. Craig aimed with his arms at the nest. Pow-pow. He'd forgotten about Paulette for a minute, but fortunately she was still inside. He put his hands under his butt so he wouldn't forget her again.

Jay had always criticized Dad for not giving squirrels a fighting chance. Dad called them nasty creatures who had no business in this world. He shot into their nests to make them run, and then he picked them off as they scattered along the branches. Jay worried about the ones that never made it out.

Paulette suddenly loomed over the hammock, her big arms wiggling over him like snakes. "Didn't you hear me call you?" she said. She grabbed both edges of the hammock and pulled them together, trapping him like a fish. He was afraid for a moment, but she laughed like this was a joke. She swung him back and forth, her double chin quivering as she kept trying to smile.

"Let me out," Craig said. "You're making me sick." She let go abruptly and he swung to the ground.

"I need some help with my groceries," she said, waddling away like some huge duck. She talked as if to herself: "I knew you were around here somewhere. Saw you come home yesterday. I looked out my back window and there you were. I wonder if you were really asleep or just hiding from me. You're sure nothing like your brother. More like that lazy daddy of yours." She turned around and walked backward. "I see lots of things out this window." She must have seen him crawling under Dad's window day before yesterday.

He followed her, shutting out her conversation. He made three trips to carry in six bags of groceries and then an extra trip for a sack of potatoes. She leaned against the refrigerator, fanning herself. He noticed that her eyebrows nearly met in the middle of her forehead. When he finished, she gave him a nickel which was better than nothing and better than usual.

Before she could think of another chore, he hurried down her steps and out the driveway, kicking fiercely at the loose gravel. One stone flew up and hit their mailbox, making a tiny dent. Dad had always meant to paint the box maroon to match the house, but he'd never gotten around to it. He walked to the end of his street and looked down on Buck's filling station in a dip in the land below. The station was on a corner lot and in the corner where their street met the highway sat Dad's car. Sometimes Dad would hang around Buck's all afternoon eating dill pickles.

Craig walked down the hill, his pace quickened by the slope and by finding Dad. There was something he wanted to ask him. Yesterday afternoon Dad had told him that the reason he never went home to Georgia anymore was that his brothers kept photographs of all their dead relatives on display. Dad couldn't stomach looking at his own mother lying in a coffin. What Craig wanted to know was whether anybody had taken a picture of Jay. That, at least, would be proof that he was dead.

Craig raised his arm at Buck like a lever, and Buck spoke to him by name. He seemed nice, but yesterday Dad had told him a story about how Buck had cheated him on dill pickles. The good part was that Buck had tried to make up for it by washing Dad's car.

"Your dad's inside," Buck said, walking toward the door. Craig hesitated. "Want me to tell him you're here?" He nodded. Somehow he wanted to see Dad out in the open. A woman in a station wagon drove up, throwing dust all over him. He closed his mouth just in time to taste the grit. She honked her horn. Dad came striding through the door like she was his best customer.

"Hi," Craig said. Dad did not look glad to see him.

"What are you doing here?"

Craig turned to walk with him. Dad put his hand around the back of his neck, but he squeezed too hard. "Ouch," Craig said, jumping away. He stopped to rub his neck. Dad hadn't meant to hurt him, but he didn't apologize, just kept walking toward his car. He'd better catch up.

Dad started jogging. Over his shoulder he told Craig not to follow him around, but he didn't mean it. He was upset about something. The woman in the station wagon kept honking for Buck. Dad climbed into the car and started it before Craig could reach the door on the passenger's side. He tried the handle, but the door was locked. He knocked on the glass. Dad didn't look. The car rocked backward and Craig jumped out of the way.

"Dad!" he cried out. Didn't he hear him? The car shot forward, passing him, and with one last lunging effort, he grabbed the handle. The car yanked him off his feet and dragged him on his knees across Buck's gravel. Then it stopped and he let go, falling to the ground. Dust stopped up his nose. The woman from the station wagon shouted at Dad to stop. He had stopped; he'd finally noticed him. Craig stood up, but Dad was pulling off again. The woman in black screamed "Monster." Three men hurried out of the service station. Buck was trying to brush off his clothes. But still Craig managed to watch the white Chevrolet, bumping over the lip of the parking lot and running the stop sign just before the highway. Dad turned right, passing in front of them, making them turn like figurines on a music box.

On a telephone pole beside the road hung a sign: TO INTERSTATE 85 SOUTH.

That evening Dad didn't come home. Craig explained to Mom that he'd stayed after school to play touch football with some of the guys. He showed her his skinned knees. She had already noticed the scrape on his chin and the tears in his corduroy pants.

"I'm not sure I want you to play with those boys anymore," she said, cleaning the abrasions with Mercurochrome. He didn't have the energy to argue even for the sake of the story. She opened a package of hamburger meat. "Is your father having dinner with us?" she asked stiffly, as if she'd just remembered last night.

"I don't know. I haven't seen him." He decided to leave the kitchen before he told her everything. He walked to his room stiff-legged since his knees ached. He didn't want to say what happened. It made it less true. Buck had brushed him off. The crazy woman had called Dad a bastard. On and on. Craig said nothing, trying to ignore her, trying to ignore Buck, but still half-listening to find out if either of them could tell him why. The woman kept asking questions. Buck finally asked if she needed gas. She walked toward Craig, her arms out. "Is there anything I can do, honey?" Her dress stopped at her knees which were thick like Melissa's ankles. Jerking away, he yelled for her to leave him alone. He fought to get away from Buck then too. He was furious, furious at Dad, at the woman, at Buck for trying to help. Buck let him go, motioning the woman back to her car. He held out his hand and Craig looked at it, a nice clean hand with long fingers and filed nails. Dad laughed at men who never got their hands dirty. "No," he mumbled. He'd wanted to shake Buck's hand, but he couldn't.

Mom called him to set the table. She didn't suspect anything. He took out two plates and two sets of stainless.

"Which one of us are you forgetting?" she asked wryly.

Suddenly he wanted her to know. "Dad's not going to be here."

"I thought you hadn't seen him." She laid the hamburgers in the frying pan.

"I just know," he said.

She kept her back to him. "Set another place, Craig, in case . . ."

Without warning tears began falling from his eyes, huge tears that made his vision swim. Mom was watching the meat. He sat there, hiding nothing, even boohooing out loud a little when she still hadn't noticed over the popping grease. When she finally turned and saw him, he threw himself forward onto his empty supper plate. Her arms came around him like a pillow. He let her fondle him as if he were a baby, touching his ears with one finger, pushing back his hair with her palm, catching his cheeks between her hands, and rubbing away the tears with her thumbs. Then she stood him up and hugged him, and he noticed that she was crying too.

She walked him to the bathroom and turned on the water. "Wash up and blow your nose and you'll feel better," she said, but she didn't stay to help. He cried again, gently now so that over the noise of the water she wouldn't hear and return. Finally, he had enough. The stretch across his nose was swollen and his eyes were pink—pussy pink, as Dad would say. He let the cold washcloth linger on his face sucking out the heat. Supper was ready, but Mom was giving him plenty of time.

They ate and talked about the new electric typewriter at her office and how it would go flying across the paper if she simply poised her fingers above the keys. She said her fingers felt like ballerina legs, but that sometimes the music got ahead of her brain. To illustrate she jumped up from the table, her hamburger barely touched, and danced around the kitchen floor as if she were a miniature dancer hopping from key to key. They both laughed until their sides hurt, longer than it was funny. In the quiet that followed, Craig asked if she wanted him to tell her anything. She shook her head no and rose to clear the table.

5

MELISSA

He was dopey-eyed and thin-shouldered and hadn't even bothered to shave that morning, and *he* was telling *her* that she couldn't have a job in this rat hole where there was a sign plain as day saying waitress wanted. And she had on her best dress and new stockings, and she'd painted the rubbed places on her black high heels with a laundry marker. So, who was *he*? The floor was even filthy—beige linoleum as gray as the sky. There were no customers, of course. He was sweeping half-heartedly when he should have been scrubbing. She leaned against a barstool whose split Naugahyde covering had been taped together and tried bullying him: "What the hell are you looking for?"

"Somebody who ain't stuck out to here," he said, not bothering to look at her, but jerking his sweat shirt out to where his broom stood.

"I won't be this way for long," she said. It felt good to lean against this stool. This was only her second stop of the day, but she felt like she'd been walking for hours. The first stop had been at a taxi company where they needed a dispatcher, but the man there hadn't even let her fill out an application. "Thanks, but no thanks, honey," and she'd let herself be herded out before she even caught her breath. At least this time she'd been smarter: visiting the ladies' room of a gas station across the street from this dump of a truck stop, composing herself, brushing out the long red hair that had frizzed in the morning humidity of Atlanta in early fall.

By the time she vacated the bathroom, she looked as good as when she'd left home that morning.

She looked at his hands clutching the broom handle. The nails were broken and black, his skin stained as if he didn't wash. But he was in here sweeping and it was only ten o'clock. The room was small, crowded with a mix-match of styles of tables and chairs, but they were arranged in an orderly fashion. All the barstool coverings were taped neatly back together. Maybe he couldn't afford to replace them. If so, she appreciated the neat repair job.

"I'm a pretty good cook, if you need one," she said. She was enjoying watching him work while she sat here. If nothing came of this, at least she had talked to somebody. She was tired of talking to the baby all the time and that strange woman at the beauty shop who kept Jenny while she looked for work.

"I'm the cook," he said.

"*You're* the cook? You can't be the cook. Look at your hands."

He met her eyes finally, taking care not to look at his hands himself. She'd found a touchy spot. He hesitated, not sure what to say, and she rearranged herself on the stool as if she were taking a break between songs. Maybe she could be a nightclub singer; she hadn't thought about that.

If he would clean himself up, he wouldn't be nearly so rough looking. Get a haircut. Send his clothes to the laundry or find a good laundress. He had proportioned features. His hair was thick and healthy looking. She could spruce him up if he'd let her.

"I can cook a mean beef stew," she said, letting a teasing note barely touch her voice. Not too friendly too fast. He stood with his shoulders bent forward as if in all this heat he were cold. If she could get him to stand straight, be proud. It was enough to run a truck stop, if you were good at it. The thought stuck in her mind. If that wasn't an idea straight from Jay Mitchell's head, she didn't know what was. The trouble was, he hadn't believed that, he'd only thought it was *supposed* to be true.

"Nobody would see my stomach in the kitchen," she said. He started to speak, but she cut him off: "The food would be good for a change."

"The food don't need to be good." He glared at her, cold triumph in his eyes. He had been waiting for an opportunity to say that.

She blushed and felt her baby move. The dirty louse. He wouldn't even smile at her. Couldn't joke a little even if he wouldn't give her the goddamn job. She pushed off the stool, taking care not to lose balance in her anger. He stood in her path, watching, a bit of interest tilting his eyebrows now that she was angry and leaving. She bore down on him like a train, but he didn't move. She felt tears pushing along her tear ducts. She wouldn't let him see her cry. "Get out of my way, you creep."

He grinned at her with crooked yellow teeth. She felt her mouth twisting into something awful, her chest tightening with a sense of self-preservation. This was her goddamn future. Didn't he realize? Without thinking it out, she drew back her arms and pushed him with all the surging strength she had. For a moment he was Jay, absorbing her anger like a boxing bag. He grabbed at her to keep his balance, but he wasn't fast enough. She did not wait to see him fall, only heard the scraping chairs that he dragged down with him.

The sun blinded her, but she walked resolutely forward anyway. Her arms, strong as a man's before, felt like match sticks. Her chest felt sunken to her backbone and her breath came in short gasps as if she had been running a long time. She made her mind into a bridle and held herself closely as she walked across the street. He was coming after her, she knew. He might kill her. He would knock her down at the least. You could tell a man who beat up on women a mile away.

Across the street she felt safer. At least—even if he came

out of his restaurant running—she could reach the safety of the bathroom before he could reach her. She remembered from her earlier visit that there was a lock. Someone whistled at her and she stumbled badly. "Watch out, sister," a faraway voice said. She smiled in the direction of the gas-station door. A clot of men stood there. The last few steps, she broke into a run, unable to help herself. They might just think she was in a hurry to pee. She looked over her shoulder before she shut the door, but he hadn't appeared.

She stayed inside ten minutes, brushing her hair until the new frizz simmered down, going to the bathroom four times, stretching her arms to the ceiling so that her wet armpits would dry, blotting the spray of sweat on her upper lip that reappeared like water in a sandhole, straightening her cheap skirt which kept twisting as if it would fit better backward. She would say she had gone in to apply for the job and he'd gotten fresh with her. She pushed him away and he fell . . . no . . . he came after her, and she ran behind a table. He chased her. It was hard to keep away from him, being this pregnant: she stood with her hips thrown forward, so that her six-month belly stuck out even farther, and looked in the mirror. Anyone would feel sorry for her in this condition. He was drunk or something, reeling around the tables trying to catch her. He must have caught his foot on a chair leg because he stumbled and came flying toward her. She even tried to break his fall . . . no . . . he fell toward her and she jumped out of his way. She was no fool. She got the hell out of there. Wouldn't they have wanted their girl friends to do the same thing? She would say "girl friends" to flatter them all: men didn't like to be reminded of their wives. She wondered if these men here were friends of the man across the street. But what difference did it make? They wouldn't beat her up as a group. She peed one more time and opened the door.

He wasn't there. She walked briskly across the asphalt, dancing one hand back and forth beside her like a majorette. The sun surprised her again after the fluorescent light of the bathroom. All she could see was a pattern of black. Her eyes adjusted by the time she reached the side-walk. They were whistling at her again—all three of them—now that she was leaving. What in the world would they do if she turned around and picked one of them out? Said she would take *him*. They'd go to heaven, just him and her. And maybe she'd come back on her spaceship for the other two tomorrow. She added an extra wiggle to her wiggle and heard one of the boys clap. Her exhilaration tripled: she was glad to know that even pregnant she looked good to some men. In her periphery she could distinguish nothing about the nut who ran the diner. Was he bleeding to death from a gash across his head? Was he peering frightened at her from one of the smoky glass windows? Was he down the block waiting to slug her? The whistles followed her a few more seconds, but then they stopped . . . or else she walked out of hearing range.

She tried to relax. Job hunting this month was hopeless. She would have to wait until she had her figure back. She paused at the bus stop, but the bus didn't come right away so she decided to walk and save the dime. Soon she wouldn't have to be counting dimes: Sergeant Jester had promised that her widow's benefits would start this week. She walked past a bakery, realized she hadn't had lunch, and turned around now that she'd thought of her check coming. She chose a cream puff and a jelly-filled doughnut and ate them out of the bag as she continued on her way. Perhaps Sally would offer her a Coke out of the employees' drink box when she reached the beauty shop. She would say she was thirsty and hope that Sally offered.

She had never had girl friends and she felt odd having one now. They had met last week in a slow grocery line. Patting Jenny's head and eyeing Melissa's stomach, Sally had complained about the difficulty of getting pregnant. Melissa had shaken her head about being extra fertile. Then

Sally had offered to keep Jenny at the Modern Beauty Nook where she worked if ever the need arose. She lay a cool hand on Melissa's forearm, and Melissa felt herself stiffen. Maybe that was how friends were made: assuming friendship until it finally came true. She had called on Sally because she had no other choice. When she brought Jenny to the beauty shop this morning, she noticed something odd: Sally wore no wedding band.

Melissa swallowed several times to moisten her parched throat. In the unnatural light of the windowless parlor, three operators, including Sally, worked on three heads of hair. Jenny sat on the floor, emptying a round basket full of permanent curlers. Yellowed photographs of women in out-of-date hairstyles hung at odd angles on the walls. Melissa gathered Jenny's things and stopped at Sally's booth. She forced her voice to intimacy long enough to whisper, "No luck." Sally offered to keep the baby again tomorrow if Melissa were going to job hunt again. "Maybe I'll bring her back Friday," she said. "I'll call first." She wasn't going to look for any more jobs, but perhaps on Friday she would go to Columbus to see if the powers-that-be had signed her check yet. Did anybody realize that except for the money from Jay's watch, some small change—really small—that Gurney had given her, and the little bit Mac left when he went away, she did not have one red cent. There was twenty dollars total. She might even have to sell her furniture.

Jenny had not looked up, which irritated Melissa. She was filling the basket back up. It was too bad Jay hadn't gotten to see her walk. She'd taken her first step exactly a week after he died. "Time to go, Jenny." She spoke patiently as mothers were supposed to do. Jenny worked, as if she hadn't heard. Being so pregnant, it was difficult to lift her. "Clean up your mess, honey," she said, but the sweetness in her voice faltered. There was a pause in the rhythm of Sally's snipping scissors. The girl she was working on was losing five-years' worth of hair. Sally had no children: she didn't realize that things weren't always sugar and spice, that you don't pamper anybody all the time, not even a boyfriend. "*Now*," Melissa said, bolstered by her own thoughts.

"I don't think she understands you," Sally said through teeth clenched over bobby pins.

Melissa closed her eyes and sighed. "She understands." It would be so easy to pop Jenny one. "Her hair looks nice," she said, just noticing. Sally had made ringlets in the auburn hair.

Jenny raised her arms over her head and yawned, twisting from side to side. She grinned shyly, first at Melissa, then at everyone else. They each smiled sympathetically back at her. What a little flirt: making her mother look mean. She had a good mind to pop her bottom anyway. She picked up Jenny although it strained the little monkey on the way.

Over her shoulder Jenny said, "Bye, bye," opening and closing her hand like she was counting by fives.

The heavy glass door of the shop reminded Melissa of the door at the diner. The horrible thought again occurred to her that the man hadn't chased her because he was hurt . . . or even dead. By now somebody must have found him because she had smelled the cooking oil warming for lunch. She'd paraded in front of the men at the gas station; they knew her looks like they knew their own. How many knocked-up redheads were there in Atlanta? How could she hide? Maybe she would have the baby early, maybe this week. She at least had to get this hair off. And not after the story appeared in the newspaper . . . before. She turned and asked Sally to cut her hair tomorrow, and Sally, her anemic face curling at Jenny as she spoke, said, "Gladly."

Did anybody in this gigantic country ever find somebody they'd lost? All the times she'd come to Atlanta, hoping to find Mac, she never had. He might not even be in Atlanta, but then he might. Maybe if her picture were in the newspaper, he would see it and find *her*. At the trial he could wave a gun at the judge and carry her away. Rescue her like she had always expected him to do. She had thought he would save her from Jay, but Jay did that. She was sorry, she was honestly sorry, but killing himself had been his idea not hers.

She put Jenny down as soon as they got outside and together they traveled slowly under the store awnings. She was lucky that the place where they were staying was nearby. She was lucky that Jenny didn't talk yet. She kept one eye peeled for Mac—you never knew who was around the next corner—and the other peeled to see if any decent-looking men walked these streets. She decided to make an agreement with herself. For a time—a month, say—she would direct seventy-five percent of her efforts toward finding Mac. The rest of her time would be spent keeping an open mind toward other men she might encounter. If she didn't find him, she would reverse the time spent—twenty-five percent on him and seventy-five percent on whomever else she might meet. She guessed after a while she would stop looking for Mac totally.

She knew you met men in small decent places, not in bars in big cities. But on the bus or in line for the pay phone or at a diner. So the first time she got angry enough to walk out on Jay—about a year ago—she'd driven across the state line to Opelika, Alabama, where she found a little short-order restaurant called the Baker House. She'd sat on a stool at the counter, not really reckoning on meeting anybody the first time, but finding herself talking to a nice young man over a bowl of homemade vegetable soup and chocolate pie. She'd established herself right away as a respectable woman by saying that she was only there because her husband was out of town and that she hated to cook for just one but thought you should eat well regardless of where your husband was.

She said: "This is such a nice place that I eat here a lot."

His shirt collar was open, and the sleeves were rolled up neatly. His tan hair fell smoothly back with just a touch of oil. She'd figured he was in college or just out because of his manners. He rose slightly off his stool when she sat down. He passed her the napkin holder without her asking. He waited until her vegetable soup came before he began eating.

"Are you just out of school?" she had asked.

"No ma'am."

Her face stained red thinking he imagined her so much older. Then she realized it was his country manners.

"I finished six years ago, first in my family." He was a high-school graduate, like her.

Before she left she had found out his name and address, that he was a mechanic saving to open his own garage, that he used to have a girl but no more, and that he would be happy to be friends with her and her husband. He didn't know too many people either, not his own age anyway. He'd grown up in Opelika, but all the people he used to know had moved away. He ate here a lot himself, three times a week maybe, and was surprised he'd never seen her. She said she thought she would be coming here often. Her husband was going to be traveling more than ever.

"He . . . he sells children's clothes," she said, choosing quickly. "Sometimes it gets pretty lonely."

She felt him slide away from her then although he didn't move a fraction in his seat. He paid closer attention to his soup and took a long peek at the menu to see what else he might want.

"I have a daughter at home to keep me company," she said. But then she realized that that was wrong too. Where was the daughter? "Her name's Jenny and tonight she's spending the night with her grandmother." She took a bite of soup. Did he believe her?

He turned and gave her the kindest smile she had ever seen. His eyes seemed to pick up her heart and lift it to the sky like a child with a piece of glass. Yes, he believed her.

They were friends then and she started talking more softly to him, letting her words caress, and he let himself smile in response but not—she could tell—too much. She could see him holding back because she was married. He laughed at her jokes but not close with her, keeping the distance of friendship. So she left first, although it was difficult, withdrawing a little before she stood up, sitting back in her seat instead of leaning toward him, bringing her voice back to its natural volume. So that he would understand for sure that they were only friends. She hoped soon to see him again, and he said the same. She made a mental list of her lies, so that she wouldn't forget: a traveling husband selling children's clothes, a nearby grandmother. Anything else?

She'd come back again a week later while he was standing up paying his bill. Unable to stir up a fight with Jay, she'd just had to leave, stating angrily that she was tired of being cooped up all day and all night with a baby. She hadn't meant *him*, she meant Jenny, but he took it that way and huffed off to the bathroom to read or whatever he did. She said goodbye through the door. He hadn't bothered to ask what was for supper, a good thing since she hadn't cooked.

She opened green dewy eyes to Mac Godwin. The top of her head came to the bottom of his chin. She had to stand close to talk so that everybody couldn't hear. "I'll bet you don't remember my name," she said.

Looking down on her, his eyes closed part way. She could see the long blond eyelashes that blended into his skin. He seemed large and commanding beside her, unlike Jay. She wanted to touch him. "Yes, I do," he said, and she knew she didn't need to ask what it was.

"Sorry I didn't get here soon enough to keep you company," she said cheerfully. Men, she thought, didn't like too much seriousness. She traveled on to her seat with an over-the-shoulder parting smile. He followed, saying, as he straddled the stool beside her, that he guessed he could use another piece of pie. Love grabbed at her throat like a strangler.

After they became lovers, he admitted that the extra piece of pie was his third and nearly made him sick. But he couldn't resist her. She asked him to say it again. He couldn't resist her . . . couldn't resist. . . . She wanted to hear it more than that he loved her, and sometimes when he neglected to say it, she would prompt, "You can't resist me, can you?" He did not feel guilty when they first started, so she wondered why it happened later. She had wanted to leave Jay and move in with him, but he had said no. He wanted her to leave Jay first, set up her own place with Jenny, and then they would see. But she was no fool. She wasn't going to be without *anybody*. Then she got pregnant. It had worked with Jay, so why not with Mac? She swore to him that it was an accident. But she had stopped using her diaphragm. He left her. He met her in a motel room in Opelika to tell her he was going.

"I never thought I would sin like this," he said. He sat carefully on the bed as if afraid of messing it up. He'd put her in a chair across the room. His eyes were rimmed with misery.

"*Sin?*" she said contemptuously. He was curling up like a worm, saying he was sorry for something afterward. If you're *that* sorry you don't "sin" in the first place. "What sin?" she shrilled.

"Making a married woman pregnant." He looked directly at her, all the guilt in his eyes looking like it wanted to jump into hers. She refused to take it. She didn't even feel guilty. What were you *supposed* to do when your husband wasn't a man anymore?

"It was your choice," she said bluntly, and he nodded that it had been.

He said he would come back when he understood himself better, but he refused to tell her where he was going. She knew already. He had talked for hours and hours about being a mechanic in a big city where there were all sorts of cars to work on. He was not content with Fords and Chevrolets. He wanted to get inside some foreign cars, some Ferraris, some Jaguars. He wanted to work on the Mercedes engine. He was going to Atlanta.

Home for her now was a furnished garage apartment that in damp weather still smelled of charred wood from a fire that had failed to destroy it fifteen years ago. It stood behind a two-story brick house on Avalon Street, facing a screened porch where her landlords, an elderly couple, sat and rocked and watched the garage as if it might still be blazing. Her comings and goings, in other words. There was no fire yet, she could tell them. She lived above a yawning hole which would have held one or even two cars if anybody in that family were still allowed to drive. Her own car, the one Jay had bought in college, had fallen apart on the trip here. She had had to be towed to town. She hadn't known what else to do but strike out walking. A few blocks from the tow-truck parking lot, she had spied this place. She'd crossed her fingers that nobody lived here and she'd lucked out.

Turning down the driveway, she instructed herself to be friendly to the old couple even though she was all pooped out. After all, they had said she could live here free until she began getting her checks. They appeared to need money badly. Excess hair crawled down the neck of the Mr. and stains marked the Mrs.'s clothes. She could never remember their last name. Pats-voras, or something like that, even though they didn't have a foreign accent. As always they waited on the porch. As soon as she and Jenny went inside, they would move into their house too. It struck Melissa suddenly that there was something unused about all four of them: no present purpose to their lives. Unless she and Jenny had become their purpose. They had taken them in, perhaps, for something to do.

"Hello, folks," she said. Their eyes searched for more. She tried to think of something. "Had a nice day?" She'd already passed them, so she turned and walked backward. They were like magnets, wanting to pull things from her.

Mr. seemed to fade into his chair, but Mrs. sat up strongly, in full focus. Her white hair was pulled tightly back and she wore mother-of-pearl glasses frames. She looked something like Jenny's Terry Lee doll. "Any luck?" Her voice always surprised, deep and guttural as if she'd had a throat operation some time.

"No ma'am," Melissa said, turning to help Jenny up the steps. "I'm going to Columbus Friday to try to pick up my check. Cross your fingers."

Mr. leaned forward then with the fingers of his right hand held up like a salute. She could see they were crossed.

"No hurry," Mrs. said. "We're not worried one bit."

At the top of the stairs, Melissa claimed back her privacy, taking her time to find her keys and unlock the door without acknowledging them again. A week ago her hands would shake, trying to turn the key before their hopeful gaze. But now they were like the lawn furniture they were sitting on, which she didn't need to wave to before she went in. As soon as she found Mac, things would be better. She only wished this were ten years ago when Atlanta wasn't so big.

The apartment was still a wreck. Somehow she thought Mrs. might have straightened up for her. She had no proof, but she felt fairly sure that each day after she left they would inspect things. Maybe they were checking that she didn't drink too much or knock holes in the walls or hide men here in the daytime. She had straightened up for their prying eyes every day she'd lived here, until today when, for the first time, she'd left the place a wreck. She had hoped Mrs. would think about how conscientious she normally was and lend a helping hand on a day she really needed one. No such luck. Red cotton spreads, the Mrs.'s taste, lay at the end of each bed. The sheets were old and slightly gray and the normally colorful room looked sour. Too late to make them now; they'd be back in bed in a matter of hours.

She started two hot dogs in the kitchenette in one corner of the room, and her stomach lurched like a tapeworm toward the smell. Her two pastries at lunch hadn't lasted very long; she wondered for the first time what Jenny had eaten. The apartment had a pretty two-person dinette set, and on it she set two plates, one fork and one spoon, and one napkin that they could share.

She liked the style of this dinette set better than her own, but anything would look better without a gash down the middle. This set included a dark-stained pedestal table and two Early American chairs, much nicer than the styles she'd had to choose from in Columbus. But this was Atlanta. Big City. Where there were lots of Lincoln Continentals and Cadillacs and foreign cars to work on if you happened to be a mechanic. Lots of dinette sets to choose from if you happened to be a wife. Maybe there was some truth to what Jay had said about her taste in furniture, but it was clear to her that she had been limited by what was available.

Jenny was growing truly fretful now: she wanted her daddy; she wanted something to eat; she wanted to be picked up. Melissa began humming above the whining. She could almost tune Jenny out. She had left their portable television set in Columbus on purpose because it reminded her of Jay; she needed it now to entertain them. Jay had thought near the end that Sergeant Jester was tuning in on their life through its Army-green screen. Often he would sit in front of it, pretending for the sergeant that he was somebody else.

"Who am I now?" he would ask, making it a game for Melissa too.

If he were slumped in his seat drinking a beer, gargling when an imaginary Audrey walked by, swinging his leg over the chair arm, whistling if someone pretty appeared on the screen, he was Merle. And if he sat like a mouse on a stool, eyes inches from the picture, feet and arms tucked close like something dead, he was Rosie. And if he leaned back and went to sleep, dropping a full beer on her rug, he was Gurney. He'd made a stab at imitating Mac, whose name he'd never guessed, after he found out she was pregnant. Then, he forced her to stand by the television set. He tiptoed from the closet, head pivoting like a thief, ears stretched alert like only he could make them do. He bowed to her, sat debonairly in the chair, and pulled her to him.

"Come here, sweet. Sit on Johnny's lap." Johnny, Charles, Robert, Larry, Jeff, and even Merle and Gurney, as if. . . . He'd tried every man's name he could think of but hadn't hit on Mac. If he'd ever guessed right though, she was ready. She could make her expression as unreadable as stone.

She sat with him, afraid not to, allowing him to rub her back. She would let him abuse himself. Not having Mac's name didn't keep him from pretending he was him. "What a pussy you must be married to, hon." Or, "When are you going to kiss this dump goodbye, baby doll?" Always with terms of endearment tacked to the end. She'd stare ahead at the screen and he'd stare at her. If she tried to get away from him, he would detain her by her long red hair.

She'd have to sit with him sometimes an hour while he concocted a new version of her relationship with her lover. Where Mac was from, what he did, how they met, where he got her pregnant. Whispering details in her ear the way lovers recall memories. Giggling at indiscretions. Claiming terror when there was a prostitute raid at the motel where they were spending the night. He came close to facts only once when he guessed that Mac was a mechanic. But he changed his mind as soon as the words hit the air. "Nope, not good enough. Let's call me an automobile salesman. Honey, can I drive your car?" He was drinking and didn't notice her agitation until several remarks later when it was too late. He couldn't tell which fact was the dangerous one.

There were other moments when she played the game herself. "Let me guess who you are," she would call loudly from the kitchen. "Two-day stubble, breath like horse shit, a noodle for a dick . . . Jay Mitchell." He'd be too drunk to get out of the chair, and she'd creep forward a few steps into the living room. "Am I right, Jay?" She'd ask if she were right until Gurney beat on the adjoining wall or Jay nodded his head. And then she would walk out the door and drive a hundred and fifty miles to Atlanta to see if she could figure out where in the hell Mac had gone.

While she was chopping one hot dog into bite-size pieces, Jenny came up behind her and clasped her arms around her legs. At least somebody needed her. She turned carefully with their plates so that Jenny wouldn't fall down. Maybe the television would help them both. She had not planned on moving any of her furniture until she had her own place to stay. But Friday she would drop by the apartment. It would be nice to bathe without having to worry about a kid.

6

MERLE

Melissa left the apartment complex the week after Jay died, her former next-door neighbor told Merle. The sturdy breath of fall which already touched North Carolina in the mornings and the evenings had not reached southern Georgia. Merle felt like he was back in August. Sweat formed around his neck and under his arms and ran down his chest and back. The sky was white like window blinds. He and the neighbor stood on either side of a screen door that the neighbor did not offer to open.

"I felt right sorry for her," the man said. "Carrying one in her arms and another in her stomach." He wore a T-shirt stained pink on one shoulder and had not shaved lately. In the dim-lit room behind him, Merle could see a woman sitting on a wooden stool, back bent forward, watching television.

"Who are you, anyway?" the man asked, not offensively.

"Jay's old man," Merle said.

"Well, I'm sorry, Mr. Mitchell . . ." The man reached behind him for the edge of the door even though it had been open for the breeze when Merle first knocked.

"Wait a minute," he said. "You got any idea where she went?" He swabbed his forehead with the sleeve of his shirt. His eyes were burning from perspiration.

"Nope." The door started coming closed as if without help. The neighbor moved back into his hole.

"What's your problem?" Merle asked sharply, and the door stopped.

"I don't get involved in nobody's mess," the man said. For some reason, though, he waited.

"What mess?" Merle asked.

His face turned scared. "If you don't know . . ."

"I know," Merle said authoritatively, biding his time. "I already know." He waved a dismissing hand in the air and changed the subject: "She take everything with her?"

"Now that part I don't get."

The woman on the stool inside the apartment whined, "I can't hear, Gurney. Go outside." Gurney pulled the solid door closer behind him and stood between it and the screen.

"Wanna come out here and talk?" Merle asked.

He hesitated. "I don't know much more."

"What about the furniture?"

"I think she left everything but their clothes. Landlord come by here last week asking if I knew where she'd moved. I don't. Didn't even know where you folks lived except in . . . Carolina, is it? The landlord wasn't sure what to do with the stuff. Ain't done nothing yet. I haven't been anywhere and nobody's come to haul nothing away."

"I appreciate it." Merle put his hands on his hips and squinted over the roofs across from this section. The sun bore down like a spotlight. "You know who her boyfriend was?" he asked softly.

"So you *did* know," Gurney said. He moved to close the door. "No use looking . . . he's gone."

"Run away?"

"You could call it that. He left four or five months ago, right after your son found out."

"Did Jay catch 'em?"

Gurney shook his head. His mouth twitched like he was trying to stop himself talking. "I don't know. I don't think so."

Merle shifted impatiently.

"Rosie"—Gurney jerked his thumb in the direction of the TV—"Melissa told her there was no way to keep it from Jay because he never . . . you know . . . himself. . . ."

Merle looked at the cement walkway. Suddenly he wanted to smash his hand through the screen and grab this jerk by the neck. Goddamn lying bastard. "Can you give me the name of the landlord?" he asked stiffly.

"I figured she'd come back for it," the landlord said.

Merle stood in a smothering pay phone booth on the highway. Whenever traffic thinned, he opened the door for air.

"She called me just yesterday from Atlanta. Asked if I'd done anything with her belongings. Said she was upset when her husband hanged himself and couldn't think of anything but leaving town. She'll be back here this week. Said to hold the stuff until Friday. I'm not even charging her for storage, seeing how much she's been through."

Merle looked down the highway to where it vanished like a waterfall. "You know where she is in Atlanta?"

"We don't take forwarding addresses. Too much trouble. They move in and out of that complex like they were niggers. Post office might know. But people are funny. They more than likely don't want anybody looking them up. One reason is because of bill collectors. We'd have to hire somebody full-time just to send the mail on. I had two on your daughter-in-law already."

"What for?"

"Aw, furniture, drugstore. Suppose I should let them in, especially that furniture man since the stuff's still there. But I thought, what the hell. Let the little lady live in peace for a while. I don't know, but more than likely she deserves some."

"Friday? She'll be back Friday?"

"Don't hold me to it. You know these gals. I told her I wasn't in any hurry. I got loads of empty apartments. I say let the little lady live in peace. She said something about being pregnant—what was it?—oh yeah, that she'd be here Friday if nothing new came on the scene."

Merle said nothing.

"Get it?"

"I get it." Merle opened and closed the phone-booth door several times to create a breeze.

"You gonna wait around?"

Merle grunted.

"If you aren't, I'll be glad to give her a message. She's a nice one. They never did pay on time and every once in a while I'd have to sic the sheriff on them. I never would have done it if I'd known they had trouble. But, you know, I gotta eat too. I didn't even know they had trouble."

"What do you mean—trouble?"

"You know."

"No. . . ."

"Well, he killed himself, didn't he? I call that trouble. I never would have called the sheriff, is what I'm trying to say, if I'd known he was getting crazy about it."

"Crazy about what?"

"Sheriffs. You know. I figure people that live out there are used to having sheriffs knock on their doors. Always some kind of squabble going on. I thought I'd shake them up a little. They were way behind."

"Upset him, huh?" Merle asked.

"They said he flew out of that apartment swinging a baseball bat like he was Mickey Mantle. From what I heard, the deputy tripped him and jumped on his back. They thought he was having some kind of fit or something." He paused, but Merle offered nothing. "Anyway, your son told the deputy that he thought he'd heard a prowler. I never did believe that, but the law did, so they didn't arrest him. Even assigned a car to cruise the neighborhood for a few nights. I got my money that week, so I didn't bother them again. Then I heard he'd got kilt."

Merle closed the door for the sweep of a tractor trailer rumbling by. "How much later?"

"A few weeks. Maybe more."

"Yeah, well . . ." Merle thought he was going to throw up. Hot phone booth.

"You want me to tell her anything? She don't know it yet, but she's going to have to come by here. I had the lock changed." His tone was gleeful. "I didn't want anybody walking in and stealing the stuff or junking it up. It's a policy we have. No telling who your old tenants will give their keys to. I'll tell her you came by. Or are you going to wait and see her yourself? I can tell her to look for you."

"Naw," Merle said. "I can't stay. Wish I could, but I've got to get back to work. I had a couple of days off and thought I'd drive down, see how she was doing. Don't even tell her I was here."

"If you say so." He sounded as if he didn't care either way.

"You sure you don't know her address in Atlanta?"

"I didn't even ask."

It was only Wednesday and she might or might not be back here Friday. He thought he might drive up to Atlanta for a couple of days. Maybe he could catch a college football game. Or latch onto some Atlanta girl who'd show him the town. He might even run across Melissa if he searched out her kind of place. Atlanta was supposed to have grown a lot in the last ten years. He probably couldn't find her if he tried.

The undefined haze of morning had turned into billowing clouds, as if by afternoon the artist of this sky had finally made a decision. Merle's foot lay heavily on the accelerator. The highway was young and fresh-looking as if it had been recently poured for a city which had sprung up as fast as a crop of corn. Merle didn't remember the roads to Atlanta being like this. He and Jenny had vacationed here once and the drive had been long and treacherous over a narrow pockmarked road.

What had been so memorable about Atlanta? The year

was 1942; Jenny was pregnant with Jay. She kept asking if Merle was going to join the Army. He promised he'd wait a while, but she didn't believe him. To take her mind off it, he laid out of work on Thursday, put her in the car, and started driving.

His speed felt much faster than the speedometer read. Why didn't he settle in Atlanta? Do enough work to get by. If he could *find* work. Although he was getting used to his hand, it might cause a problem. Not that it hurt so much now, but that he had stopped relying on it for hardly anything. A doctor he'd seen on the way down here said he could tape it up, but unless he operated, the hand wouldn't be useful again. "Not ever." Some nerves were smashed and most of the bones that worked his fingers were in pieces. Well, he could get a job doing something else. Moonshining. But that was a lot of work. There were times you needed to be able to protect yourself. Lots of times. He guessed he could set up his gambling room here. But he didn't know a Chunny who owned his own building or who had a deal with the law.

He registered at the Ponce de Leon Hotel because of what was across the street—Ray Lee's Blue Light Tavern. The desk clerk, a frizzy-haired woman with lipstick applied like crayon scrawl, gave him a room key attached to a rectangular piece of metal the size of a ruler. "That's so you won't walk off with my key," she said. She looked like she had a lot stored up to say about keys and key stealers if he uttered one word, so he nodded and trudged up the stairs. At the first landing, he stopped and asked her what time Ray Lee's opened. "Oh, one of those," she remarked before answering Seven o'clock.

Usually the thirst of dehydration wakened him, but he had not drunk as much as usual last night. By the brightness of the window shades he could tell it was late morning. Not a woman had walked into Ray Lee's last night who didn't already know whose lap she was going to sit on. Of course they hadn't known he was going to be there, and he'd gotten some sexy looks. And if he felt like hanging around one more night, he was sure there would be comers. But he was taking a chance. If Melissa arrived early . . . if the landlord called her . . . hell, if the landlord was the one laying her, he'd better get back to Columbus. Sleep hung onto him, although he'd gotten plenty, and he shrugged to get it out of his bones.

A sink was attached to the wall beside his bed, but there was no john in the room. He wet a washcloth and wrung water over his head. Then he ran the refreshing cloth over his entire body. He felt the six-day growth of his first beard, wiry as pubic hair. For the trip down the hall to the toilet, he put on his clothes which after so long seemed like a size too big. He should have thought to bring another set, but he hadn't really known he was leaving.

While he took a leak he looked into the unframed mirror hung by wire over the commode. His mouth, chin, and cheeks were dark and squarish as if someone had scribbled over a picture of him. He wondered whether Melissa would recognize him. He didn't return to his room although he thought it would have been funny to steal the key that lay with its unstealable ruler on his bedside table. But . . . it was more advantageous to get out of this place without paying. On the second floor he met Frizz-Face with a guest.

"Leaving, Mr. Mitchell?" she asked sing-song.

"I'll wait for you at the desk," he said politely. He could see her trying to decide whether or not to follow him, but then she turned back to helping the guest get his key unstuck.

He swung through the lobby like a doctor on call. The night here hadn't been so great anyway. No woman to bring home. If it had been worth his while, he would probably have paid.

Two hours later he was back where he ought to be, watching a poorly constructed red brick building through the windshield of his car. It was midafternoon and hot. The last beer of a six-pack he'd bought on the way was tepid. He drank it anyway. There was no parking space with shade, so he backed into the space directly in line with Jay's apartment. The building was styled like a beach motel with five units on the first floor and five on the second. Jay had lived in the end apartment on the second floor, 117-F.

The only trees left on this whole tract of land grew behind this particular building where construction had ended. Jay's luck. The forest was young so that only a few treetops showed over the roof. Everywhere else the ground was flat and dry. There was no shrubbery. A vague attempt had been made to plant grass but only patches had survived in the packed red soil. Around the base of the building, the brick mortar was stained red. Jay's blood, you could say, but all the buildings were like that.

He needed to stand up. His clothes were wet against him and his ass had gotten numb. He needed to take a leak. He needed some air. A stringy-haired girl came out of Gurney's apartment and sat on the sidewalk in the sun. Merle judged her to be thirteen or fourteen years old. The door slammed, startling her. Someone must have been pointing out that she'd forgotten to close it. After a few minutes she began playing some sort of game. She wet her fingers in her mouth and pressed them against the white cement. Drawing, he supposed, and watching the wet places evaporate. The sun was making its last swipe at them before it traveled farther away. Merle reached across the car and opened the door. Then he opened his own. The girl didn't look up. Only the slightest of breezes stirred through the car. The red brick began to look pink in the heat. The car was an oven cooking him. She stood up, walking lethargically down the steps. In the distance he could see the sun bouncing off the metal parts of a small playground. She headed in that direction.

With Gurney's door closed and the drapes pulled, Merle thought he could walk around the building and relieve himself in the woods. No sign of life had shown itself at any other apartment. His legs were aching to move. He slid out of the car, ass prickling from the disturbance. He rubbed it with his good hand, first one flank, and then the reach for the second, until the circulation flowed again. He unfastened two buttons at the top of his shirt. Still no movement from Gurney's, but what difference did it make? He was legitimately there to visit his daughter-in-law. If he wanted, he could probably drink beer all afternoon with Gurney. Then Gurney's wife—what was it, Rose? *Rosie*—might let a little more information pass between those whining lips of hers.

He had wondered earlier about which tree Jay had used, but in his haste to move without being noticed, he'd forgotten what he was approaching. He came full stride into the woods and stopped, surprised. He was on the opposite end of the building from Jay's apartment. The trees here were little more than saplings. Only deeper in the woods could he see some larger oaks and an ash or two. He struck a straight path through the trees where he could observe without being seen. Fifteen yards in, he stopped and let out an extended stream that made his bladder shrink painfully. He walked parallel to the building, stepping on the old piles of leaves that had had almost a year to mulch. He did not make a sound. Hunting seasons were planned for a reason, and it wasn't just to do with the animals. When he judged that he was even with Jay's apartment, he cut back. Each apartment had three windows. The view through Jay's was cut off by the unfinished side of three pairs of curtains. Merle bet that when Jay did it, he had left them all open.

Young dogwoods, maple saplings, and an uncharacteristic

pine stood outside the windows. It had been the pine. There were no low branches, so Jay must have had to shinny up. Bits of bark would have stuck to his clothes; his hands would have been sticky with resin. To have to shinny up a tree like a bear, on the way to hang yourself, seemed grossly undignified, enough to make you change your mind. Only it hadn't.

The pine, without doubt, even though he could see no telltale sign: no broken limb or worn bark. No other tree nearby could have held Jay's weight. How had he done it? Tied the rope around the branch, then placed the noose around his neck? Had he at the last moment changed his mind when he was already falling through the air? Merle leaned against the tree, feeling its rough bark prick through his shirt sleeve. He was short of breath. With his good hand he picked at a section of bark until it fell off. He studied the ground around the tree but saw nothing but two bottle caps, still shiny, and a piece of green glass. Nothing to indicate Jay. It was cool here and quiet. The pine tree had a firm resolute smell that might have been a nice last memory. He leaned against it again to enjoy the shade a few minutes more. He had thought he would collapse by this tree, but he hadn't. Suddenly, the smell of resin nauseated him. He lit a cigarette to blot out its odor.

A car drove up on the other side of the building. He came around quickly, walking a direct path to his car so as not to startle anyone who might not be Melissa. No one was in sight. The new car in the lot was a yellow Falcon. Not Melissa; she would still be trying her key in the new lock.

He opened his door less circumspectly than before and stood in the crack it made, leaning against the roof. The heat had lost its bite. She was bound to come soon. Lowering himself into the car, he pushed the glove-compartment button but the hinge stuck. He slapped it hard with the stump of his injured hand and a surprising fresh ripple of pain burst through his arm. The door dropped open. Ignoring the burning sensation, he rummaged through the mess—hundreds of bottle caps, some dirty napkins, a Coke bottle, pencils, a map of Connecticut, and a half pack of peanut-butter crackers. He gobbled them and was immediately sorry. Even though they were stale, he should have separated the halves, eating each one slowly so that his stomach would think it had had more. When he was a kid, he did Oreos that way, except he would teethe off the icing, put the halves back together, and offer the cookie to Otto.

Gurney's daughter wandered in sight from the opposite direction in which she'd vanished. Her hair was limp from the fierce heat of play. She trudged to the second floor, stopping at Jay and Melissa's window to peer through the crack in the curtains, something he ought to do. Her straight thin legs knobbed at the knees like bamboo. At her own door she opened the screen and twisted the handle but the door didn't open. She knocked and waited and then knocked again. Finally she leaned against the door, suffering from her tiredness, and tapped a steady tattoo at the highest point her fist would reach.

He had played the same trick on Otto many times, but Otto always took the cookie from him anyway. Why hadn't he ever refused? He would cram it whole into his mouth and say, "Where's the icing?" and then he would slug Merle or spit the chewed-up cookie in his face or tear his bed apart so he would have to make it up again. The worst was when he had run to their mother, stuck his finger down his throat, and thrown up on the floor in front of her white support shoes. Momma was cooking supper. She worked a split shift as a waitress and was supposed to leave again for work in twenty minutes. Unexpectedly Otto had puked a second time, and this time he soiled her pinkish-orange uniform with chocolate crud. She yelled angrily at Otto, but when she threw the hot pot of water, she aimed at Merle. "You bother him again and I'll kill you," she screamed. Bits of her hair trailed shabbily out of the net she wore. The top of his arm glowed red, but he didn't yell. His mother's wide gray eyes still menaced him, not Otto, refusing to be sorry, holding the empty pot high like a weapon in case he ran at her.

"I hate your guts," he said. The generous lips in her large flat face softened. She dropped the pot and knelt in front of him. He backed away, step by step, and then turned and ran, glancing back to see her curse the mess and slap Otto across the face. Tears had finally filled his eyes, but not from the pain.

From the woods next to the small frame house his grandfather had built at the edge of a pecan grove, he'd watched her leave for work. She hollered out the back and front doors for him to come, but he only sat and watched, building an acorn town on a slab of rock which had probably been in those woods since before the Indians. She finally left, but he kept on with his play until the woods began to dim. Several times Otto came out on the porch to call his name.

As the evening descended, Otto stood inside the house. His voice trembled slightly, reaching into a higher register with each new plea for Merle to return. Merle dug into the brown leaves and found ants to people his city. He dropped them one by one into the streets and under the houses, careful not to squash them. On the porch Otto whimpered. In a while Merle moaned, a deep animallike sound that moved like a wave up and down the scale.

"Merle!" Otto shouted once more before he slammed the door. The house lit up like a mansion at dusk as he ran through the rooms flipping on lights.

Well after dark Merle had let himself in the window of the bedroom they shared. He climbed onto his thin bare mattress on the floor in one corner and pulled the single muslin sheet over his head. In the living room the radio—Otto's only companion—crackled the "Tennessee Waltz."

Otto blubbered for a time but then there was only the static of the radio wandering off the channel. Maybe something in the night would get Otto sometime, smush him like Merle had smushed the ants one by one with his thumb against the granite floor of the town, leaning close so he could see, his breath a heat wave for them. He had left one alive to wander around the maze of acorns and leaves, finding his dead companions, then looking on and on for some life, some company. He was Merle and he was free forever to wander the country alone, unhampered by a blubbering brother and a mother that was nuts.

At midnight he woke to hear Momma leading Otto to bed. She came to his bed and kissed his cheek, her face lingering over his. He smelled the lilac odor in her hair fighting with the grease and smoke of the restaurant. He knew that she knew he was awake, but he would not open his eyes and she would not speak. He did not forgive her. Because she was sorry didn't make up for what she'd done.

Merle felt itchy again, ready to burst out of the car, knock down Melissa's door, wait for her to turn the key in the broken lock, and say Come in, good-looking. His hunger had returned full-steam. Only two o'clock and no sign of her and she probably wouldn't arrive for another day. At any rate the probability that she would have to come twice because of the keys grew in his mind. He would leave for food and return quickly. Someone finally opened the door for Gurney's daughter, but she turned at the sound of his motor starting and flattened her nose against the screen. As he pulled away, she waved, and without thinking, he waved back.

At a small curb market four blocks away, he found sandwiches and beer. While he was paying, he broke the plastic off a chicken salad sandwich and bit deep into it. He had a church key on the dash of his car, but he was thirsty now so he asked the cashier to open a can for him.

"I can't," the girl said, her eyes a dismal black. Blue

veins ran down the insides of her skinny arms. An opener hung from her belt by a looper clip.

"Sure you can." He pointed his finger like a pistol at the opener, dangling down her hip, and she stepped behind the cash register. They were the only two in the store. "*Now,*" he said, glancing around. "While I take a piss." He went down the last aisle where he had seen a bathroom. The room stank of urine, and no wonder, for when he shut the door he couldn't see to aim. He cracked it for light.

At the front counter one of his beers was neatly jacked open. So that he could be ready for anything—even spending the night in his car, he bought three more sandwiches, half-a-dozen packs of Cheese Nabs, potato chips, a case of Miller Beer, and an ice-cream sandwich that she forgot to ring up because he was eating it. He took his cache to the car and returned once more for a bag of ice and a Styrofoam cooler to store beer in.

He drove back into the parking lot as the yellow Falcon was leaving. In it sat a woman with black beehive hair and severe make-up—not Melissa. She looked dispassionately at him as together they passed their cars slowly over the asphalt bump in the road. He nodded as if tipping a hat, openly surveying her. They were close enough to touch, and he observed where the line of make-up stopped at her chin, revealing a darker dirty neck. She glanced at his car, but the look was meant for him.

After a couple of beers he fell asleep, propping on one arm so he would awaken easily. An hour later he opened his eyes. Sweat was streaming down his body and the air he breathed seemed to come from an oven. Then he heard it again, a voice softer than his own waking-up noises.

"Mister."

He tightened in his seat, startled. It was the girl, Gurney's daughter. She stood pressed against the hot door of the car, watching him focus on her.

"Gurney says you oughta come in out of the sun." She

showed no shyness, watching him through light brown eyes. Her eyebrows were faint and pale, drifting back from her eyes so that her face had a lack of definition.

"He does, does he?" Merle stretched, looking over the steering wheel at Gurney who leaned against the metal guard rail on the second floor. He wore the same stained T-shirt he had on yesterday. He made no sign to Merle, only ducked his forehead to wipe against his sleeve. "How'd he know I was out here?"

"I told him." Her thin shoulders straightened under her cotton shirt. Her breasts were just before needing a bra.

"You don't know me," Merle said. He wiped the sweat off his face.

"Yes, I do. I watched you through the curtain yesterday. You're Jay's daddy." She went on in a lazy voice: "Gurney says you can sit in our house if you want. He thinks it's too hot out here, but it's better here than in there where it's dark and hot too. He says if you don't want to come in, wave. And I'll bring you some water if you want some." Merle considered. "You don't want to come in, do you." A statement, not a question.

"Guess not," Merle said. He threw up a hand at Gurney, and Gurney, waving stupidly, turned back to his airless apartment. The cast of his shoulders showed relief.

The girl waited, unready to move, it seemed, but he didn't know what to say. He looked at his steering wheel, at the dash, at the white numerals of the speedometer, the 112,062 miles that he and somebody else had traveled in this car. Finally he grinned as he thought about his attractiveness to women, even, say, thirteen-year-olds. She made a slight noise, the beginning of a laugh perhaps, before it was cut off by self-consciousness. Then she dropped out of his periphery so quickly that he wondered if he had imagined all this. She had squatted like a drooping flower on the slight bare bank beyond the curb. Her toenails were outlined with red dirt. She cuddled her knees in her arms. Her underpants showed mud stain through the space between her legs. She did know there was a space.

"How old are you, honey?" he asked, looking at her with a frankness meant to scare her home.

"Fourteen."

He let his eyes wander searchingly over her folded-up body. Her skin bruised easily, he could see. A blood mark disfigured one knee and on her arm were printed the fingers of an irritated mother. They had to be Rosie's; Gurney didn't have that sort of thing in him. She didn't scare off. Now he was thinking of asking her to come sit on Daddy's lap, but what would he do if she said okay? Something funny about this kid. He hadn't quite figured it out, but something funny.

"Jay was my best friend," she said, knocking her knees lightly together—opening and closing that prettiest of sights. "He took me off every Sunday."

Merle pushed in his lighter and readied a cigarette. "Where to?"

"Lots of places. The park, fishing, the lake for ice cream." She grinned as she said "ice cream." Still part-kid. "We don't have a car," she said. Merle had thought that a rusty black Fairlane was probably Gurney's.

"How do you get places?"

"Taxicab," she said, raising her chin like she was special. "We've been to church in a taxicab before."

"That so." Merle lit his cigarette, puffing several times. "What's your name?"

"Marty. Used to be Martha. Jay said Martha sounded too old, like I had already finished with all the fun stuff." She was repeating something she didn't quite understand. "He even took me to Atlanta one day. They thought we were going fishing, but he took me to Atlanta. We got home real late and everybody thought that we'd run away."

"I'll bet."

Some life came into her vapid eyes. "They *did*," she insisted. "We didn't want to come back, but Jay thought we'd get arrested." She pulled a blade of grass from its socket and chewed the fresh end. "We were thinking about going to Alaska."

"He was going to run off with *you*?"

"Yes," she said. "He was going to *marry* me when I got old enough."

Crazy kid. He tried to stare the lying out of her. Her chin jutted out of her face like a small fist. Tears clouded her eyes.

"He hated her." She tossed her hair in the direction of the apartments. "We were going to leave this summer. He gave me his watch and told her he lost it—and then he asked for it back. He said nothing had changed. But he *knew*, and he sold it and left the money for her."

Merle opened the door for air. Now there was no metal wall protecting her. No cover on the book of her fairy-tale. "Gurney know all this?" She squatted again, not bothering to wipe her tears. "Don't you think there's something wrong with taking a man away from his wife and baby?"

She stared at the sky above his car top. "We were taking Jenny with us," she said quietly. The anger was gone from her eyes and her face looked plain, even boring. Merle swung his legs out the open door and propped his feet on the curb. The girl swatted at two sweat bees playing around her toes. The treetops behind the apartments looked painted on the sky. The red dirt looked hot enough to burn. She turned toward the place she lived, her mouth self-indulgent. "Now I'm stuck here," she said.

"What's your name?" he asked suddenly as if that would make things clear.

"I already told you. Marty."

"Oh yeah, used to be Martha."

Her eyes crossed his without expression like he was the blank blue sky. She unfolded herself, her muddy underpants disappearing under the checked dress, and walked away. Her neck was stiff and unyielding.

"You can go with *me*," he called to her, wanting to see what she would say.

"What would I want to go with you for?" She stopped but didn't turn around, her erect shoulders waiting for his dismissal. "You ain't going to Alaska, are you?" A whisper of hope rippled her voice. He didn't answer, and in a moment she walked away.

He listened to the radio as long as he could stand it because he didn't want to go to sleep before he was too tired and ruin whatever night's rest he might get in the backseat. His body cooled when the sun went down, but then he warmed up again. He turned off the gratingly cheerful Mouth of the South, and sat in the dark trying to dredge up some old interesting memory. Nothing came to mind. He felt as if long beautiful arms were pulling him down, down to bed. He slid over the seat into the back, quietly so not to disturb too much his semiconscious state. He thought about taking off his khakis. He lay down, his head on the armrest. His neck was uncomfortable, but finally it grew numb and he slipped into a dreamless sleep.

He was sweating when he awoke to the stink of sandwich wrappings, his clothes, and a leftover fried apple pie. He climbed into the front seat. The birds were taking advantage of the last sunless moments. Immediately, his muscles felt tired of sitting. If he were to live in this car in any permanent sense, he would have to have a regular exercise program. He ate the apple turnover, washing away its greasy taste with swigs of warm beer. The sun popped up, warming the car quickly. If Melissa had any brains, she would come early to move her furniture. By ten o'clock everyone who was leaving had left. Merle wondered what Gurney did for a living that let him stay home all day. He took one more walk in the woods. Thirty minutes later, Melissa drove up in a bright red Volkswagen Beetle which he had never seen before.

7
AUDREY

The weekend, two melancholy days of drizzle that could not faze Audrey's high spirits, passed without word of Merle. On Sunday night Paulette took supper to an invalid friend and Clayton wandered over. After joining their meal he sent Craig to his house to collect the portion of meatloaf Paulette had left him, and the three of them sat on the side stoop and fed it to George, a neighborhood dog. Clayton sent Craig back to his house for the green beans and corn. Craig climbed the steps dejectedly. He didn't smile when George swallowed whole the fatback in the green beans or when he nosed into but refused to eat either vegetable.

Over their heads the gray clouds pushed together like dough. A mist enveloped them, but no one moved. Craig said he would like to have a dog of his own, and Clayton said he saw no reason why he couldn't. Audrey could think of one—money—but she didn't comment. Mist changed into beads of water on their heads, making Clayton's and Craig's hair look webby. Hers too, she imagined. Clayton mentioned that it always seemed to rain on weekends. Except last, Audrey thought, but maybe he'd forgotten. Looking at her, Craig said that if he couldn't get a dog, maybe he could get a couple of hamsters. Clayton said a dog would be all right.

"Mom?"

Clayton glanced at her but didn't wait for the opinion in her eyes. Which was yes, she thought, getting used to the idea. Clayton seemed settled here, as if this stoop and this family were already his.

"Can I, Mom?"

The changing grays of the sky were fading into the spread of night. Audrey leaned back on her elbows, feeling the solidness of the cement stoop. Could Clayton simply switch houses? Craig's question hung in the air, nudging her back to the moment. "No hamsters," she said, "but a small dog might be nice."

Excitement shot red through his cheeks and he looked with awe first at Clayton and then at her. Which, in this case, was as it should be.

"You'll have to earn money for its food," she said, pressing Craig's leg with hers. "He has to be your total responsibility."

He knew he knew he knew he knew. . . .

"Good grades," she added.

He nodded. Anything.

"Help me carry in the groceries. . . ."

Around the corners of his mouth his smile began to strain. Clayton looked at her, his eyebrows raised into question marks. She struggled against him again. Craig's grin faded, waiting for the rest.

"I'm just kidding," she said, putting her arms around his narrow shoulders. "All I want you to do is feed it." She sent him to do his homework.

Clayton wanted her to come over to his house for a few minutes, but she was afraid Paulette would come back, so they stole across the rain-softened ground to the backyard. She leaned against the dying oak tree and he leaned into her. She needed this gentle loving. By now the mist had wet their faces. He rubbed his cold smooth cheek against hers. She felt him trying to comfort her in this sharing of Craig, as if the wetness on her face were the tears she hadn't shed. She wanted a man for Craig, she honestly did. Now that Jay was gone, he needed a good man's influence. Clayton comforted her a long time before he asked her for the rest, which she warmly gave.

It was nine o'clock and he didn't expect Paulette back until ten, so she invited him in for coffee. He walked back to Craig's room immediately and she heard them discussing homework. Clayton's tone was offhanded. She plugged in the percolator and joined them. He was leaning in the doorway talking about his experiences in math. When she ducked under his arm into the room, Craig was laughing.

"What's so funny?" Her neck was near, but not too near the crook of Clayton's arm. She felt his warmth.

Clayton explained; she laughed; Craig laughed again, less heartily, but it was his second time hearing the story. There was an awkward pause when they all let up, and she added an extra giggle to fill the space. They were deep inside the house. Craig looked at them, and she could see in his eyes the knowledge that something was new. That Clayton here like this was something to be considered, judged. He cocked his head before remembering that they were watching him.

"I'll start your bath," she said, breaking away. Clayton turned for the kitchen. When she had the water temperature right, she returned to Craig's room. He was still twisted in his chair, looking at the door. "Don't forget to turn off your water in a few minutes," she said. He nodded, half-hearing. He seemed to be waiting for something else. She lowered her voice confidingly: "Some men just don't know what to do with themselves if their wives leave the house for an hour." Craig turned back to his work as if he weren't listening. "Don't forget the water," she reminded in her normal voice.

Clayton had gotten out her heavy white ceramic mugs for them and stuck a spoon in the sugar bowl. He took up a man's space in her kitchen, a space vacant much longer than the three days Merle had been gone. She liked having him here. Under the table rested the blue metal toolbox which she would move tomorrow out to the shed or to the crawl space under the house. Over the stove the cat clock ticked, chipping away at the minutes. The longer he was gone, the longer it seemed he would stay gone. Until eventually she might summon the nerve to move his clothes out of his closet and his half of the chest of drawers. The coffee pot gurgled like a baby, a homey, soothing sound. A homey, soothing smell. If she didn't know better, if Craig were not in his room—the physical proof that he was a fourteen-year-old boy—she might think that this moment was years later, that Merle and Paulette were out of their lives, that only she and Clayton remained. She patted his back as she walked past to take the chair facing the dining room. She settled her eyes at the height that a grown boy might appear, walking in like a miracle, white-shirted, pink-faced, forgiving. Grown, and all this time over with.

She found his eyes searching her, demanding answers again. In a moment his question would come between them: "*Now* are you ready to leave?" Before he could speak she said, "I feel like you already live here."

The question backed out of his eyes. "I do too." He reached for her hand, but she shook her head no, directing her eyes toward the back of the house. Could she make an honest decision without knowing what had happened to Merle?

He drank a second cup of coffee, lifting her chin from where it had drooped near her chest. Perhaps he'd decided that they did not need to talk, that today was too perfect to stain with decisions. She smiled patiently at him, masking the confusion swirling inside. Without any experience at all he was good with her child. Without much experience he was good with her. There was calm at this table, calm in this kitchen, calm in Clayton's eyes. Those eyes that were trying to magnetize her. She felt terribly unsettled. He was somewhere in a future that she could only imagine; she was somewhere in the past of now. She still hated to mess up Paulette's life.

Nine-thirty came and he pulled her by the hand to the back door. "If you'll get me a piece of glass for this, I'll replace it," he said, pointing at the door pane patched with cardboard. He reached for the light switch and threw the kitchen into darkness. Taking her face in his hands, he kissed her forehead, then the tip of her nose, then her lips. She abandoned herself to the deep stomach-trembling sensation, trying to make her mind crawl into her breasts and lips. To make it feel and not think. The moon and stars were still hidden, so his face was not illumined for her. She had thought she wanted him because he was so calm. She had found that he was as exciting a man as she had ever known.

He left in the dark and she leaned against the door, genuinely weak, watching him bend for the two cooking pots on the ground near the steps and hurry through the rain between their houses. He turned on the porch light for Paulette. She was still there watching ten short minutes later when Paulette drove up on the grass to get as close as possible to the stairs. Outside the car she struggled with her umbrella but failed to get it open. She held it over her head anyway, for whatever use it was, and heaved up the steps stiff-legged. Clayton let her in. How could he have ever married a woman like that? What did it say about him? But then, how could she have married Merle?

On Monday when there was a slowdown at her window, Audrey called Otto and told him Merle was gone.

"Gone where?"

She didn't know. She didn't know why either, but she suspected it had something to do with Craig.

Otto's voice turned suspicious. "When did he leave?"

She thought sometime Friday.

Otto groaned. When Merle visited him on Thursday, he'd collected his pay check once before he met with Otto, and again after their conversation. He'd told the bookkeeper that Otto said it was all right to give him an advance, and the bookkeeper believed him. Two weeks pay, and he'd vanished. "I don't suppose he gave you any of it?"

"No." She had not taken time to think about her finances without Merle. She was still three months behind on their house payments, but her boss had worked out a plan with the Savings and Loan to spread the delinquent payments over the next year. The plan was based on Merle's having an income.

Otto was silent.

Audrey asked if he thought anything might have happened to Merle.

"Hopefully, yes," he said. "Realistically, no. Someone would have called you." Silence again. "Do you need some money?" He sounded as if she were a pesky fly.

Carol stood at her desk, waiting to ask a question. She seemed oblivious to Audrey, smiling to herself now and then as if deep in her own thoughts, but Audrey knew better. Perhaps this money matter was something she needed to see Otto about anyway. The house payment had been made for this month, but any day the fuel company would be filling their tank with oil. If Otto were to lend her money, they would need to discuss how she might pay it back.

"May I come by this afternoon after work?" she asked. For all Carol knew, she could be going to the doctor.

"Of course, of course," Otto answered effusively. She imagined his plump features spreading like a balloon.

It was Carol's fault she was having to do this, she thought, as she joined a thick wave of traffic headed in the westward direction of Otto's plant. She propped a hand on top of the steering wheel to block out the sun when she turned curves. For the first time today she felt too warm in her corduroy jacket. It was Carol's fault; otherwise she could have handled everything over the telephone.

She turned into the neatly painted parking lot. Otto's Cadillac, its top showily lowered, straddled two parking spaces. The upstairs lights were off, so Audrey walked to the basement where Otto's office used to be. A swirly green linoleum wrapped itself efficiently down the stairs and disappeared into the dimly lit hallway. Merle had told her that Otto had moved upstairs to the presidential offices, but he'd lied. A doorway of light shone out of the opening. Audrey stepped into it. From his desk Otto caught her with his eyes. She felt pulled into the room. A huge jar of lemon drops, half-empty, sat on one corner of his desk.

"You must have heard me coming," she said teasingly. She wished there were some other people here, but her footsteps had echoed emptily all the way down the hall.

"No," he said in a considered tone. "I've been waiting like this since you called." He stood up. "You think I'm exaggerating, but I'm not. I've been waiting for you right here." He grinned the peppy grin of a cheerleader prodding you to cheer. She noticed that he had slimmed down since she last saw him. His shirt tail was tucked securely, his hair smoothed as if he had just combed it. Perhaps he *had* been waiting these six hours. He pulled a small leather chair around to his side of the desk and motioned her to it. Stale tobacco fumes along with the light smell of lemon drops pleasantly scented the room. Audrey could not help a glance once again at the wallpapered wall where Marilyn Monroe was supposedly sealed away forever. An oil painting of a buoy in a storm now hung there. He offered her a cigarette from a silver box. When she reminded him that she didn't smoke, he said he thought she might have started by now.

"How's Theresa?" she asked.

"Theresa—business—everything is fine," he said, sweeping away all the questions she'd thought of asking.

"You look thinner," she said. He stared at her longer than was comfortable. Finally she pulled her eyes away, glancing around his perimeter, reaffirming what she knew of him: his balding head, his white sweaty shirt, his small plump hands. He still sweated like a stock boy; even his forehead was damp. She glanced back at his eyes, trying to break this strange silence, but he only kept staring. He seemed to be trying to make up his mind about something.

"Otto!" she finally said in mock exasperation that was actually quite real.

He smiled. "You don't believe that I've been waiting for you all day. Do you?" She shook her head, giving him the answer he wanted. "I have been. And now it's hard to believe that you're actually here. You look more beautiful than ever."

"Thank you," she whispered. She ought to tell him to stop. She ran her fingers through her hair several quick times. "Look, Otto, I need to borrow some money." She leaned forward. "I don't want you to give me any. Even with all you have, you shouldn't have to give twice."

He said nothing.

"But just this once," she continued weakly. Perhaps he had decided to give her nothing. "If you can give double to our family this month, then maybe someday I can do something for you. Or Theresa," she added quickly. She doubted the occasion would ever arise. "I'l pay you back too," she added, her voice more intense in case he thought she were asking for charity. "I can't say how because I don't know." Her lips twisted with emotion. She sat up straight. "Will you, Otto?"

"I love the way you say my name."

She looked questioningly at him.

"Do you know how many people say 'Oddo'? Even Theresa."

She laughed once and then thought about it—Merle said Oddo too and probably didn't realize it. She would have to tell him sometime. She laughed more, too much, but she couldn't seem to stop. He grinned, a wide toothy grin, and his nostrils flared slightly. She recrossed her legs, relaxing. He glanced quickly at her knees.

"Otto," pronouncing the *t*'s crisply. "Can you help me?"

His face brightened, but he didn't smile. With a pencil he made silver scratches on his black ink blotter and then began flipping the pencil back and forth between two fingers. It looked nervous. "You know I will," he said.

"I'll repay you. I want to."

He waved one hand at her. "Don't even think about it."

"I insist," she said.

"I won't let you."

She accepted the favor. She would try to convince him once more before she let the subject drop forever. He leaned forward seriously as she had done a moment before, hands cupping his knees. He looked as if he might fall out of his chair. If he did, he would land at her knees. No telling what he would try with opportunity so close. She imagined him kissing her knees, touching her feet, sliding his fat hands up her skirt. What would she do? She saw his lips move, and in her imagination the words sounded: "I want to make love to you."

"Audrey?" he said.

She lifted her eyes carefully to his. "Yes?"

"Did you hear me?" She looked at his thin hair which revealed the sickly pink plain of his scalp.

"No," she said.

"I said I want to make love to you."

The imagination rarely repeated itself. She jumped up, the way one does in emergencies.

"Sit down, sit down," he said, irritated. Like an animal trainer. She sat. "Answer me," he demanded.

"Don't talk that way, Ot—" She stopped before she said his whole name.

"Why not?" he barked. He rolled his chair off its platform onto the carpet and took both her hands, caging her. His voice changed to a murmur: "I've been wanting to talk this way for years." She sat stiffly, not letting him pull her hands too far into his lap. "Did you know it?" he asked.

"No."

"Surely you've realized how I felt."

She shook her head.

"Well, I've tried to hide it," he said, explaining to himself. "I didn't *want* you to know really. Or Merle or Theresa. But seeing him Friday made it all clear for me. The whole weekend I could think of nothing but how miserable my sweet little Audrey must be. And how I wanted to help you, take care of you." He pulled at her hands, but she would not relax them. "When you called this morning, it was as if my prayers had been answered. You finally *needed* me."

She pulled back from him involuntarily, but his grip had the strength of electricity. This was the craziest story she had ever heard. Theresa must have refused to sleep with him this week. He breathed heavily as if he were exerting himself.

"Tell me, honey, is it Theresa you're worried about?" He rubbed the tops of her hands with his thumbs. "Sweet thing."

"Merle would kill you if he found out." Otto grinned smugly, and she realized that she had misstated herself. "Found out"—as if something were going to happen between them.

"I can handle myself. Besides, he doesn't have to know. Nobody has to know." Then he knelt at her feet, pushing his chair out of his way with his buttocks, reaching around her back. A ring of keys fastened to his back belt loop clicked as he moved. Before he got a firm hold on her, she jumped up again.

"What if someone's still working?" she asked from several steps away. He waited on his knees by her chair.

"Shut the door and come back here," he ordered. She shut it and came halfway across the room.

"Get up, Otto," she said firmly. "If you don't want to give me the money, that's fine."

He stood up slowly, his face angrily betrayed before it went blank. Pushing his chair back in front of his desk, he sat down and motioned her to her seat. He picked up his letter opener, a silver blade with a swirling mermaid as the handle. Then he started again as if this were the beginning and he hadn't been on his knees at all.

"I care about you deeply, Audrey. Whether my feelings are shared or not, I don't know. Money does not . . . I repeat, does not . . . enter the picture." He grimaced. "What I give you, I give from the love I have for you." He paused, twiddling the letter opener. "And the love I have for Craig. He's the nearest to a son that I have, you remember."

She watched the mermaid roll from one fleshy pink palm to the other, wondering whether or not she believed him. Craig was his only nephew. Otto could help him a great deal if he were so inclined.

"Do you care for me at all?" he asked.

"Of course I do. But I can't make new problems for myself before the old ones are solved." She sniffled a little and he offered his handkerchief. The tenseness in his face relaxed, and his cheeks and chin looked plumper. The phone rang, but before he picked it up, she knew it was Theresa. He stuttered that he'd be home shortly, that he was attending to some business. Said, in fact, too much.

"You see?" she said when he hung up. If she could just find enough things that would show him the futility of a relationship without turning him against her. He could help Craig so much.

"I don't see anything," he growled, speaking to her much as he had spoken to Theresa on the phone. As if she were already his property.

"Otto," she said reprovingly. She slurred the *t*'s slightly.

But he was no longer imploring. "I love you, Audrey." He made a note on his scratch pad, perhaps an errand to run for Theresa. Still writing, he said, "I want to be your lover. I will be your lover." He sounded as if he were telling a potential client what a good builder he was. Rolling his chair out of the kneehole, he folded the note and put it in his breast pocket. She wondered if she dared ask what he paid mistresses. But this really wasn't funny.

"I care about you too, Otto. But this is the wrong time. I don't know if there will ever be a right time." Her hands felt weak.

For long seconds he didn't speak, and then for minutes. Looking at him, she thought it could very well be true that he had waited for her all day. He was waiting now, as patient as a cat, the letter opener falling from one hand to the other. Gradually her ears picked up its dull thud thud thud. She noticed the fluorescent light buzzing and heard Otto faintly sucking at a handful of lemon drops hidden under his tongue. He was not, in other words, planning to open his wallet.

"Oh, Otto," she said, moving meekly to him. "How can I get you to understand?" He did not collapse toward her as she expected. A plastic picture cube, obscured previously by the jar of lemon drops, sat on his desk. The pictures she could see were of fish Otto had caught. She touched the back of his neck lightly with her fingertips, but still he didn't respond. The hand that held the letter opener was clenched tightly. She touched it. Finally, he turned the chair on its rivet, took her around the waist, and pulled her into his lap. He put a clammy hand against her skin at the open neck of her blouse and slid it jerkily down her chest until it hovered above one breast. With the other hand he began pulling her blouse out of her skirt. He kissed her neck, up under her chin, and behind her ears. She looked behind him at the paneled wall.

Upstairs someone working late shut a door and began walking down the hall. She jumped off his lap, pushing quickly at the tail of her blouse. His face flushed as if he had been drinking. "No more," she whispered.

He looked at his hands folded importantly on his desk and chuckled, but not meanly. "Oh yes," he said. When the footsteps were gone, he came to her and unfolded her angry arms from under her breasts. He grabbed her up against him, and she felt his penis pushing into her stomach. Finally he kissed her, swabbing his mouth into hers like a puppy. When she didn't fully respond, he pushed back to see why, but she grabbed his arms and pulled him toward her. She didn't want him to see her face.

"*Here* is a horrible place," she said, breaking away for a breath. How far was he going to make her go? She let him pull her close once more, and then stepped determinedly back. "Otto, we must stop." He stood there, smiling at her like a bragging boy, not trying at all to hide the wet spot on his trousers where he had ejaculated just knocking against her. She tucked her blouse and straightened her off-center skirt. It was hard now to believe that this would help Craig.

Otto returned to his desk, finally aware, she supposed, that she knew what had happened. Opening a bottom drawer, he pulled out a green metal box and unlocked it with one of the keys off his belt loop. He peeled through a stack of money five inches thick to pick out six twenties. "Is this enough?" he asked. "I can give you more if you want."

"I never knew he got this much." Merle usually gave her thirty-five dollars a week.

"He doesn't."

She blushed; the extra was for cooperating. Still she was excited about the money, excited about Otto's inclination toward Craig. She really hadn't had to *do* anything. He folded the bills and handed them to her. He opened another box on his desk, rewarding himself with a cigar. She stuck the money in her purse and then moved it to her jacket pocket. Merle could always be there when she got home. He had walked out the door with her wallet before.

"Goodbye, Otto," she said fiercely. She wanted him to know that she wouldn't "pay" every time, maybe not ever again. Not even if it meant summer camp for Craig or college. Not even. When she was at the door, he called her name.

"Will I see you next Monday?" he asked carelessly, puffing at his cigar.

"I don't know." Increasingly, she felt tricked.

"Or Friday or Tuesday . . . or Wednesday or Thursday." He leaned back, surveying her. "Wednesday, Friday, *and* Monday, if you like. In fact you can visit me every day."

"I don't think so."

"I'll be waiting," he said. She studied his soft beige carpet. An image of her lying naked on this rug with Otto bouncing around on top forced its way into her mind.

"Wait then," she said venomously. She hurried down the hallway, her heels tap-tap-tapping the floor. The moistness in her underwear disgusted her. She felt guilt painted in red all over her face. Please don't let her see anyone. They would know everything by her eyes, her trapped-animal eyes. Behind, she heard him locking up and starting down the hall after her. She would not go through this again. If he tried to force her, she would threaten to go to Theresa. Or to Merle. That would scare him. It always had.

When she arrived home, Clayton was in her kitchen, helping Craig heat up some frozen spaghetti sauce she'd made a couple of weeks ago. Water was boiling, ready for the noodles. She fought back an urge to push past them both to privacy. "Hello, everybody," she said. She had meant to sound warm, but her voice had come out cool and suspicious.

"Hi, Mom," Craig said.

Clayton turned from the stove where he was stirring sauce. "You're very late," he said, leaving space for her to explain. As if she had to. He didn't even *live* here. He'd never even said he wanted to marry her. He was another Otto for all she knew.

"Honestly, Clayton," she said, pride affecting her voice. "If I owe anybody an explanation, it's Craig." She went on: "Honey, I had to work late. You were helpful to get things started."

"It was Clayton's idea," Craig said.

Clayton wiped his hands on a dish towel and said to the room that he was glad to have been of help. He threw the towel into the sink.

"Won't you stay for supper?" she asked, but it was too late and too false.

"Thanks, but I believe that that place is set for someone else." The table was set for three. She glanced quickly at his eyes but they were unreadable.

"That's for Dad, in case he comes back tonight," Craig said. He looked innocently at each of them before dropping spaghetti into the boiling water. Clayton moved toward the door.

"I appreciate your helping Craig," she said, her eyes pleading for his understanding. She had moods like anyone else. But as he left, his eyes lit on nothing. She watched his shoulders move erect across the yard. She went absently to the refrigerator. A freshly made garden salad sat in a bowl on the top shelf, shaming her. Why was she always so stupid? Why could she never reject what was bad and open her arms to what was good. She would be served right if the money had vanished from her pocket on the way home. But the small folded wad was still there. Why did she even need money if she were going to leave with Clayton?

"Mom?" Craig called from the stove. He looked at her knowingly. "I've been thinking that I want a special kind of dog. Not just one from the pound."

She looked blankly at him. "What are you talking about now?" she asked.

"You said I could have a dog."

Children could be so cruel, not only to other children, but to adults. Why hadn't he invited Clayton for supper? And Clayton patiently chopping his lettuce, finding a meal in the freezer for them. "I've changed my mind," she blurted. "No dog."

8

MERLE/MELISSA

From the way the Volkswagen bounced over the bumps in the road and the tires wheeled around the parking-lot islands, Merle knew it was Melissa before she had even alighted from the car. She must have already had the baby. Her door flew open before she turned off the motor, as if she were going to run into her apartment. He opened his own door quickly, ready to intercept her. She sat, leaning to her rearview mirror, and for a moment he thought she had discovered him. She was only applying lipstick.

Marty came out of her apartment and stood at the railing looking down. Heat waves rose toward her from the rear motor of the car. Her hair was pulled behind her head. She must have been coming to see him. She looked his way, and then at the red roof of the car. Melissa was heaving her way out of the seat, the unborn baby still huge in her stomach. She had not seen Marty. Light-footed, the girl hurried back into the dark apartment. She braced her feet to slam the door as hard as she could.

Melissa looked up to the second floor. She wore white shorts and a pink smock cut low on her bosom. She had clipped off her long curls and her hair formed a single shock of red, fluffy on top but smooth in the back like the breast feathers of a bird. She shut the car door, still looking up toward the slam, and pulled at the back of her shorts, loosening them from the sweat of her legs. She was too pregnant to move anything, too pregnant to escape him. She walked slightly swayback, holding the baby up with her shoulders. Her legs were heavy, but firm and fine-looking. Halfway to her shuffling figure, he spoke, not wanting to startle her.

"I heard you were going to be here," she said flatly, turning to give him one quick glance. She trudged on toward the steps.

She didn't seem to expect a response, so he didn't give one. No need to ask about the new key; he'd bet fifty dollars she already had it. He followed her quietly. She passed Gurney's door without pausing and stuck a shiny gold key in the new deadbolt, bending slightly so that the shorts flared invitingly from her ass. Blue veins bulged in the back of her knees from the baby's weight.

They entered a long dim room that smelled of carpet cleaner although the shag carpeting was soiled in large areas. In the antiseptic air Merle was briefly aware of his own sour odor before it blended. He preferred to leave the door open and open some windows, although it was cooler here than outside.

"This apartment stinks," Melissa said. The sun strained at the edges of the curtains, but she turned on lights instead of opening them. The room became only vaguely brighter. On the near end was a sitting area of shabby furniture and on the far, an area for dining. Three doors led off the room, one for the kitchen and two for bedrooms. A white paper lantern hung over the small dining table. "These places are so goddamn gloomy," she said.

Without the dead air, the apartment could have been vacated only a few minutes before. A stuffed rabbit and several other toys lay on the floor. Magazines and old newspapers covered a glass-topped coffee table. Melissa set the rabbit on the chair and began to reassemble the paper, paying less attention to him than she would a child. She motioned toward the furniture finally. "Have a seat unless you're tired of sitting."

He chose the near end of the couch and she took the

chair, pulling the rabbit into her lap. "Well?" she said, her tired eyes focusing on him for the first time. Her arms rested on the arms of the chair and she stuck out her bare feet and crossed them on the table top, leaving her sandals on the floor. She looked ready to sit there all day.

"Where's Jenny?" he asked.

"With a friend."

He wondered who.

"What happened to your hand?" she asked, finally noticing. She halfway uncrossed her feet, but then changed her mind and set them back on the table.

"Answer *my* goddamn question," he snarled. He had showed his feelings too soon, but with her lazy face, it was hard to maintain the pitch of his anger. She leaned her head back against the chair, half-closing her eyes. There was something fortresslike about the mound of her stomach, which rose to protect her from him. He wondered if Marty stood at the common wall of the two apartments, her ear at the open end of a drinking glass trying to amplify their voices. He relaxed; it seemed absurd to do otherwise.

"It's a long drive from Atlanta," she said. "Especially with these legs." She turned over one leg to examine her varicose veins. Then she looked at the other one. "What are you doing here?" she asked. She followed an especially dark vein with her pink fingernail. Then she folded her hands in her lap and asked the question again with her eyes.

"Came to see *you*," he said, not able to resist the old challenge. She had once found him very attractive.

"Oh yeah?" she said sleepily. She turned her face to the side, showing him the graceful line of her chin and neck. "How about dinner at the cafeteria and then the double feature at the drive-in? I like my steak ra-a-are. Or whatever . . ." she said, shrugging like a girl.

"Whore," he said abruptly, but the expression on her face didn't change.

"Son-of-a-bitch." Quietly then, but in a voice scratchy

with emotion, she told him that she could play any game he wanted to play anytime he wanted to play it. And she would win. She was going to be here one hour, one hour and no more, and if he had anything important to ask her, he'd better ask it now.

He leaned back against the sofa, letting the tension in his body disperse into the cushions. When he spoke again, his voice was without challenge. "I want to know what happened to Jay."

"How many days have you got?"

He sat forward slightly. "Enough," he said, his voice still even.

"I wasn't here when it happened," she said, dropping her sarcasm. He nodded. She dug her fingers into the gray fur of the rabbit. "But I'll tell you like I told the cops *and* the Army . . . he had gone nuts. I was honestly afraid that he might hurt me. Look what he did to that chair." She pointed her thumb over her shoulder.

Merle refused to look now, but he had noticed the broken chair in one corner when they first came in.

"Why aren't you looking?"

"I already saw it."

"Look again, goddamn it. He almost killed me with it."

"Come on, Melissa." Hard to let that pass.

She snapped forward in her chair. "What do *you* know? You hadn't seen him in eight months. I say, he tried to kill me with *that chair*."

"Too bad he missed." It was easier to be in control when she wasn't. He crossed his legs to try to overlay the edginess he felt. She sat almost prone, humming in a light soft voice while she danced the rabbit around on its hind feet. He knew who was crazy. She kept on and on, and he knew she wouldn't stop until he made her.

"Cut out the crap."

In a high singsong voice, she tittered to her rabbit, "Cut out the crap."

"I'm going to count to three."

"One-two-three, one-two-three," she said.

He came out of the chair at her and she threw the rabbit across the room as if *it* were his target. "Stay away from me," she said, squirming until she was upright in the chair. When she saw he was going past, she cried defiantly, "You always thought he was so smart. What do you say to your brilliant son sleeping with a fourteen-year-old?"

He wanted badly to connect with something like another windowpane or the front of her refrigerator. Instead he swung his left fist several times in the air. "I don't believe either one of you," he said with effort from behind her, and then he vanished into the kitchen. He found two six-packs of beer minus one can under the sink and put them in the freezer compartment, wondering if the missing beer was Jay's last. In a corner was a green plastic trash can and in it was the missing can. He did not pick it up. He poured a beer over ice and watched the cubes writhing in white suds. Melted to death. She yelled to ask him what he was looking for.

When he sat across from her again, she said, "Thanks for bringing me one."

"Anytime."

She went for her own, but when she came back she brought ice water. "I'll catch you later," she said, raising her glass as if to toast him. "When the beer's cold." She slid down in her chair again, more supine than before, her legs stretched on the table like marble columns. Her stomach was at an odd angle so that it looked to Merle like it lay just under her chin. "So, you've met Marty," she said, her voice as casual as her position.

"Yep. A knock-kneed dirty little kid. Who you trying to fool?"

"He might as well have slept with her. He would have sooner or later. They were going to run away together.

Gurney read all about it in her diary. They were even planning to steal Jenny."

"You believe that?"

"Why not? In a diary you tell it all."

"Or you make it all up." He drained his glass in one gulp, letting the nearly melted pieces of ice slide down his throat. Melissa patted the nape of her neck. Merle figured her hair had been cut only recently.

She caught his stare. "Like my new hairstyle?" she asked. Her green eyes gazed intimately at him as they once had teasing Jay.

"Sucks," he said.

"I don't like your beard either."

She laughed, but it was a laugh full of hate, like she was spitting. "Anyway, I guess he probably wasn't sleeping with Marty. He said he wasn't, and usually he told the truth." She looked at her hands which lay silent in her lap. "You should have seen him that day. He hadn't been to work in a week. Hadn't brushed his teeth in three days. He smelled like a zoo. His hair looked like a bird's nest. He said he wasn't going to eat again until I took the new dinette set back. I had just *got it*," she said, eyes suddenly flaming. "I wasn't going to take it back." She leaned over the arm of the chair to look at the damaged furniture. "My mistake was I waited an hour too long. That was my mistake. If I had left when he first started whining, maybe he wouldn't have torn it up." She fanned herself a couple of times with her hand.

"Other people know more than I do about the rest," she said. "Marty found him. She heard Jenny screaming and came over to help Jay calm her down. *Supposedly*. Jenny was sitting in her crib with bowls of food spread all around her. When she carried the bowls to the kitchen, she saw Jay hanging from that pine tree outside the window. I don't know why he didn't go back further in the woods. I *do* know. He thought I'd find him. He wanted to leave me something to remember him by. But all he did was send Marty to the hospital. They moved Jay to the funeral home before I got back, so I never had to see him. Then Audrey came and took him . . . but you planned that."

He asked dully how the police had located her. "Wait a minute before you answer." He unfolded slowly from his chair, thinking he might need to throw up. In the kitchen he pushed the curtains back from the window and gazed outside. To his left stood the pine tree, but he didn't look at it. The rest of the trees were so still that they hardly looked alive. He waited for something to move, but nothing did. Not even a squirrel appeared, to spring life into the branches. When his eyes no longer could stand the temptation of the pine tree, he moved to the refrigerator. To open a beer, he had to anchor it between his stomach and the edge of the counter. He poured each one slowly, trying to avoid a head, but it was difficult when he didn't have a second hand to tilt the glass. He had better have his hand operated on after all. Too many things he couldn't do. To carry the glasses, he had to press them against his chest.

She was asleep, her mouth slightly open, chin sunk in rolls against her chest. She looked worn and tired, much older than at Christmas, the last time he'd seen her. He wondered if, before he died, Jay had aged so much too. Off her guard, her chest was sunken instead of at its alert best. He noticed her hands, folded around the toy rabbit. At least she did not neglect them. Her nails were painted carefully and her skin had been oiled to healthiness. Her hands had a strong masculine sense combined with a grace that he found compelling.

His hand tightened across the two glasses. He noticed her navel protruding through the fabric of the shorts, forced outward by the baby. The next Mitchell. According to the law anyway. He felt a craving to touch her, but suddenly she awakened. She moved quickly to straighten her slack body. He wanted to stop her, keep her exactly like she was.

Almost like an accident, one of the glasses began sliding from his hand. It fell into that sweet tempting lap of hers, a not-so-cold shock, but plenty wet.

"Jesus Christ," she screamed. Her white shorts went opaque and her dark pregnant nipples poked curiously through the pink smock. He took the second glass of beer and poured it over her head. Her bright red hair gave off a light shampoo smell. "Stop it," she yelled, flailing both arms at him. He backed behind the chair to avoid her, letting the last suds drip out of the glass. She bounded for the door, but he caught her arm and pulled her around like in a yard game.

"Sit down," he said brutally. "I haven't finished talking to you." She was angry, but he had scared her enough so she wasn't going anywhere. Already her face was dry of the beer, and the heat of her body was drying her shirt. Only her hair was totally wet, sleeked down against her head like a swimmer's.

"Thanks one hell of a lot," she said. He headed toward the kitchen. "Get me another goddamn beer, and bring me the roll of paper towels."

"You look kind of funny," he said as she wadded up some of the towels and blotted the wetness.

"You look kind of old."

He winced, not expecting her to recover so quickly. "Getting older every day. Just like you." He picked up a magazine. "Look, why don't you go in the bathroom and straighten yourself up a little. Get a few of your things together. Late this afternoon, I want you to go on a little trip with me."

"Where?" she asked. "If it's to Fort Benning, I'm not going." He didn't change expression. "I'm not going to Atlanta with you either. Or anyplace else."

"None of those places. I thought we might just ride around the country for a few days."

"Around Georgia?"

"Hell, no. The *whole* country."

"Are you nuts?" she asked. "I'm supposed to have a baby in two months. You can't go places when you're this pregnant."

"You just came here."

She sat forward. "I won't go with you." Her voice grew more anxious as she saw his obstinate face. "I won't and you can't make me."

He smiled at that.

"I have a little girl with a babysitter. . . ."

"Tell your boyfriend to go get her."

"No." Her hair looked like sparks around her head. "I don't have a boyfriend."

"See what you can figure out." He motioned her toward the bedroom. "While you're getting your things together."

She stood, flushing deeply. "I'll make a deal with you. I'll do whatever you want, tell you anything you want to know. I'll even stay until tomorrow so you have time to hear everything." She guessed she could keep Sally's car overnight. "But then I *have* to go."

He nodded.

At the doorway she stopped. "If you make me go with you, I swear I'll have you arrested for kidnapping."

He nodded again.

He thumbed through *True Confessions*, stopping for fun to examine the bust-improvement advertisements. He guessed it was tough being a woman if you weren't born with decent-sized knockers. Melissa could have fifteen nice legs and it wouldn't mean anything without her tits. He wondered if she were changing clothes. He was ready to get back in a car sooner than he expected. He lit a cigarette, his first of the day. For some reason he had forgotten about smoking, although now that he remembered, he had a craving that seemed to have been with him for days. He stretched forward to look into the bedroom and saw her standing at the window looking out into the woods. She'd better get her ass in gear. He glided over the shag carpet to the door. Nothing had been done. She was bound to have heard him by now, but she didn't move except to lean her stomach more heavily against the windowpanes. The bed had been made by tossing the spread over disordered sheets. Someone's last night here. Jay's or Melissa's. Or Jay and Marty's. Maybe Melissa and Gurney. No telling whose really.

She walked to the dresser, a flimsy piece of furniture made of a material like wallboard. She jerked open all the drawers and returned to her post at the window. There were a few things inside, but not many. "I gave all Jay's stuff to Gurney," she said, more to the outside than to him. "If you want any of it, I'll get it back."

They stood for so long that his legs began to tire. Every once in a while, he could see her catch her reflection in the glass and start slightly. The room had a fresh paint job, he noticed, one applied with skill. Jay's work, taking after his father.

Then without planning, he began walking toward her. She turned to watch him, his good hand working his belt and zipper, his bad hand trying to help. Her face was as blank as the walls. She didn't resist while he jerked down her elastic shorts and underpants. He undid her bra and pushed it up near her neck. He started to pull the bedspread away so that they would lie on the softer cooler sheets, but he hesitated. She lay down obediently, her green eyes staring in the area of his neck.

"Don't hurt my baby," she said. "You bastard."

He grunted, but it was a grunt of passion, not assent. He curled the midriff of his body up around her belly, lay his mouth on her soft flabby bosoms, and entered her. Only a few thrusts and he would be finished. He looked at her white neck and the soft chin turned away from him and saw what Jay had first wanted. Trying to be gentle for his grandson's sake, he sucked in his stomach, forming a natural cave for the mound. Then he came. A moment later she threw him aside and went to the bathroom to clean herself.

The bedspread was rough with cotton tufting. Merle wanted to pull it aside and find some comfort in the soft old sheets, but Jay was in them—his smell, his last lay with his wife, his last lay with Marty, maybe his first and last lay with Marty. If he looked, Merle knew he would find tired pubic hairs, dried spots of semen, sweat-scented sheets, signs of life, dead signs of life, dead signs of a dead life. If he looked. As he lay on his side listening to Melissa's noises in the bathroom, he grew used to the rough bedspread. He smelled Clorox in the covers and saw dustballs around the edges of the closet doors. What had Melissa done with Jay's books? He had seen none here. Given them to Gurney?

He wished he hadn't done it, but it was over with and too late and besides it wasn't lust but a desire to show Jay—if he could see from wherever he was—what he himself had known all along. It was the fault of the heat, the long time without a woman, the sweltering days in a car waiting for this one. "Don't hurt my baby"—shit. Somebody had banged her last night, the night before, the night before. Who'd she think she was kidding? He would never have screwed Melissa—he *swore*—if Jay had been alive. He would never have lain in Jay's bed like this, his pants loose around him, his penis pink and limp, his shirt raised because he'd wanted his stomach to touch her firm swollen one. It had reminded him of Jenny when she was pregnant with Jay. He would never have done this at all except to show that Melissa was a whore.

Perhaps he could doze here for a few minutes while she took her bath. She would not expect him to be asleep so she would wake him with her splashing, the drain, the door opening. But if she got away now, he would never be able to find her again. He grabbed the pillow from under the spread and, fastening his pants, carried it into the living room. He would sleep on the couch. She might still slip by. He would have to lie across the pathway of the door. Not so comfortable, but he wasn't so tired either. He had slept well in the backseat last night. He would not mind having a shower himself, but the only way he could do that would be to lock Melissa in the bathroom with him.

She shook the last of an old box of Comet evenly around the bathtub and scrubbed the porcelain with an old nail brush. She rinsed the tub with the shower head, turning off the water several times to let all the dirtiness drain away. She was in no hurry. Two towels hung on the rack. With one she dried out the tub. When she finished, she lay its fresh side up on the floor as a mat.

She filled the tub with hot water only and steam rose to make a cloud at the ceiling, settling fog on the mirror and the white fixtures. The air was like cotton, and every few minutes she felt as if she were going to suffocate. Then the desire for fresh air would subside. She laid out her toilet supplies and from under the sink she brought old facial and body creams and powders. She picked up the towel from the floor, using its soiled side to wipe the mist from the mirror. Leaning close, she looked at her eyes, at various angles of her nose, at her pores, at the pores filled with blackheads. When the mirror clouded, she wiped it clear. She smeared white cream under and over her eyes.

The water looked as deep as a river. She tested it with her toes but it was too hot. She sat on the closed top of the toilet, leaning back against the sweating tank to support her stomach. Its coldness relieved her momentarily. Without testing this time, she stepped into the bath, pretending her feet were someone else's. It was the only way she could stand the pain.

Her feet and ankles grew numb from the heat and she began a slow descent into the lovely gray water: first onto her knees and then a luxurious sway back onto her buttocks like an exotic dancer. Her skin tingled and sweat dripped from her face. Her scalp itched. Finally she lay completely submerged except for her face and where her stomach broke the surface.

No, he couldn't try one more time. She was sorry but she was tired. Her body was bored—did he hear her?—bored. She was cleaning herself now of all the wasted perspiration, unused lubrication that was, *tell the truth Jay*, sweated and oozed for nothing. Would he please leave or go to sleep? Anything, just get away from the door and stop whimpering that this time you'll be able to.

She submerged her head past her ears, drowning out his voice with echoes from other apartments: the fits and starts of appliances, the mutter of distant conversation, the humming lives of the water pipes themselves. The water let loose the beer smell in her hair.

"What would you do if I did come out?" she whispered hatefully. "Nothing." She lathered her hair. She lifted her feet to survey the deltalike network that the water was making of her skin. No matter what he thought, she didn't stay behind that locked door to punish him, but to recover herself. She wondered if he knew what caused the dead skin on her toes to turn white. Why did wrinkles come on some parts of her body and not others? Her elbows and not her stomach, for example. She doubted that they taught you stuff like that in college, but maybe they did. Could she lie here for twenty-four hours and make everything wrinkle? Even her stomach?

She was surprised Merle hadn't knocked on the door by now, wanting her out so that he could piss, or bother her some more. Maybe he was asleep, and if he was, then she could sneak away. She didn't want to go anywhere with him. She dragged the washcloth across her body like a scarf so that the rinse water would skim quietly down her body. She sank in the tub to rinse her hair. She stood slowly and for a second felt dizzy, but the sensation disappeared, and she dressed quickly. Her neck and face perspired again as soon as she dried them.

He wasn't on the bed. The bathroom exhaled steam into the bedroom. Perhaps he had even gone somewhere. She carried her shoes to the doorway. He wasn't on the couch. She walked quickly out of the bedroom toward freedom. She had retrieved her purse beside the chair and was reaching for her keys on the coffee table when she saw him lying in the shadows at the front door. She turned back toward the bedroom, but he was up moving just as fast. He could break down the door if she locked it, but maybe Gurney would hear and call the police. She pushed, but she was too late; his loafer wedged there.

She let the door fall open. "That the best place you could find for a nap?" she asked haughtily.

He leered at her. "Not the best place, honey."

"Cut it out, Merle."

He looked around her into the bedroom at the rumpled spread. "Where's your stuff?" He seemed bouncy, excited, revived by his nap. "I'm ready to go."

She resumed her post at the window. Before he could stop her, she raised it a few inches, but she didn't try to signal anyone. Hot fresh air streamed into the room. "I told you I'm not going anywhere," she said to the woods. She seemed to be staring directly at the pine tree.

"Aw, come on." He grinned pleasantly at her, his puckish face free of secrets. His sandy hair fell innocently across his forehead. "I won't pester you anymore. I just want to look around a little. Let you show me Atlanta." He looked in the open drawers of the dresser. "You have some clothes here, don't you?" He shut the drawer with Jay's socks in it.

If she were in Atlanta, perhaps she'd have a better chance of getting away. She would at least be back home. And the more places she went, the more likely she would run into Mac. "Have you totally forgotten Jenny?" she asked. He paled at the name. He thought she meant his Jenny.

"No," he said slowly, the color returning to his face. "No, I haven't." She wondered what the sudden responsiveness meant. Had he been in touch with Jenny about Jay? Had something started up again between them? Two months ago she and Jay had spent one whole night calling up hospitals all over the country, asking if a nurse named Jenny Mitchell worked there. Merle had always told Jay she wanted to be a nurse but didn't have the brains, and Jay had had some crazy notion he could find her. Thank God, she had moved out before that phone bill arrived.

"I have to pick up Jenny . . ."—she paused to look for another response—". . . at five." His face was impassive. She checked her watch, a small dial on a black band as thin as a rubber band. "It's two o'clock now."

"We'll pick her up," he suggested.

She went to the closet, feeling his thinking gaze on her back. Once she walked through that beauty-shop door, she was home free.

"On second thought, forget it," he said.

"Forget it?" She whirled to find him looking as if he could read her mind. "You can't forget my child. Your own grandchild."

"Have some girl friend pick her up."

"I don't have any girl friends."

"That's for sure." He advanced a step, and the shock of hair that fell over his forehead looked menacing. "Call a girl friend." He lifted his foot and shoved the remaining drawers of the dresser closed—bam, bam, bam.

"I-I guess I can ask the girl who's keeping her to let her spend the night. I'll have to call."

"Be my guest." He blocked half of the doorway so that her arm brushed his chest. "Just step on it," he said, laying a cupped hand lightly on her ass.

She telephoned Sally with Merle's finger poised above the

disconnect button. What could she say anyway? That her father-in-law was coercing her to take a vacation? Who cared that she didn't want to go? Certainly not Sally, who said she would be delighted to keep Jenny for one night, two, three. Melissa had assured her it wouldn't be that long. She sensed that Sally would like to keep Jenny for good.

In a way this was more exciting than cooking her feet on the hot Atlanta pavement. Than calling every garage in town looking for Mac. Than watching a couple of old people outside her window watch her, wondering why they had ever agreed to this arrangement. She might meet some new people. She might find her lover. For sure if she didn't go, Merle's car would break down and coast into the very repair shop where Mac worked, and she would never know.

Sally asked when she would be able to bring back the Volkswagen. "Tomorrow," she said. Merle shook his head vehemently. "Nothing will happen to it. I'll park it outside the apartment where I used to live." Then he cut her off.

She opened her closet to the old clothes she had left behind. A pair of Jay's fatigues hung there guarding two dresses that she'd thought she'd never wear again. The closet had used to be crammed with Jay's books, and even though she'd directed the emptying of it the week after he died, the space still surprised her. She had hated them for one reason because they took up the only storage she had in the whole apartment. She had called the local home for drunks and sat on her sofa drinking beer while two pale-faced ex-boozers carried the piles to their truck outside. She couldn't help but feel that the whole apartment was unburdened with the weight of the books gone. A sag had remained in the closet shelf, but gradually it was disappearing.

In case they went somewhere nice, she would wear this navy dress that showed off her red hair. For riding in the car she could use her apricot housedress with pretty stitching on the yoke. In the chest she found a couple of pairs of shorts and tops, one of which she had been looking for. She was happy to have it again. Her oldest underpants were here too, the pairs she had felt weren't worth packing. Merle brought an old grocery bag from the kitchen for her to put her things in.

"How do you like this?" she asked gaily, grabbing up the navy dress from the bed and draping it over her stomach. Merle stood in the doorway drinking a beer.

"Fine."

She went through the rest of her clothes, fanning them on the bed like a hand of cards. He looked at her and at them and then at her again, trying not to show his surprise. She folded each garment neatly and placed the stack they made inside the paper bag. When she felt him watching her, she made her movements more deliberate.

He was finishing this beer so he could take a full one with him. His injured left hand lay against his hip and he stood with his feet wide apart. He bent forward when he threw his head back to swallow so that he wouldn't lose his balance. She had not asked him again about his hand. He nailed the bedroom trashcan with his empty and went to the freezer for a new one. She had a sudden desire to try to get away again, right when she was beginning to accept this. But too late. He closed the freezer door; he knew what she was thinking. In a quick motion he threw the unopened can of beer hard in her direction. It turned over and over in the air. She lunged to keep it from knocking a hole in the wall or exploding or both. Her body trembled as she gathered herself slowly back together.

"More tricks like that, and you'll be delivering your second grandchild." She took a deep breath.

"Might be interesting," he said.

"If you like blood."

Did he like blood? At death maybe, where it should be. He said: "I gotta take a leak. And then I'm ready to blow this place." He left the door open while he pissed to be able to cut her off if he needed to. She started for the living room to gather her things, but he told her not to move another step. She stood with one foot raised and stared evenly at him while they listened to the torrent of his beer. He came out of the bathroom still zipping his pants like he had the longest zipper in the world. He wished.

He carried the paper bag and she the rabbit, her purse, and keys. Leaning against the breezeway railing outside was Marty, wearing a yellow sun-back dress with white rickrack, her hair in pigtails coiled around her head. She looked older by four or five years. She still went barefoot, but he noticed how the red grooves around her nails had been scrubbed clean. Her cheeks were rouged. He wondered what Melissa would say if he invited her along. Then for sure he'd be arrested, compliments of Gurney.

"Hi, Marty," Melissa said.

"Hi," she said, watching Merle. "Where y'all going?" she asked in her slow drawl.

"Off," Melissa snapped.

Merle glanced back.

"Take me?"

He turned around, although Melissa kept walking. Marty had not moved a muscle, had not even turned to follow them with her eyes. She looked like she was talking to someone behind her own door.

"We can't, honey," he said.

Melissa's sandals clip-clopped down the metal steps. "Come on, Merle."

"Sorry, honey, but we've got some business to attend to."

"I'm all ready." The girl held up a green duffel bag that he hadn't noticed. He turned his back on her. Melissa was far ahead.

"You said you would," Marty said, louder now. "You promised me."

"I didn't promise you anything," he said gruffly, descending the steps quickly to catch up with Melissa.

"You did too." She faced them over the railing as they made their way to Merle's car. "If you don't take me, you'll be sorry." Tears spoiled her face.

"She nuts or something?" he muttered.

"Or something," Melissa said. She did not look at Marty even when she was facing her behind the windshield.

At least Marty had kept him from having trouble with Melissa.

Before he stepped into the car, he gave her one last long look. She stood silent, one hand clenching the rail, the other at her shoulder where the duffel bag hung down her back. Maybe she did this to everybody who was leaving this hell hole. She had done it to Jay. He threw up a hand at her and left it in the sky until she could not ignore it, until she saw that he meant it, and that it was some flag for her future, not with him, but with some man. He didn't know why, but he wanted her to feel like she was somebody. That he cared enough to wave. She had a cute ass, no question, and someday soon somebody was going to notice it. Somebody besides Jay. The door of her apartment opened and the buzz of the TV escaped into the still afternoon air. From the depths of the hole, Rosie called harshly to her. She glanced back and then turned to wave at him, her tears stopped, waving quickly while she still could, waving harder and harder as she backed toward the screen. The voice came again, telling her to stop waving, and Merle jumped into the car. As they drove away, Melissa picked up one of his magazines and began looking at her competition.

9

CRAIG

He needed a map. The Saturday air was crisp, not dense like yesterday, so the men at Buck's service station had brought their chairs outside. They all stared at the abrasion on his chin, but nobody said anything. Craig was thankful. He waited until Buck was servicing a car and then he slipped inside and tucked a map of North Carolina in his shirt. Maps were free, but they would wonder what he wanted one for. He selected a fat pickle from the pickle barrel and took three cents out to Buck, who thanked him warmly and asked how he was feeling today. Craig took a big bite so that he would only have to nod fine.

"You were lucky," Buck said. The juice ran down Craig's hand, burning in one of the cuts from when he fell. He blew on the hurt place, not answering. The map bulged under his shirt, but Buck didn't seem to notice.

At home he found Durham on the map and then after a while Interstate Highway 85. He followed it with his finger, passing through towns that really didn't mean anything to him, or to Dad that he knew of. Greensboro, Thomasville, Lexington, Kannapolis, and finally Charlotte. The map stopped at the North Carolina border, but just beyond it, printed in soft gray letters, was SOUTH CAROLINA. Georgia. That came next. Dad had gone to Columbus. He knew it like he knew that Clayton came to their house to see Mom and not him. Dad was going to see if Jay were really dead. He folded up the map and put it under his mattress. He needed more maps. He found more pennies in the drawer beside Dad's bed and walked the dusty road back to Buck's. There was a map of South Carolina in the rack but none of Georgia. Then he spied one of the Eastern United States. He was on tiptoe pulling it from the rack when Buck walked into the station.

"You like pickles about as good as your Dad," Buck said.

"Yep." Craig tucked the map under his arm and went to the tall barrel. He got out his three cents so Buck would know he was buying.

"What do you need a map for?" Buck asked.

"Is it all right?"

Buck rang up a sale. "Yeah. It's just that they cost me. A nickel apiece, but if you need one, you can have it."

"It's for history. You know the colonies? We're supposed to find out where they'd be today."

"That's easy. Same place as they were back then."

Craig flushed. "I mean what they're near and everything."

"Oh."

"My mom also said she'd like to go to Florida," he added weakly. He scooped up the first pickle he saw and walked toward Buck, letting the hand holding the three cents lead. It was an awfully small pickle.

"It'll be fine," Buck said as he popped open the cash drawer again.

He thought he would never get it folded back up. It stretched across his bed, panel after panel of squiggly red and black lines. Durham was easier to find on the smaller map. I-85 was drawn in red, except for some places where dashes showed it hadn't been built yet. He found his way to Atlanta, but then he had to search around for Columbus. It was on the very edge of Georgia, halfway down. He found the mileage scale and measured that he was about four hundred miles away. Four *hundred*. He measured again and came up with three hundred and fifty. Still a long, long way. His freshman year at Duke, Jay had thumbed home sometimes and said it was nice meeting people around his hometown that he didn't know. But the distance was only five miles.

That night Clayton came into his room while he was pretending to do his homework. Actually he was trying to memorize a list of the cities he would pass through on his trip. Clayton asked if he was excited about getting a dog, and after a brief moment Craig said yes. He had totally forgotten. Mom ducked under Clayton's arm, which was stretched across the doorway, and stood there watching him. He thought she must have found the maps, although he had moved them from under the mattress where she might have felt them when she made up his bed. They lay in a shoebox full of rocks under Jay's old bed. He had never gotten either one of them folded back correctly. She stood close to Clayton, but she didn't mention maps, so maybe she didn't know. Or maybe she was waiting for him to confess. Looking at maps didn't prove anything. He was trying to learn his way around was all. His history teacher had asked them to bring maps to school. Mom had said she wanted to go on a trip, hadn't she? He slid his math book over his list of towns as she walked across the room to kiss him goodnight. He could hear water pounding the bottom of the tub for his bath. She did not pause above him waiting for the truth, but simply kissed him and left. At the door she reminded him to stop his water in time. Burlington . . . Greensboro . . . High Point . . . Thomasville . . . Lexington . . . Salisbury. . . .

He thought he would leave Monday morning, but they overslept and Mom had to take him to school because he missed the bus. He was in homeroom before he remembered where he was supposed to be instead. That afternoon while she was still at work, he got his things together. He planned to walk out to the bus stop the next morning and just keep walking. With a knife he emptied a large amount of change from his piggy bank. Dad hadn't "borrowed" from him in a long time, fortunately. From Dad's bedside table and from the junk drawer in the kitchen, he collected pennies. He remembered to check under the chair and couch cushions and found a bonanza—a fifty-cent piece, two quarters, a dime, and four nickels. Then he checked Mom's purses, the way she did when she needed some money, and found a couple of dollar bills inside a zipped pocket. The change was heavy, so he took it down to Buck's to see if he could turn it in for bills. Buck was happy to oblige—he spotted a 1934 nickel for his coin collection. Craig left him turning over the pennies he'd brought. In his pocket was sixteen dollars and twenty-seven cents. At home he called the bus station and asked if he had enough to go to Columbus, Georgia, but the man said no. Just as he was hanging up, Clayton came over to help him find supper for him and Mom. He worried that he might slip and say something, so he decided not to talk at all.

Tuesday morning he awoke to the sound of his stomach turning wild somersaults in his chest cavity. Mom had changed her mind about getting him a dog, which somehow gave him courage. He had packed his knapsack with peanut-butter crackers, an extra shirt, and a couple of apples stolen one at a time from the fruit bowl on the dining-room table. In one pocket was Jay's address which he had copied carefully off the telephone book in the kitchen; in the other were his maps. He had an extra copy of the address in the back pocket of his pants. He laid his three bills, a ten, five, and one, inside his left sneaker. He slipped his knapsack over his shoulders so there would be no chance she might look inside. He planned to ask her for two dollars for a new lunch ticket.

Halfway through his egg, he had to excuse himself to go to the bathroom. He threw up. Even after the egg was gone, he threw up again. When he had finished, he looked in the mirror and saw a white face crowned with sweat. He wiped his lips and saw that his nervousness had turned them a chalky color. He would leave when he had gotten more used to the idea.

All that day at school, he thought about his trip, anchoring in his mind the great explorers he knew: Columbus, Magellan, Vasco da Gama, Ponce de León. They had crossed uncharted oceans, not two states filled with highways and people. He thought about the men who had climbed the highest mountains, the people who had dog-sledded to the North Pole, Lindbergh, Sir Walter Raleigh, Captain John Smith, the Wright Brothers. Once in high school Jay had thumbed to Myrtle Beach without permission. By the 3:15 bell Craig was braced for his journey. The fear that had spread through his body had become invigorating. His stomach was a brave chunk of ice.

Thursday morning he asked for Wheaties with banana instead of egg. For strength he took a second bowl. If Mom wasn't going to get him a dog, there was no reason not to leave. At 7:45, ten minutes early, he kissed her as usual and walked out the door. He slung the knapsack, heavier now by two bottles of Coke, over one arm, holding his head high. There was a certain cadence to his step that kept him moving. The morning air was nippy and he thought he was wise to have brought his jacket. He felt vaguely as if he were not himself. As if this body walking down the highway past Buck's were someone else's and he were behind the smudged glass front of the station merely watching. *He* walked proudly for *him* to look at. *He* felt sorry that *someone* was so left behind in this world. *He* decided not to start thumbing until he was out of *his* sight in case his feelings would be hurt. He imagined that most explorers thought of themselves as two people.

When his first ride pulled over, he looked back but the station and the boy inside it were out of sight. He ran to the car, a gray Plymouth, his knapsack flapping against his back. His fingers closed over the cold chrome handle, and he remembered not letting go of Dad's once and being thrown to his hands and knees. He attempted to reclaim his hand now, but it was too late. The shiny chrome held him like dry ice. A toothy smile floated from the driver's side toward him and a hand with polished fingernails unlocked the door.

"You look pretty harmless, honeycomb," she said. Her skimpy colorless hair was pinned with one large clip on top of her head. He closed his door. She told him to lock it. She got a wheel as she started up and apologized for it.

He may have talked to her. He may have told her the truth or told her preposterous lies. He may not have said a word. He never remembered. The world floated by him like a happy dream. He counted cows on both sides and when he passed a white horse, he tripled his totals. He didn't acknowledge graveyards. He saw wide open spaces for miles and miles, and he wanted to tell Jay, who had always worried about overpopulation, about them. There might be too many people in other parts of the world, like New York City and Washington, D.C., but there was plenty of room here . . . for *thousands.* He wished he had a pencil to circle the locations on his map. He devoured billboards that told him about the towns he was passing. He was invited to visit the world's largest chair. Later he rode through the land of towels and thought that he could sing a song about that. One billboard all the way up in North Carolina advertised something all the way down in Georgia—Stone Mountain. He must not be so far away after all. When she stopped, he was in Charlotte. He remembered her warning him to watch out for the state police. She wiggled her fingers through his hair once.

Gastonia . . . Gaffney . . . Spartanburg.

He was no more aware of his second and third drivers, except that he only got to Gastonia with his second ride and he had to wait an hour on the outskirts of town before someone else picked him up. He was not sorry. He wanted to stand outside, feel the rude rush of wind as someone passed him by, experience sore feet as he showed people who were lucky enough to have cars that he was trying to make his own way. It gave him time to eat his peanut-butter crackers which he hadn't wanted to do in anyone's car. A truck going to Atlanta picked him up about three o'clock, according to how he read the sun's position in the sky. A small clock mounted on the cab's dash confirmed his guess, and he began to feel knowledgeable about what he was doing. He wondered if explorers were born, like athletes. And good students.

The fact of night struck him three hours later as the highway sprung into the city almost without warning. A sports stadium, larger than life, loomed on their left. The road curled like a roller coaster that the truck was trying to master. Brightly lit signs blinked and flashed. There were possibilities to exit everywhere. For the first time, Craig turned to his chauffeur, a ruddy fellow with slick hair and tight jeans. A comb peeked out of one of the sleeves of his T-shirt which were rolled like socks. He smelled like Dad.

"Are you stopping here?" Craig asked.

"End of my line."

Craig didn't know exactly what to ask. As a field of stopped traffic appeared ahead of them, the man had to pump his brakes with both feet. He pumped harder. "Hope I don't lock up," he said loudly. Sweat rolled down his forehead from a head of wet hair. Craig hoped. The brakes wheezed and he felt the tires grab the roadway. While they waited for whatever it was to move, Craig asked the man if he lived in Atlanta. The answer was no. The man opened his window and lay his arm in the sun. On it was tattooed a heart with a snake arrowed through it. The snake wiggled when the man flexed his muscles.

"Do you need a place to stay, kid?"

Craig nodded, his heart roaring a twenty-one gun yes in his chest, which he wondered if the man could hear.

The man jerked his hitching thumb toward the back. The tip of it was missing. "Back there," he said. Craig turned to look. Behind their seat was a space almost as big as a double bed. A gray-striped pillow without a case and an olive-green blanket were wadded in one corner. "I'm going to dump this trailer first and then we'll grab something to eat. I start up to Ohio tomorrow; you can ride along if you like." The traffic began moving again, and he pumped the gas to get the truck rolling. They were on an incline and rolled back several feet, amid loud honking from the rear. "Ah, eat it," the man said, throwing his arm out the window. The honking began again, the clutch caught, but he just rolled up his window.

When Craig awoke, he knew where he was even before he smelled his pillow, sour with hair oil, and heard Sam's raucous snore. Outside the clouded window of the truck cab, he saw the unlit sign of The KitKat Lounge, a low flat-topped building, where Sam had spent most of the night. It was quiet, finally, when most of the world was just getting moving. For hours he had watched the sign talk, electricity spreading amazingly across the three words, lighting up one letter at a time. Whenever the door of the KitKat opened, he could hear the blare of a juke box, and then the music and the sign seemed to mesh in one rhythm. Fancy-dressed women had moved in and out of the doors all night.

Sam had forgotten Craig was in his cab last night, opening the door, talking to himself, smelling like the salt water around a boat dock. With effort he had pulled himself halfway over the seat, but at the crest, he seemed to go loose, like his bones had collapsed. He dropped toward the floor of the back, but Craig managed to roll out of the way. While Sam was feeling for his pillow, he discovered him again. "Oh yeah," he'd muttered, looking at Craig through eyes as puffy as pretzels. "Go back to sleep."

Craig raised himself quietly to look at the clock on the dash. Six-thirty. Too soon to be disturbing Sam. The refreshing odor of salt water had vanished. Sam smelled dirty; he exhaled a hot, rancid stream of air. The cab was growing warm from the morning sun, and Craig pushed off the blanket. It was hard to breathe. Both windows were rolled up. He stepped over Sam and slid to the front seat. Just in time—he thought he was either going to faint or throw up —he lowered the window and took a deep breath.

He was in Georgia.

The crisp air revived him like a long draught of Coke. Across the street a tall wooden fence grown over with ivy enclosed a drive-in theater. Craig would have tried to find a place to watch its movies last night, but he was afraid Sam might come out and leave him. He hadn't known they were going to park here until dawn. A heavy weight had vanished from his stomach. He felt the way he used to feel when he went to downtown Durham on Saturdays that Jay wasn't around. Sort of important because he was out there where everybody else was, and sort of unimportant because nobody knew he was there. He wondered if Mom were worried about him. He wondered if Dad were somewhere along the road ahead. Neither of them seemed to matter very much anymore. Maybe he would go with Sam to Ohio.

Sam snorted and sat up. Stubble had popped out of his face and his hair was awry. "Shut that damn refrigerator door," he said. Craig didn't know what he meant. "Shut the *window*, stupid," he said, exasperated. Falling back to the floor and jerking the blanket up around him, he rocked the cab. A few minutes later, he woke up, took Craig to a diner for breakfast, and drove him out to a junction of highways where he could find a ride to Columbus. He wished him luck and Craig said good luck back. He felt part of a sea of people going places.

He arrived at Columbus about four o'clock that afternoon with a soldier who had been on leave to bury his mother. It had been a bad day for thumbing. People were willing to pick him up, but none of them was going anywhere. He looked too young to be traveling far, someone told him, and he mumbled that he lived only a mile away. Inside Columbus, fewer people seemed to give rides. The ones who stopped didn't know where Jay's apartment building was. He walked the last couple of miles after a cashier at a curb market pointed him in the right direction. The weather was so hot that the Dreamsicle he bought melted faster than he could lick it.

There was no point to it really, Dad's car not being there, but Craig knocked gently at 117-F anyway. He moved to the window and tapped there. The glass sounded louder, more insistent, but no one came. He tried to look through the drapes, but they were drawn tightly. He went back to the door and tried the knob. Dad always left doors unlocked. It opened. Dad, Melissa, and Jenny were probably out for supper. He stepped inside, finding a light switch quickly. It lit a lamp by the couch. He wanted to be sure not to trip over anything. A faint whistling noise sounded in his head, similar to the way he thought a dog whistle must sound to dogs. He swallowed and it went away, but then it came back.

He stood in one corner of a large room that was for living in the front half and eating in the back half. A sofa with an upholstered chair on either side sat at the right wall. On the left was a low-slung chair of hemp and wood facing a television set. The dining area held a small table, undersized for the space. Three chairs sat haphazardly around; the fourth, broken into pieces, leaned in the corner. Several of Jenny's toys—a pull grasshopper, a set of blocks, some books, trailed into a room on the right which he assumed was hers. A doorway farther along the same wall led to the kitchen. On the opposite wall, another doorway led to Jay and Melissa's bedroom. All the doorways were dark.

"Dad?" he called softly, in case. "Melissa and Jenny?" And finally, "Jay?" The hope in his voice was all that came back to him. He took hold of the doorknob, his hand a fixed claw, as he teetered between staying and leaving. He had come a long way to quit now. He pushed away from the door, his momentum propelling him to the middle of the room. Suddenly he was walking faster than anyone ever walked inside a place. He flicked on the kitchen light and pulled the silver chain to the hanging paper ball that lit the dinette table. No light came on by the switch in Jenny's room, so he skipped it. He thought of firemen who prepare buildings already on fire, closing doors, yanking curtains to slow the licking flames. *They* hurried too. He ran to the window beside the front door and drew open its curtain, and then to the other end of the room behind the dinette table. He hesitated, knowing from Uncle Otto and Aunt Theresa what was there. They had talked like it was worse outside the dining room than outside a bedroom or kitchen or bathroom window. He flung open the curtain and saw it. All the other trees were thin saplings that wouldn't hold a cat. It ought to be cut down.

He was slower now, but methodic, walking into Jay and Melissa's bedroom, seeing the accordion doors of the closet, like his own closet at home. There he knew what he would find: piles of books climbing from the floor to the tails of Jay's shirts. More books weighting down the hat shelf. He would bet he'd carried fifty armloads of books to the trailer Jay had rented to move down here. He flung open the doors, aching for something familiar. A set of green fatigues, looking like a body, caused him to suck in his breath; otherwise the closet was empty. Where were all Jay's books? He stood on tiptoe to feel along the top shelf and found a faded back cover. They had been here, but now they were gone. He felt a haze of uncertainty settling in his mind. Was he for sure in the right apartment? He noticed the nubby bedspread, hanging long at the base of the bed, almost exposing the pillows. It was wrinkled as if someone had been using it as a trampoline. He walked slowly to the bedroom window that was halfway open. Nothing out there but more trees.

He was as tired as he had ever been. Returning to the living-room corner by the front door, he faced the room like a lookout man. He pushed his shoulder blades against the two walls and slowly slid into a sitting position, his knees up in front of him like a wall. The air felt unfamiliar like his coat after summer in the attic. Jenny's toys looked not laid aside but abandoned. On each end of the room, the green curtains hung like rags. Craig shed hot fast tears. His brother was dead.

They were in the kitchen again, their low intimate voices drifting to him like a gentle snore. Every now and then, a beer can would slap the table, punctuating, or Dad would choke on a cigarette, but otherwise the hum was steady. Their voices slurred and rose and fell. They talked without talking, relying on suggestion and their own common thought, sighing and heaving and grunting to make ideas without words.

He wanted a piece of lemon meringue pie, he told them, padding into the kitchen quietly, not surprising them at all because they couldn't be surprised at this hour with all those beers under their belts. They smiled faintly at him as if he were some safe but unknown apparition. A pyramid of beer cans sat on the side of the table next to the wall. Craig cut a piece of pie, poured a glass of milk, and sat down with them. Dad raised his eyebrows, but Jay was in the middle of something.

"I never believed you," Jay said gently. "Never, never, never." He shook his head for more emphasis. "I still don't."

"Get me a beer," Dad muttered. Craig had the first bite of pie almost to his mouth but dropped it back to the plate. The can opener lay on the table, and he jacked open both sides before setting a fresh can before Dad.

"If you didn't salt it away, where the hell is it all?" Jay continued.

Dad's eyes closed and he sighed. "I spent it. On things."

"That pretty well blows our future. That is, if you're serious." He took a long swig of his beer watching Dad down the side of the can.

"There's always money around."

Jay grabbed his wrist. "Where?" he demanded.

Dad moved Jay's hand off his. "People . . . banks. I'll bet you there are five hundred people in this town who would dearly love to put us in business. There are that many who hate Otto's guts. No telling who would just like to make a good investment."

He thought they might make him leave when his pie was gone, so he cut small pieces and waited minutes between bites.

"You're pure-tee dreaming. Nobody hates Otto that much. Except you." He looked expectantly again at Dad. Then he pointed Craig to the refrigerator. "All this time . . . all my life really . . . I thought you'd been saving for something like this. I thought that when we first started talking about going into business together, it meant that you had money."

"But I don't." Dad's face was taut. "Son . . ."—he bounced his chair to the floor—". . . if I had money I would have helped you get rid of Melissa."

Jay nodded and dropped his head back to drain the whole new can. He had been married for four months.

They did not talk to him even when their tempers had mellowed and their minds were ready for new subjects. Craig finished his pie and milk. He thought they had forgotten he was there. Dad propped his chin on his hand and muttered to himself that all his money had been spent on this family. Jay pulled two more beers from the refrigerator. He opened his own but not Dad's.

"I got a letter from the draft board today," Jay said. "I'm

supposed to report to Fort Benning in two weeks." Dad's face looked sick. "I should have thought about the possibility of being drafted when I quit school . . ."—his voice trailed off—". . . but I didn't."

"Goddamn," Dad said, a wetness in his voice. He shook his head and kept shaking it.

Jay turned to him then. "Hey, old buddy. Your big brother's going to be a soldier. Whaddya think about that?" He turned back to Dad. "There's one good thing about all this. When I finish, I can go to school free and Uncle Sam can take care of Melissa."

Dad hunkered over his beer. When he raised his head, his eyes were charged with feeling. "I would have given you the last dime I had. Do you believe me?"

Jay gave a short crisp dip of his head. "I thought you had plenty . . . but now I know you don't." He spoke as if repeating after someone.

"I thought . . ." Craig said out loud, and then clapped his hand over his mouth. He had been about to repeat what Jay said.

Dad rose out of his seat, one hand jerking Craig by the arm, the other giving him a sharp slap on the behind. "Get out of here," he said.

Over his shoulder, Craig shot Jay a glance, but he was looking at Dad, his brows miniature thunderclouds over his eyes. He heard Jay ask Dad what he'd spent his money on, and he heard Dad answer, "Women, what else?"

Sometime in the night he awakened, so achy that nothing but a bed seemed to matter. He tried Jenny's room first before he remembered it had only a baby bed. He went to Jay and Melissa's room, flipping on and off the overhead light, checking that everything was as he remembered. He crawled on top of the spread. When he awoke, the apartment felt familiar, like a rented room after one day at the beach.

10

MERLE/MELISSA

They drove west through Alabama where the long Appalachian mountain chain finally petered out. Up until now she had thumbed roughly through every magazine he had in the car, like she was angry at some doctor who'd kept her waiting too long. She didn't bother to notice that they were taking a trip. When she finished one, she would lean to the back for another, showing him the choice curve of her leg. He thought she could have picked them all up at once, but she preferred to stretch herself out before him.

It was too soon to say this, he knew, it might ball him up before he found out everything he wanted to know, but he was going to tell her that all this was her fault. She sat there so . . . so unmournful, like nothing had changed for her, like life with or without Jay was no different, like she was the innocent babe whose mother had died at her birth. Only she wasn't so innocent. It might keep him from learning all he wanted to learn, but he was going to tell her what she was.

"If he hadn't gotten messed up with you, he wouldn't be dead." The words slipped softly from his mouth.

She turned a page and then another. "You talk like he had a choice," she said drily.

"He didn't *have* to marry you."

"You forget, Merle." Her eyes flickered slightly as she mentioned those circumstances one more time. Her first pregnancy had been a false one that had fooled both her and her doctor. But it hadn't been her fault. She had stopped her period, the rabbit test was positive, the doctor had felt an enlarged womb . . . until two weeks after they were married. No one would have believed her, so she had said that she'd miscarried, a sharp pain one morning that she dismissed as part of pregnancy, but had actually been her losing it. "He *did* have to marry me," she said. "But killing himself had nothing to do with me. He just hated the Army. If you'd given him a little bit of your goddamn money, he would never have been drafted." Often as she said things, she found out what she thought; this was one of those times. Merle was getting at something, and she thought she knew what. She kept on precariously, but she kept on. "Jay said you didn't have any money, but I never believed it." She paused. "He didn't believe you either."

It seemed so logical now that Merle should have helped them. It seemed so logical that if he *had* helped them, Jay wouldn't be dead.

When she had first learned that he had hanged himself, she thought it might be over Mac, but before the phone call to Gurney was through, she knew she was wrong. Jay hadn't believed there was a Mac, not really. They had had the fight about the dining-room set, but they'd always had fights like that. On the trip from Atlanta to Columbus, she figured out that he must have had another run-in with Sergeant Jester. Two weeks later when she went to the base to sign papers, she had intended to ask the sergeant about it. But he was so hopeful about the Army giving her money to take care of Jenny and the new baby, that she didn't bother. It was the Army that Jay had hated anyway, and in her opinion he was in the Army because of Merle.

They passed the crest of a tall hill and viewed a small community, punctuated by three church spires, below. She had never thought about how much she hated small towns until she moved to Atlanta. As they descended, the spires appeared to recede and the thick humidity pasted her apricot dress to her. What was the point of living in the mountains, if you settled in one of these fire pits? If she had to live in the South, she wanted a place with a decent night life. She had almost decided to look for a job as a cocktail waitress when she got home.

On both sides of them rose cool bluish hills. She rolled down her window all the way, letting what wind there was grab at what hair Sally had left her. She told Merle that she wished he would go to Florida, but he said he had another place in mind. He wasn't telling her where because he didn't want to get her hopes up. Besides, he said, the country seemed to choke in the direction she wanted to go. Florida was a big net that might just close at the top if you drove too far down. He knew that someday she probably wanted to go home. Didn't she?

Someday, she thought, she wanted to kick him in the balls.

So what was west? she wondered to herself. A big sandy sinkhole that might swallow them up. Countryside that stretched past where she was willing to go. Unless he was taking her to California. Could she be on the way to a brand new life that forgot this one completely? If she were, that was okay. The things she'd left behind weren't worth walking across the street for, except perhaps the new dress she'd bought last week. Mac was hiding out like a criminal, which, in a sense, she guessed he was. Sally would be glad to bring up Jenny. She could let go of everything but one—this baby waiting in her stomach, making her legs ache, her breasts puff up, her back weaken. She would be glad when it was outside her, and she had a choice of what to do with it, which would be to give it to Mac if she ever stumbled onto him again.

Merle groaned from the heat and pulled to a stop at the town's one intersection. The stores were too plain for window shopping. Along the sidewalks everyone turned to look at what was new in town—them. They watched, picking out what details they could. A thin squinting woman and two uncombed children crossed slowly in front of the car. Merle whistled sarcastically under his breath. "Nice specimens." One of the children, a tow-headed boy, turned his head to keep staring, his mouth a sour slit, but when he reached the curb he lost interest. The stoplight changed finally, and Merle followed the road that beelined out of town.

"I never had any money, and Jay knew it," he said.

"Sure." She laughed the word into two bitter syllables. "All those nights talking about running Otto out of business and nothing to back it up? Tell another one." She heaved back in her seat so that her belly rose like an insolent wave. This monkey also made her hot.

"We were going to *borrow* money. People would have run to us with it. That whole town hates Otto Mitchell."

She wiggled to a straighter position and wondered what they were going to California on if he didn't have a wallet full. Not her eighteen bucks. "Jay thought if he could get you to admit you had money, he could get you to give him enough to stay at Duke." She was sure now that Jay had thought this, although he had never said those exact words.

He studied her, his eyes marked with questions, until she feared that he was going to run off the road. Just in time he glanced where he was going and kept from sideswiping a metal guard rail. "You're nuts," he said.

"Am I?"

"He wanted us to go into business together. Mitchell and Son Construction Company."

She laughed bitterly. "Did you believe that? Did you really think Jay Mitchell wanted to build houses?"

He stared angrily at her. "You can't pin a thing on me," he said. "His whole first year at Duke was free. He only quit because you tricked him into marrying you. *You* were the big price tag. We never even talked about Duke. He wanted to ruin Otto as much as I. . . ." His voice trailed off. He'd spoken falsely about Jay's feelings for Otto and it dirtied everything else he'd said.

She didn't answer, letting the worry in his voice be his own contradiction. Closing her eyes, she allowed the regular mountain curves to lull her, but, like after coffee, she felt too energized to fall asleep. Her mind saw the woods passing by, the scenic hills stretching before her like rooftops she could dance across—missing those hot valleys—if her legs were long enough. She saw lovers picnicking on fried chicken from wooden baskets and lying on blankets for naps. Who gave a damn why Jay had quit school? She was just glad that he had. It was degrading, his devouring books with more feeling than he ever devoured her, groaning over them, laughing like they were more real than she. Sometimes at night when he had awakened her with his laughter, she would demand to read the funny part, and it was never funny, at least not funny enough to be waked up for. So then she'd suspected that he simply wanted to bother her. The light bothered her enough.

"The only time he ever wanted money from me was when you needed an abortion," Merle said.

"When do we eat?" she asked, wanting to change the subject. She was starved. The sun was already halfway down the sky and she hadn't eaten since breakfast. When she wasn't pregnant, she could last without food all day.

Merle turned the radio dial to a hillbilly station and lit a cigarette. After he thought about it for a few more minutes, he reached under his seat and brought out a pack of crackers. She didn't like cheese crackers but she took them anyway. "Can we stop at a service station for a few minutes?" she asked through the stale taste. A few curves later he pulled into an old whitewashed building with one unlabeled gas pump and rows of empty vegetable bins. "It looks closed," she pouted, but he turned off the ignition anyway and disappeared behind the building. She followed since the main thing she wanted after fresh food was to go to the bathroom. The women's lavatory was unlocked and paperless. There was no mirror so she smoothed her hair by her faint reflection in the metal door of the commode stall. She hated the waxy taste of her cheap lipstick, so she didn't put any new on. The commode seat was clean but, fastidiously, she squatted above it.

In the car, she wondered if he would let her stop explaining for a while. She needed to plan what things she was going to say and what she was going to leave out. Talking all the time didn't give her much chance to think ahead. He had taken the keys with him, so she couldn't turn on the radio . . . or leave, even though she doubted she'd drive off if she had the chance. Hell, what else was there to do? at least while she awaited this birth. He strolled back from the woods in his slightly unbalanced gait. He had taken so long that she was already hot again. Her legs felt as cramped as they had before she stretched them. "Move it," she said toughly. He slowed his pace by half. "Come on, Merle, it's hot." They rode less than a mile before he wanted to hear about life at Fort Benning.

"You'll have to wait a few minutes. I'm hungry and hot and tired." She looked at her stomach. Less oppressively, the sun hung across from them in the sky instead of above. He seemed unruffled by her refusal, so she relaxed too. Now that she had time to decide what she was going to tell him, she didn't feel like thinking. She didn't like to reconsider the past, not because it was sad, but because it was over. She guessed she would have to tell it this once, but never again.

"He told me a million times that the Army wasn't so bad," she said. "That he'd get it over with and then go to school on the G.I. Bill. But it was all a lie. Jay hated Fort Benning—the town, the heat, the guys in his division. Sergeant Jester. Especially Sergeant Jester." She was careful now not to mention the compensation the sergeant had promised her. "The day Jay reported, Sergeant Jester asked him in a class of three hundred men how he expected to stay in the Army if he couldn't stay in college. Jay answered that he doubted the Army would be much of a challenge. He knew he wasn't supposed to talk smart, but, I guess, the first day, off guard and all, he forgot. They put him in solitary confinement for a week and he was in trouble from that day on. He didn't seem to learn. Sergeant Jester would ask him who the smartest man on the base was and he would say himself. I thought maybe he was trying to get kicked out, but being enlisted ain't like being at private school." She smiled and Merle, in a rare response, smiled back. What she said was true, he knew from having heard Jay talk.

"It went on like that for the first year. Every few weeks, Sergeant Jester would throw Jay in the guardhouse. At Christmas we almost didn't get to come home. We had a leave due us, but the day before, Sergeant Jester said Jay couldn't take it. I begged him to go apologize for whatever it was he'd said.

"When he came home the next day, he said we were going to Durham after all. He hadn't apologized; out of the blue Sergeant Jester told him his leave had been restored. He didn't tell Jay why, but I expect the doctor had something to do with it. Sergeant Jester had sent Jay to the base psychiatrist to try to work out his hatred of the Army." She glanced discreetly at Merle. She hadn't meant to mention the doctor but he appeared not to have noticed.

"After Christmas vacation, he seemed to get better. He said he thought he could endure anything for two years, which was the time he had left. He even started talking about going back to Duke, which he hadn't mentioned in months. I really didn't like to hear it," she confided. "We'd been poor so long and now that we were just getting going again, he wanted to grub for three more years. I let him talk. At least he wasn't going to jail on weekends anymore. Then he started trying to find Jenny. At Christmas he'd decided she was dead, but suddenly he thought she was alive again. He began writing letters to every newspaper he could find the name of, and he found lots because he went to the library on his day off."

They were leaving the mountains finally for the quicker rise and fall of the foothills. The trees looked tireder here, more saddled by the heat. The road had been deserted for several miles. She stopped watching the countryside and began picking at her fingernails.

"For three or four months, he stayed about the same. He spent less time with Marty and more with Jenny and me. Then I got pregnant again. I don't think he wanted me pregnant." He looked at her coldly. "It wasn't my fault. I didn't get that way by myself." She stopped fiddling with her fingernails because the urge was becoming strong to bite them, and she had just gotten them pretty like she wanted. "He got worse and worse and worse," she said softly. The evening light was soft now too. "He started sleeping through guard duty. I'd try to wake him up, but he wouldn't wake up. Or he'd jump out of the covers to scare me and then go back to sleep. He would act like he was going to hit me." Her voice dropped. "But then he wouldn't. He said he didn't think we should be having another baby. He started spending more time with Marty." She looked out the window, thinking she had told enough.

"And?" he prodded.

"At first I thought it was because he missed Craig. He did miss him an awful lot. He would take Marty to the park and to the library. He helped her with her schoolwork. But she got so she was jealous of me and wouldn't let us be alone. She practically lived with us. I tried to tell him he couldn't treat a girl the way he treated a brother, but he didn't listen. After a while I began to feel like the outsider. I was getting ready to tell him to choose between us, but the day I decided that, he had his nervous breakdown."

She looked at Merle, but he didn't look back. His guts

began trembling when she mentioned the breakdown. He knew Jay had had one, but what were they? Melissa had called to tell them, but he hadn't been able to ask, *What happened?* He imagined Jay rolling around on the floor, screaming in words he couldn't understand, knocking his head against the walls. He wasn't sure he wanted to hear the truth; it was probably worse.

Through Merle's side mirror Melissa watched a moving patch of the scenery they'd left behind. He looked tired and sweaty . . . older too. Before this, nothing had ever really bothered him, she guessed. Before this, he seemed more of a man.

"I came home one day last May," she said, slowly restructuring the day in her mind. "The oven was open and the coils were red hot. Jay's feet were propped on the door. He said he was dying, freezing to death. It was ninety degrees outside. The life was seeping out of his body, he said. He had closed all the curtains; the apartment was as stuffy as a closet. He said somebody had stolen the sun, and he knew who it was."

Merle raised an eyebrow.

"I asked why he didn't turn up the heat, and he said he was afraid to go into the living room where the thermostat was. He said Sergeant Jester had rigged up a way to watch us through our television set whether it was on or off. I got him a sweater but he wouldn't put it on. He said that he'd seen a peeping tom a couple of hours before . . ." If she told something dangerous, he would come closer to believing. ". . . and that he knew it was the man who made me pregnant. He was crazy. I couldn't get him to believe anything I said. I swear to you, I tried. Finally, he said that he knew Sergeant Jester was the one. I had never even laid eyes on Sergeant Jester.

"I made him go to our room and put on some socks, and when he crossed the living room he ducked down low to peek out of the draperies. He said somebody was standing behind the pine tree. I opened the curtains and told him nobody was there, but he said he knew I would say that because I was in cahoots with them. He crawled back to the kitchen on his belly. I tried to get the telephone from him. He pushed me back into the living room." Melissa's voice rose. "Told me to go behind the pine tree if I wanted to see my lover." She struggled to control herself. "He called the police and then he called Sergeant Jester's office, but they wouldn't put him through. Jay said that *proved* that he was out there, and they were trying to cover it up. When the police came, he started swinging a baseball bat at them. I watched from the window. One of them tackled him and threw him to the sidewalk. When they let him up, Jay was normal again. He told the policeman that he thought *he* was the peeping tom." She looked carefully at Merle. "Maybe I shouldn't have done it, but I went outside and told them what had really happened. They probably wouldn't have believed me, but Jay tried to shut me up. They took him to the base infirmary for two weeks. They should have discharged him."

For quite some time, Merle didn't speak. She felt him sympathizing, understanding finally what had happened to her, what had happened to Jay. She had never told anyone, not even Mac, what Jay had done that day. It was too humiliating; it told more than she wanted anybody to know. When it was all over, Gurney had opened his door, standing behind the screen, to ask if everything was all right. But he stood behind his screen. Even after Jay had ridden off with them, looking accusingly back at her, he hadn't come over to ask or to offer or to talk, and neither had Rosie. So she knew how other people would be.

"Who knocked you up?" Merle asked abruptly.

She bolted upright in her seat. "Nobody did." Her mind searched wildly for what she might have implied.

"Gurney says different." His voice chilled her.

"Gurney's lying." She regained control. To her own ears,

she didn't even sound worried. They drew up suddenly behind a flatbed truck with three men in the back. Merle drove on the truck's tail. Somehow she felt safe with the men ahead watching. He grabbed for her hand but missed and didn't try again. He dropped back slightly from the truck.

"I want to know who by." She imagined the burning where he would have twisted her arm and might still when they were out of sight of the men.

"My husband," she said lightly.

"Your husband . . ."—Merle summoned his strength—"... was impotent." His voice combed her like knives. And she gasped, not able to stop herself. He watched her, not missing a single detail of her face, knowing the road only by the feel of the steering wheel.

"Watch where you're going," she cried, but she was too late to try to cover up. The truck in front of them slowed to turn down a dirt road choked on each side by thick bushes. Merle swung left to keep from clipping it.

"I'll find him," he said, in a low promising voice. "Don't think that I can't."

"Like you found Jenny?" She breathed rapidly.

"I never looked." He grinned at the empty road ahead, pleased with himself.

No matter how much she wanted Mac found, she couldn't trust him to Merle. The man was a rattlesnake, ready to strike. He'd just sounded his warning. She lied then because she could think of no other way to save him, and he was the only thing she'd ever loved. "Jay found her," she whispered, her words barely audible above the noise of the engine.

He heard. She saw his skin grow dark and his eyes twitch painfully. "You're lying," he muttered, the words deep in his throat, unwilling to come out.

"I don't think so," she said skillfully.

"Where is she?" he demanded. He had a hand on his side—only one, but one was enough—that could twist hers. And he had feet that could kick her until she told him anything he wanted to know. He wouldn't mind using them one bit.

"I don't know where she is. He wouldn't tell me. Maybe it was part of his going crazy," she added for protection.

His eyes were wild now, big circles that showed white all around. Like hers a few moments ago. "Did he say a town or state? Did he write her or talk to her on the phone?"

"None of that. He just told me he knew where she was. I don't even know if he was telling the truth." And then with calculation, "Maybe she's dead and he saw her in heaven. Maybe he went to join her."

He glared at her, his face grim with want. "I would know if she were dead," he said.

"Did you know about Jay?"

"No," he said, "but it wasn't the same." So she knew he hadn't.

The car seemed to slow of its own accord as they traveled the seventeen miles to the next town. She had had, she thought, a narrow escape. Merle looked like a man under water, his hair wild, his eyes bloodshot, his mouth tightly closed. Every once in a while he would murmur to himself or mouth something to someone invisible. Not someone . . . Jenny. His face grew tender in phases, and color would cross it the way shadows do. He was oblivious to her. She could step from the car, she felt, and he would never notice until the shock of what she'd said wore off and he had more questions.

She would need more answers. She would have to tell about last Christmas when they had left Durham and driven to Charleston where Jay had felt mysteriously drawn. She would tell about the night-long search through the Charleston telephone book, the calling of all the Mitchells and

Heaths, Jenny's maiden name. The absence of any positive sign. She wouldn't say that she thought Jay's dizziness was flu.

Then she would tell about the hundreds of letters mailed out to letter columns of newspapers, the hundreds of calls made to cities that Jay "got a feeling for," the negative responses, the positive responses—all lies, and the lack of responses. Jay said a town's heart could be judged from its letters, for some towns sent many and some towns sent none. She would say you could tell the number of crazies in a town in direct proportion to how many people wrote. Jay had burned all the letters, lighting them one by one like a cigarette against a red-hot stove eye, blowing them to turn the coal to a flame, turning them while a scrap of white still remained, singeing his fingers on purpose each time. He dropped the thick charred ashes in the sink; the apartment smelled of the sour flames. He had never found out anything. When Merle began to turn back to Mac, she would make up more.

They checked into the Paradise Motel and went to a nearby restaurant for supper. He didn't speak because he wasn't over the shock. She remembered that of the hundreds of letters Jay had mailed out, he'd never duplicated a single one. Each was original, written in a new way, using new words for the same thoughts. It was only meaningful that way, he said. She'd thought he was wasting his time, but now she had more to talk about.

Over coffee she drifted into her own dreams of Mac and found that they were tinged not with her general anger but with that same luminous fever flowing from Merle. Mac was the best man she had ever known. Jay and Merle were roaches on the huge white floor that was him. He left her because he was good, not because he was bad. And someday she'd find and forgive him.

They watched television for two hours because there had to be something in front of their faces, something—like their supper—that kept them from having to talk. When the news came on, he switched the set off, not wanting to be drawn into the world. She undressed by the bed, her back to him like he hardly existed. After she took off her bra, she put her slip back on to wear as a nightgown. He removed everything but his shorts. She watched as he climbed into bed. The lamp was on her side and as she reached for it, she decided to ask him about his hand. With one set of fingers she touched the light switch; with the other, she pointed at the broken mess of flesh.

"Tell me what happened to it," she said.

The hand held a cigarette which it had grown limber enough to do. "I smashed it through a window the night they called about Jay." He nodded at her to go ahead with the light. He preferred her not to ask anything else. She stood, the boss, her fingers at the switch.

"And it looks like that?" she asked, incredulous.

"Yes," he said, nearly unnerved. "I ain't interested in your flabby tits, so turn off the light."

In the dark she asked when he would be able to use it again.

"What do you want to know for?"

"Go to hell."

They lay there, the rough edges of reality coming around them like teeth. He hated her and she hated him. He loved Jenny and she loved Mac.

"Will you *ever* be able to use it again?" she asked through the hot menacing darkness. She was like a vulture picking at him.

"I don't know," he answered, knowing it was easier than to listen to the question again. "Probably not." He turned to his pillow, pulling it to him like it was *her*. He didn't want to think it, but it was true. The doctor who had drained the blood said it could be operated on, but only right away with payment in advance. Two weeks had passed. Was that right away? Where could he get six hundred bucks? A week ago he had imagined bragging about this.

He tried to think about Melissa lying in this bed, probably a little worked up from just being so close to him. He bet she'd enjoy it a little more the second time. They always did, and the man always didn't. But his stomach said no. He didn't want her. He wanted the person he wouldn't think about right now. He would not think about her. He would think about Audrey or Jay. Audrey, who was a nice little cunt. What else, what else? Jay. Dead by his own hand. Hung by the limb of a pine tree. Climbing up there, coating his clothes with resin, wrapping the rope. . . . She kissed him on the forehead and put on her dark blue blazer. She was going to get cigarettes, she said. He didn't look up. Lucky it was their eyes that always did it. Their eyes that would lock together not like a chain because there was always that one selfish link, but like a circle, their eyes one circle together. Not two of anything. She had stood slightly to the side of his chair, so that he would have had to stretch to find her eyes. And that day he had worked hard, he had tried to do good because she loved him and she wanted him to. So he was tired because of her and hadn't stretched his aching neck that short distance to find her eyes. *Because* of her. What would she say if she saw his hand? The pain in his stomach spread upward like her fingers on his chest. He wanted so much to cry.

11

CRAIG

He searched the apartment for hours, starting so early in the morning that the light outside was gray and mysterious. Since the apartment was not big enough or filled enough—nearly all the closets and drawers and cabinets were bare—he searched most places many times. But after one or two scans through a chest or desk, he stopped only looking and began to feel for secret drawers and levers as well as deep down the sides of furniture where no one had ever been but an upholsterer. He found no secret hiding places, but he did find a fair amount of change, which he put in his pocket.

He kept trying the closet in Jay and Melissa's bedroom, thinking each time he opened it that the emptiness was a mirage that would have filled up. The pair of green fatigues hanging there brought his heart to his throat each time.

Gradually it occurred to him that he was looking for Jay's will. He went through the desk again and found nothing but a couple of pencils and some paperclips. Jay had always kept envelopes full of things—used stamps, quotations clipped from newspapers or copied carefully from books, ticket stubs from movies, and even rose petals that he'd crushed once trying to make perfume for Mom. All of those things were gone. Craig sat down at the desk thinking, what else? but also pretending that he was Jay studying in his Duke days, hunched over papers and books, eyes bleary, pen faltering in an aching hand. Suddenly he remembered their old habit.

He reached under the desk and slid his hands carefully across the splintery underside of the pencil drawer. No luck. Then a hunger pang struck him, and he hurried to the kitchen for another handful of Sugar Smacks which was the only food in the house. As he passed the dinette table, he thought he might look under it too. He washed down the sticky cereal with water, felt the smooth underside of the dinette table, and found an envelope. And then three more. They were taped carefully, like instructions for assembly. The first one that he disengaged carried his name.

There was also a fat one for Dad, one for Mom, and one for Gurney, whoever that was. They were sealed, tighter, he thought, than any envelopes he had ever seen. He looked at the one addressed to him. His name was printed in bold capital letters. Below it was drawn a fancy curlicue line. The same curlicue was under all of them. They seemed odd, like ornamented sympathy cards.

He had decided—from the apartment being so empty—that perhaps Dad and Melissa weren't coming back at all, but now he felt that they were only minutes away. He took the four letters into the bathroom and hid them in the cabinet underneath the sink. This room, in contrast to everywhere else, looked very *used*, with bottles of creams and lotions sitting open around the sink. He went to the front window and peered out, not seeing Dad's car in the parking lot. He had time to find a better hiding place. He retrieved the letters and laid them side by side on top of the closet shelf. He looked out the front window again.

Perhaps they weren't coming after all. Perhaps he could steam open the letters, read, and reseal them. He took the one addressed to him to the kitchen and got some water boiling. He would practice on his own letter. The first thing he did was spill a drop of water on the envelope, which ruined the ink of his name. At least now he knew what water could do to this kind of ink. He was holding the envelope over the kettle of water, watching the heavy paper wrinkle unexpectedly, when the doorbell rang. He stuck the envelope inside his shirt where his map had been and went to answer. The dampness of it clung to his chest.

A girl stood there, a girl about his age with straight tan hair pushed behind her ears and eyes like cat's-eye marbles. Her skin was very white except for several bluish places on her arms where it had bruised. She wore pink shorts and a thin cotton blouse with sleeves that rolled up. She opened the screen door to come in, and he didn't know what to say to stop her.

"I don't live here," he said.

"I know that." She didn't smile, she just watched him as she pushed the door gently closed behind her. She was barefooted. "I know who you are. I just don't know how you got here." He decided that to ask "who" would be foolish. She walked into the done-up baby's room, talking as she went. "I've been listening to you bang around all morning, and I thought I'd warn you that Gurney will call the police if he hears you." So Gurney was someone she knew.

He followed her into Jay and Melissa's bedroom where she stared pointedly at the open closet. He wondered if she could possibly guess the letters were there. She walked over and sullenly pushed shut the accordion doors and he relaxed somewhat. She led out into the living room, and he thought of locking himself in the bedroom until she left. But that seemed silly.

"Who are you?" he asked. He was less scared by her thin back.

She turned around so fast that he almost walked into her. "Don't you know?" He backed up a couple of steps, embarrassed that he was supposed to know and Jay hadn't told him. She was not scary so much, he thought, as she was definite. He had never before met someone his age who was so definite. And he hadn't exactly met her yet.

"Where is everything?" she asked.

He shrugged his shoulders and when it didn't seem enough, he spoke: "I don't know." He wasn't exactly sure what she meant by "everything." It was true: there wasn't much here.

"Where are all the books?"

Those he knew about. He had loaded all those boxes of them in the trailer when Jay moved. But he shook his head.

"Where did *they* go?" she asked.

"Who?"

She curled her lip at him. "You don't have to hide anything from me." She tucked her hair tighter behind her ears in two darting movements. "I know more than you do." She gave him a superior look.

"Are you talking about Melissa?"

"*And* . . ." she said, pausing elaborately.

He knew for sure now that Dad had been here and that *he* was the answer she expected. For a brief moment he wanted to say "Melissa and *Jay*," but he was afraid of what she might say if he did. There was no point to it anyway. He knew Jay was dead. "And . . . my father?"

"Merle," she affirmed, triumph in her voice.

It made him angry that she knew all of them and he didn't know her. Maybe Jay had mentioned her in a letter, but if he had, Craig didn't remember. Maybe he'd mentioned her in the letter he'd been about to open. At least he knew Dad had been here and would probably be back. He would have to bring Melissa home. "I wasn't sure . . ." he began.

"You weren't sure what?" She cut him off, not even knowing what he was going to say.

"That Dad . . ."

"Weren't you with them?"

He looked angrily at her so she would know not to interrupt again. He waited, and she covered over the impatience in her eyes. "I only got here late last night," he said.

"What have you been doing all day?" she asked, her voice more friendly, but still he flushed. "You've been nosing around, haven't you. You didn't find anything, did you." She didn't give him a chance to answer, but then they weren't really questions. "I already looked," she offered. "I thought he might have left me a letter or at least a keepsake, but he didn't."

"What's your name?" he asked again.

"You know it," she said disdainfully.

He frowned.

"I'm Marty," she said, shaking her face at him like he *did* know and jiggling one knee nervously. "Now do you know?"

He nodded.

"Did you find something for me?" she asked.

He shook his head.

"Are you sure?"

He shook his head again, feeling color return to his face. "I honestly didn't," he said. She watched him closely, her eyes unblinking, hard as rock. She tucked back her hair again. "I didn't find anything addressed to you," he said and was immediately sorry.

"Are you saying you found *something*?"

He didn't answer.

She stepped one pace toward him. "You better tell me the truth."

He didn't seem to be able to shake her off. "Did you say you know someone named Gurney?" he asked. Her face showed excitement which she tried to conceal by biting at her bottom lip. "He's my stepfather," she said. She held back now, waiting like she should since these were his letters. He felt kindlier toward her. She had a right, he guessed, to see a letter that Jay had written to her family.

A letter which shouldn't matter to him anyway. He didn't even know them. "There's a letter for Gurney," he said. Not even a very thick one. "I'll let you have it, if you'll promise to take it to him."

"I promise," she said too quickly.

She followed him to the bedroom, but at the door he turned to face her. The letter inside his shirt had dried, and it crackled when he moved, but she didn't notice. "*I'll* get it," he said. She let him close the door. He coughed loudly when he opened the closet and coughed again when he closed it. He put his letter on the shelf and brought the one addressed to Gurney out to her. She snatched it from him, but he ignored that too. He shut the bedroom door behind him.

"What else do you have in there?" Her tone was more difficult now that she had what she wanted.

"Nothing. Nothing for you." He would fight her if he had to over possession of the letters.

"Where did you find them?" she asked, trying to trick him.

"I found *it* . . ."—he paused for extra emphasis—" . . . under that table." They both turned toward it.

"Under that table . . . ?" she said suspiciously. "I would have seen. . . ."

"Taped," he interrupted forcefully. "On the underside." She didn't know as much as she thought she did. Not about him *or* Jay.

She frightened him then, advancing on the table, like it was some barking dog that she was going to kick. He saw one of her hands tighten into a fist. Her mouth stretched back showing her side teeth. "It figures," she muttered. Her hands closed along one edge and he thought she was going to pick it up and throw it. Instead she lifted it and bent over to examine its belly. He could have told her nothing was there except the manufacturer's tag which she grabbed at greedily and then flung aside. She let the table drop back on all fours. When she turned, her face was white. Her hand holding Gurney's letter flapped like a wounded bird at her side. "Where's *my* letter?" she demanded.

He stood his ground. "Jay didn't leave you one," he answered, his voice brighter than it should have been. He was glad there wasn't a letter for her. Why did she dare think there would be?

She moved toward him. His eyes blinked uncontrollably and he felt his body bunching up the way it did before Dad hit him, but he didn't turn away. She said she would kill him if he didn't give her what was rightfully hers. She said just because he'd found something didn't make it his. She said if he wanted to know anything about Jay, he should ask her and not depend on other people's letters.

When she was close enough, he snatched Gurney's letter back out of her hand.

"Give me that," she shouted and then stood deadly still, watching the wall shared with the next apartment. From behind it came a scraping noise like someone moving furniture. She whispered harshly, "Don't say a word." Her eyes darted to the door and back to the wall.

He smirked, knowing how to get rid of her.

"Please," she begged.

He'd let her stay until she got on his nerves again and that was all. The noise in the other apartment subsided. The tight fearful line of her mouth relaxed.

"Will you let me have Gurney's letter back?" she asked in a mewling voice.

"Maybe."

She turned her back on him and dropped into the nearby chair, heaving a long tired sigh. Her shoulders slumped to almost nothing. They each waited. He thought he might want to read Gurney's letter himself, but he didn't exactly know how to say it. Even to someone like her, who probably didn't know what it meant to feel *wrong*. You were wrong no matter who you were wrong to, weren't you? It was her letter, or Gurney's. Same thing.

He thought of the writer then, who should count as much as the receiver. Jay wouldn't want him opening this letter. Jay, who would never read your homework or ask questions about it, only whether or not it was done. Never checking closely. Which had been the reason it was always so easy to fool him. Jay, who would let you be private. But Jay didn't have any more say-so. The idea crowded into his mind before he could stop it. Jay didn't have say-so over him. It spun through his head like fire. He felt mean, but at the same time he felt honest. Jay would never again tell him what to do. He was sad about it, but he also felt relief.

"Well?" she asked. Hope had withered in her voice, and she seemed not to care as much whether or not she won this battle. Her eyes were lifeless and her eyebrows, so active before, were vague chalk marks above her eyes. He wondered why Jay had never told him about her. Maybe she wasn't that important.

"I'd like to know what it says," he told her.

"Why?" Her voice was as sharp as a knife again, but then she leaned her head back against the chair. He saw the white, almost translucent skin of her neck. The trunk of her body trembled, one time and then again. Then her body jerked many times in a row. He looked at her face. Tears dribbled out of her closed eyes. Her arms lay tense along the arms of the chair. He had *said* "maybe" about the letter, but in truth he was planning to give it to her, so she didn't need to cry. He watched, not telling. His stomach felt as if weights were attached. He wished she would shut up.

"I'll give you the letter if you'll stop crying," he said. Her eyes flew open like he'd sprung a secret drawer. "After I read it," he added.

"You can't. It's none of your business."

He knew that. But on the other hand, whose business was it, if not his? Jay was his brother, not hers. She acted as if it were the other way around. His fingers trembled against the envelope. He occupied his mind with persuading her, so that nothing might alter these thoughts he was having about Jay. He reasoned with her that she would never have known about the letters if he hadn't found them. That they would have remained under the table forever if. . . . She was lucky actually, he said.

Finally, he told her that he didn't have to give her the letter at all. It wasn't, in fact, even addressed to her, but to Gurney, who might not even be her stepfather, for what he knew, and he thought that maybe the best idea was to find Gurney and hand it to him. With that threat, since the alternatives had disappeared, she said, *All right you can read it*. Her face burned with anger.

Craig turned the letter over and over in his hands, not looking at her, but teasing her with it. He felt he had some sort of permission now to open a letter not addressed to him nor to anyone he knew. She had said all right, open it, even though she was nobody really.

He ripped it open. He wasn't as careful as he'd planned to be and the envelope split across the middle. His insides trembled, but outside nothing showed. He unfolded the tight unyielding paper, holding it in both hands, so that the corners pricked his palms. Earlier he had been afraid of what he might discover, but now he felt that this letter contained information he was supposed to know.

Possession flowed in his veins, taking hold of him. What was Marty here for? Jay hadn't written a letter to her. She strutted around this apartment as if she owned it, as if because she lived next door and Craig was up in Durham that she was more important. He felt uneasy. She had known Jay when he died . . . and he hadn't. But a year of knowing someone was nothing compared to fourteen. *Nothing*.

His body moved without him telling it to. He took her skinny arm and made her stand up. She struggled but he forced her toward the door. Her bare toes grabbed at the gold carpeting. She tried to shake free of him, but his grip was too strong. "You don't belong here," he said, working to keep the hate out of his voice. He tried to understand what was happening, and then he realized. He was getting rid of her for Jay. Jay had tried to do it himself, but she kept coming back, even after he was dead, feeling sorry for herself, wallowing in the misery that belonged to Craig, and not to her at all. He locked the door and listened while she drummed on it, until someone came out of the next apartment and dragged her inside. He heard yelling, but he was almost certain she wouldn't tell that he was here.

Looking around the room, he felt a surge of elation. He saw Gurney's letter, arched smartly on the sofa where he'd dropped it. Jay's presence fairly jumped from it, flooding him with a light bubbly feeling. He looked at the bare walls and the old beaten furniture and they seemed to glow with confidence. He had done Jay a favor, and he felt triumph, a sad triumph because Jay was gone. But Jay was his again. He hadn't left Craig. He understood, thinking of that sniveling girl and holding this telltale letter in his hand, that Jay had come back to him.

He smoothed the paper to make it hang straight. There were two pages of dark neat writing. He looked to the end where Jay's name was and saw that the letter was signed "love." He felt chastened for a moment, a trespasser. Jay had loved this person Gurney. But "love" could mean many things. Clayton loved Paulette. His eyes locked on Jay's name, a broad familiar signature that he'd never thought about before now. He read through tears that, like a magnifying glass, made the ink more distinct than it was.

Now that he had started, he moved like a roller coaster. Scanning Gurney's letter, he ran to the bedroom for the next. He opened, read, and scattered the next two in seconds. Then he got to his own and it wasn't as bad as he'd expected. An admonition to behave differently than his "older?, smarter?" brother had. A suggestion to "widen his options, not narrow them like me"—whatever that meant. Jay said he loved him and would miss him, *had* missed him, in fact, these last two years. He said he hoped that his "final situation" would allow him to watch over Craig and even help him in times of crisis, if that were possible. Craig hoped Jay couldn't see him right now. He imagined that it could be as hard to be watched over by a dead brother as a live one.

He needed to read all the letters again. Gurney's hadn't said much that he understood, except that Marty was mentioned a lot more than he would have wished. Jay had wanted *all* of them to go to Alaska—Alaska?—not just her, but she had misunderstood, and then everybody had misunderstood. Craig wondered who "all of them" included. Jay had wanted to form some sort of colony, like the colonies in early America. "Not the Lost Colony—ha! ha!" he wrote. They would all work and they would all play. He had wanted everyone to share with and love everyone else. He was just sorry Marty had misunderstood.

The letter to Dad talked about all the people who weren't to blame, which was everybody and especially Melissa and Jenny. The fault, Jay insisted, was his own. He also said that for a long time he'd wanted to tell Dad how much he hated hunting, but he hadn't been able to bring himself to say it. He suggested that Dad treat Mom and him better, but Craig thought that was a little unfair. Dad had been treating him fine. Almost fine, except for that time at the gas station when he must have been in a bad mood. Dad had been fine, Jay just hadn't been around to notice.

Mom's letter was short, less than a page. Jay said he wished she had been his real mother. He thanked her for sharing the love she had for Craig with him, and said not many mothers could do it. He said if she ever met his real mother to tell her the good things and, if her conscience would allow it, not how he died. He said he liked the way she ironed shirts and he put another "ha! ha!" at the end of that.

Craig still didn't know why Jay had killed himself, but maybe Jay didn't either. Maybe it was Jay's fault, like he'd said. How did you judge such things? Anger still floated in his mind like garbage in water, scattered and aimless. He had thought it would stay attached to Marty, but it hadn't. He could blame Melissa, he supposed. She was the only one who didn't have a letter, and she was Jay's wife.

He folded the letters as one, placing them inside his shirt. He was faint from having not eaten all day. Perhaps he could bribe Marty for some food with Gurney's letter. Or maybe he'd walk the two miles to the curb market where he'd asked directions here. He didn't know whether he could walk that far right now. He felt scrawny and weak, like an explorer at the end. He finished the crumbs in the Sugar Smacks box, but they didn't help. He rummaged through the cabinets for the sixteenth time, finding nothing but a half bottle of ketchup and some sugar folded in a plastic bag. There were lots of beer cans in the trash, and he wished that whoever had been here last had left a full one for him. He picked a can from the garbage and heard beer slosh in the bottom. It smelled all right, just hot. It couldn't be too old. He took a swig, thinking that he would drink anything right now, and got a mouthful of ashes. Almost anything. His stomach churned with the billowing sensation of hunger. He would give the letter to Gurney and ask please if he could have something to eat.

He fixed the door lock so he could be sure to get back in, but in the parking lot a policeman was stepping out of his patrol car. That traitor. She'd called the police on him. He saw her standing inside her screen door, grinning like a cat.

"Why did you do that?"

"I didn't," she said, the grin still lighting her face.

"Liar." The policeman looked up at them. He wanted to tell her what a miserable bitch she was, but he'd never said that word out loud. He tested it softly. She heard that he'd said something, but not what. "Bitch," he said, louder.

She frowned. "Jay didn't think so," she said. "He thought I was smarter than you are."

"That's a lie." He tilted his head knowingly. Thank goodness he had chosen the letters over the junk she would have told him. He could hear the policeman's footsteps.

A big arm moved in the darkness behind Marty, pushing her aside, and then a man stood there. He was fat and dirty and his hair scattered out from his head. Craig guessed he was Gurney. If only there were a back door to this place. Gurney looked at him long enough to place him and then shut his door. The lock clicked into place.

For his last few free moments, Craig ran to the bedroom and threw the empty envelopes under the bed. He checked two or three places where he might have missed something. He looked once more at Jay's pine tree. When the policeman knocked, he opened the door and went with him to the patrol car. He looked back, but nobody was watching him leave that he could tell.

12

AUDREY

"I love you," Clayton said, his arms circling her waist as she stood at the stove frying chicken for Craig's coming-home dinner. The kitchen was hot and damp and she felt like she was caught in a sort of pan too. Perspiration itched along her hairline and her eyebrows were saturated from catching the beads of water rolling toward her eyes. Clayton buried his nose in her hair and found her ear with a tongue that was normally hot with eagerness, but tonight in this kitchen only lukewarm. Now that they had found Craig, Clayton wanted to go to bed, and she didn't feel that she could turn him down. She didn't *want* to turn him down, no matter how dangerous it was with his wife across the yard. Paulette had walked in on them several times in the last two days to check how the search was going.

He had been with her nearly every minute since Craig had vanished, not touching her even though the sheer energy that had grown in them both seemed to be waiting for just one spark. The phone would ring, and it wouldn't matter whether there was news of Craig or not. She would go to him and press against him, so tight that she felt she was becoming a part of his vast protective body which was hardly bigger than her own.

But he said no when she said that she would like to, genuinely, she needed to, she wanted to, please. He was afraid that later she would think it was wrong, and if, for instance, they found Craig dead, which both of them knew would not happen, she would blame herself.

He cupped her breasts in his hands, and she warned him about the popping grease as she turned the chicken.

They had found Craig late this afternoon. He was in Columbus, or had been; now he was on his way home. When his picture appeared in yesterday evening's paper, the new young man at Buck's service station telephoned and told about the squabble in his parking lot last Friday. A semihysterical woman called, saying she'd witnessed a scene with the lost boy. She kept calling Merle "that monster," and Audrey found herself grinning. The young man at Buck's called back and said that Craig also had taken a map of the Eastern United States, if that helped.

So, the Eastern United States covered a lot of territory, and Merle had disappeared into it and now Craig. Probably Craig was trying to follow Merle, but where? She let her mind roll through town after town, like she was planning a vacation herself, but nothing stuck. She centered on Florida for a while before realizing that Florida was where *she'd* like to go. If Jay were alive she'd say Columbus, but he wasn't. Clayton had no ideas. So finally she called Otto who said where else *but* Columbus. And meekly, she said perhaps Cairo, Georgia, which was where the remaining Mitchells lived, but he said Merle hadn't corresponded with the family in fifteen years. She called the Columbus police department, even though Otto offered to, and they sent a man out to check. A few hours later Craig was on a bus home. He was due to arrive at nine o'clock.

"How do you think I should punish him?" she asked, watching the chicken turn a rich brown. His hands were on the poking out bones of her hips. She thought of the round knobs of the drumsticks. He grew still but did not let her go. His embrace was comforting in the way cooking this meal for Craig was. She thought of Paulette surprising them. They would hardly hear her with the sizzling grease. But Clayton had said she was busy cooking their supper.

"Why do you want to punish him? Maybe you should wait and see why he did it." He began stroking her again now that the thinking was out of the way.

"I know *why*. He was chasing his no-good father."

"Maybe not," Clayton said. "Maybe he just wanted to see where Jay died."

"Damn, Clayton."

"I mean it. Like visiting a grave."

"Jay's grave is here."

"But it happened down there."

How did *he* know so much? He hadn't even thought of Columbus. She stopped considering his opinion. Craig was going to be punished. In the back of her mind, a voice that she tried not to recognize told her that she needed punishing too. She snuggled into Clayton's chest which fit the roundness of her back like a coat. She wished she knew that Clayton would be angry. Then it would be easier to confess about Otto. But would he punish her or would he just forgive her? She would tell him that Otto had forced himself on her. But then would he offer her some of *his* money and murmur that she couldn't possibly have helped it? She backed him away with her elbows while she piled the chicken on paper towels.

Being like this with Clayton reminded her of when she and Merle used to go to Myrtle Beach. Before Otto had started getting promoted. He'd had only her to worry about, and, like now, they would play while she cooked in the efficiency apartment that they'd rented for a week. Craig and Jay were with them, but it was almost like they were alone. The boys would spend all day at the ocean and then at night they would go to the boardwalk where they spent the evening playing pinball. She and Merle would make love for hours. But those trips ended five years ago when Otto became Merle's boss. What money Merle made began dribbling through his fingers weekly instead of finding its way into their savings account. He got so he couldn't save up for pleasure; it had to come every day. And not necessarily from her.

She set the chicken on the table and checked the potatoes and peas. She was going to make biscuits and gravy closer to the time of Craig's arrival. "Are you going to eat with me or with her?" she asked, peeved because she knew the answer.

"You," he said, smiling at the surprised jerk of her eyes. "And then I'm going home to tell her." He looked over her shoulder at the cooking vegetables. She studied his intent profile.

"Tell her what?"

He pulled her away from the stove. "That I'm leaving, that I'm taking the car and she'll have to rent one when she wants to go see her mother. That I have to be able to drive in order to work so I can make money for her alimony." He paused for a deep breath. Her arms lay stiff around his neck. "That I'm moving into a trailer out on the highway."

She pulled quietly away, but he kept one of her hands. "I don't want you to," she said.

"Which?"

"Move away."

"You can move with me." He pulled her face to within inches of his own. "I want you to come now." She wondered why they couldn't just stay like this. They didn't have to move; they didn't have to do anything different. One day, after Paulette had gotten used to the idea, he might even move over here. "Craig's on his way home, and there's nothing to hold you here," he said. "Nothing."

She looked over his shoulder at the piece of cardboard stopping the hole in the kitchen door. "I bought a new piece of glass for that," she said, inclining her head toward it. Gently, she added, "You said you would fix it."

He let go of her hand. He wouldn't look at the door. "Audrey," he said in a low patient voice.

She didn't listen. "The glass is in my car and the hammer's in that toolbox." She cut her eyes to the rusty blue box under the breakfast table. She would move it to the shed tomorrow.

He tightened his grip on her arm. "Do you still love Merle?"

Her chin was turned into her shoulder. She shook her head without looking up. She didn't love Merle, but she didn't love Clayton either. She wasn't even sure she loved Craig. Oh, she *did*, but right now she felt so betrayed. "I'm confused, Clayton. I love you . . ."—she had to say so—". . . but I'm confused." She looked at the cat clock's tail, wagging away all her time.

He raised her chin with his fingers and kissed her. She closed her eyes, trying to think of nothing else. Just then a car pulled into the driveway. She moved to the window and saw Merle's white Chevrolet. Wings of mud were spattered along its fenders.

"Merle's back," she said. They looked at each other across the short width of the room, stunned. "I do love you, Clayton, I do," she said. "You're just too good for me." A car door opened and then another. Who was with him?

"What do you mean by that?" He moved away from the door, his face an angry flush. "Don't tell me, I don't want to know."

And they had to leave it at that because Merle had already reached the stoop and was turning the handle to the door of his house where Clayton King really shouldn't be at all. There was nothing new, she could tell him: the door pane was still missing; she was still putting Clayton off; his brother was still trying to get what was Merle's. There was one thing new: Craig had left home to find him. Gone halfway across the country for a father who didn't know he was alive.

Merle, bearded, rushed into the kitchen like something

escaping. "God, it's hot in here." His blue eyes gleamed out of his face like eggs in a nest. Hands on hips, he looked with amusement at Clayton. "While the cat's away, the mouse will play," he said.

"Hi, Merle." Clayton picked up a piece of chicken and began eating it. Merle inspected the pots on the stove. Someone else was coming up the steps.

Merle announced: "And while the cat's away, the *cat* will play." Which meant, Audrey supposed, that this was a woman. Which meant also that Clayton's being here could hardly be a problem. Merle looked expectantly at the door. Clayton squirmed in his clothes as if they had shrunk. She wished he had not taken a piece of chicken; it seemed so familiar not to ask. And then the door opened and Melissa walked in, leading with her pregnant stomach, and Clayton said, "That was fast work, Merle." Merle hee-hawed for the first time seriously at one of Clayton's jokes.

Audrey reintroduced Melissa and Clayton, for they had met most recently at Christmas, with as much cool dignity as she could summon. She shot Clayton a dark glance. She could understand him not recognizing her, she guessed, but she couldn't understand his crudeness. She squeezed Melissa's hand, which wasn't particularly responsive, and led her to the table. Clayton was trying to apologize about what he said, but she tersely told him to forget it.

"I'll bet you two are hungry," she said in her cheery bank voice. Everyone was thinking about that poor baby, she guessed. Merle took a seat at the table, and Audrey knew he would notice the three settings Clayton had placed. "Who's not eating?" he asked immediately.

"I'm not," Clayton said.

"You *were*." While he waited for an explanation, Merle fumbled through the chicken pieces and set a breast on his plate.

"Craig ran away," Clayton said quietly.

"He did?" Merle chuckled softly. "Have you two found

him yet?" His tone was mocking. He examined his piece of chicken for a fertile spot to sink his teeth.

Clayton continued unperturbed: "We just got a call from the Columbus police department that he's on a bus coming home." Clayton moved toward the door.

"We just came from there. Didn't we, doll?"

Melissa looked up startled and then reached for a piece of chicken herself. Audrey went to the stove to mash the potatoes.

"Paulette's probably got my supper ready," Clayton said.

Merle spoke through a full mouth: "You can't leave now." Grease rimmed his lips but he didn't bother to wipe it away.

Clayton hesitated, his hand dropping from the doorknob. Audrey had just as soon see him go. She wanted to talk to him about the trailer and whether it was really big enough for her and Craig, but later, tomorrow perhaps, from work. "We'd love to have you stay," she said, barely hesitating, but he was smart enough not to.

She added vegetables to their plates and then to hers, deciding not to wait for Craig. She asked Melissa how Jenny was, when this next baby was due, was she going to get a job, and who would take care of the children. She did most of the talking because Melissa offered only one-syllable answers, pretending like her chewing was the reason.

Once Merle broke in and said "butter" and she got him some. "I don't know how Craig knew where you were going," she said, setting the dish before him. "Did you tell him?" He shook his head. "Are you even interested?" she asked, irritated.

"Why should I be? He's on his way home."

She told Melissa that she'd take her out to Jay's grave tomorrow. It was a lovely place on top of a hill overlooking a small lake where children could play with ducks. She said she thought it was nice that they had ducks at graveyards. She said that then children didn't dread going.

Melissa studied Merle. "I don't want to go," she said.

Merle pushed his plate into the middle of the table, sucking loudly at his teeth as if he hadn't heard her. His napkin lay folded by his plate and he swabbed his greasy hand against it. "I've been thinking," he said. A grin cut across his face like a knife through meat.

Melissa arched back in her chair.

"I think. . . ." He stopped abruptly. In a new tone he began again: "I think I'll go pick up Craig." He scraped his chair roughly against the linoleum. They listened without speaking as he went to the back of the house. Audrey wondered if his hand were any better. Except for some puffiness, it looked normal, but he hadn't used it to eat. In a few minutes he reappeared in clean clothes. "What time's that bus due?" he asked.

"Nine o'clock."

It was seven-thirty. In twenty minutes her whole life had collapsed. The telephone rang and Merle grabbed it. He stood with his injured hand on one hip like this was wasting his time. "What do *you* want?" he asked the caller. But he didn't listen, thrusting the receiver toward Audrey. "Talk to him," he said bitterly. She was afraid it was Clayton, but Otto answered. He was calling, he said, to tell her that he wanted to come over and give Craig a talking to, but he saw that that would be impossible.

"When did *he* get back?"

Merle stood at the door, swinging his key chain on his index finger.

"He'll arrive on the nine o'clock bus," she said.

"Oh."

"He was where you said he'd be," she added, although she'd already given him that information.

Otto cleared his throat. "Is your boyfriend still there?" Clayton had answered the phone earlier today. "Never mind. If you'll come by tomorrow, I have something for you."

"Thanks for calling," she said and hung up.

Merle stood before her, his face suspicious. "What was that all about?" He kept twirling the keys.

"He wanted to know about Craig. Most people have been concerned."

"He was surprised to hear me on the phone."

"I was surprised to see you at the door. You disappeared, remember?" She went back to her lukewarm supper and he left, slamming the door so hard that the piece of cardboard fell out. It lay on the floor like something to walk on. The food was dry and tasteless, but she pushed it down anyway, not wanting to have to talk. Melissa kept eating too, although she had finished the food on her plate. She picked at the bits of clinging flesh and sucked on the gray bones. She chased a pea around her plate for what seemed like a long time.

Audrey thought of Clayton eating Paulette's fried chicken instead of her own and wondered if he had taken that one thigh just to make her feel good. Sweet of him if he had. Maybe he would stay next door for a while now that Merle was back and it would be more difficult for her to leave. At least give some support when she announced her intentions. With Melissa around Merle might let her go more easily. Why had she even come here? And why didn't she want to visit Jay's grave? She looked tired, like she hadn't wanted to make this trip at all. But here she was. There was nothing left on either plate that they could possibly eat.

"Coffee?" she offered. Melissa nodded. In silence she cleared away the plates and started the percolator. She wiped the table where Merle had sat and laid a fresh place for Craig. If they all lived here, they would have to eat in shifts or else in the dining room. She brought cups and saucers to the table. Melissa played nervously with her cup.

"How long is he going to make me stay here?" she blurted.

Audrey perched on the edge of her chair. "Make you?"

"He made me come here," she said.

"I thought you'd moved."

"I went to Columbus to pick up some things. He was waiting for me."

"What for?" Audrey still felt that being here was Melissa's idea. She rose to pour the coffee.

Melissa said, "He told me we were going to take a trip, but he wouldn't say where. We drove through Alabama and part of Tennessee, and then he turned in this direction. I want to go home, but I don't think he's going to let me."

"How can he stop you?"

Melissa sniffled. "I had to leave Jenny with a beauty-shop operator I hardly *know*. I don't *feel* very good." She gave certain words a whining twist. "Merle *raped* me." She stopped whining to look at Audrey.

Audrey did not drop her gaze.

"I hate to tell you that, but you ought to know." She set her chin self-righteously. Picking up her cup, she drank the rest of her coffee in one slow swallow.

Audrey's cheeks reddened. Melissa must have tempted him. Merle wouldn't do that with his own son's wife. The faintness in her chest turned to anger. "I don't believe you," she said.

Melissa coldly answered, "That's your choice."

"You're lying," she insisted.

Melissa sat perfectly composed. "God, I've got to go to the bathroom." She rose slowly and padded toward the back of the house, leaving her shoes under the table.

Either one of them could be guilty. Not too many seven-months pregnant women asked to be raped, but not many fathers went to bed with their sons' wives. Maybe it never even happened. Maybe Melissa was getting back at Merle for last Christmas when he finally had to tell her to get her parading ass out of his face.

Melissa reappeared, a worried look on her face. She sat down, tasted the new cup of coffee Audrey had poured, said it was cold, asked if Audrey would mind getting her a fresh cup. It was so hard to keep getting up and down in this condition.

"I'd better call and see about Jenny," she said.

"Sure."

"Hand me . . . could you hand me the phone?" Audrey brought it and the coffee to the table. "And my purse."

She tried to be generous-spirited, but it was hard. "Would you like me to dial your number?" she asked.

But her meaning was lost. "I can do it." There was no answer, and the concern in her face deepened. "Where are they? Where the hell are they?" She let the number keep ringing. "Can you give me bus fare?" she asked.

"I don't have it," Audrey said curtly.

"*Audrey. . . .*" she implored.

"I don't have it, Melissa." There was sixty dollars left from what Otto had given her, but that was hers, the money that freed her and Craig whenever they might need it. Melissa would have to figure out her own transportation. Maybe *she* could visit Otto tomorrow.

With her last swallow Melissa fumbled her cup, but it didn't break. Audrey wondered if the baby in her stomach was as wild-eyed and jumpy as its mother from the caffeine shooting through its young veins. She wondered if the umbilical connection was this very minute transmitting feelings of rage and bitterness. If bitchiness and sloth were moving from mother to child. She didn't like this coming baby in the same way she hadn't liked Jenny. Not—as they all thought—because she carried Merle's first wife's name. But because she seemed so irrevocably a part of Melissa. Even when they became two, they would always be one.

"Get up and help, you fat bitch": Jay's words to Melissa at the Christmas meal. Audrey wanted to repeat them now. Melissa still let the phone ring; she lifted her empty cup to

Audrey for a refill. She had never removed one plate from Audrey's table or washed one glass.

"I'm going to bed. . . ."

"Sh-h-h," Melissa interrupted. "Never mind, I thought someone had answered. What?"

"I'm tired and I'm going to bed. Hang up and I'll show you where you can sleep." Melissa recradled the phone reluctantly. "We have only so many beds in this house, so you'll have to sleep in Jay's old one." She didn't look to see if Melissa minded or not. "And, unfortunately, we have only one bathroom, so please take that into consideration when you're in there." She knew she was being mean, but she couldn't help herself. She didn't want to give her the money; it was all she had.

At the door to Craig's room, Melissa said, "Craig's going to sleep in here with me?" She looked down the hall to the other bedroom.

"Um-hmm."

"What about Merle?"

"He sleeps with *me*," Audrey said, a bit fiercely. She felt a sudden surge of jealousy like she hadn't felt in a long time. Maybe she couldn't control what happened outside her house, but she would certainly control what went on inside.

"I meant could Merle sleep with Craig and let us sleep in there?"

"No thank you." She could see a drunken Merle coming after both of them. "I want you to get one thing straight, Melissa. While you're in my house, you stay away from Merle."

"I've always stayed away from him." She moved toward the bed. "All my clothes are in Merle's car," she said. "I don't have a nightgown." Audrey had only one herself. "I said I don't have a nightgown."

Audrey smiled. "I'm sorry."

"I can tell," Melissa said hatefully. She pulled her dress

roughly over her head. Audrey watched because this was a show for her. Melissa dumped her bra and underpants on the floor at the foot of the bed. She put her slip under her pillow and slid naked into the covers. She wanted Audrey to know that she would be lying this way only a few feet from Craig.

"You better watch your fanny," Audrey said.

It was *her* house, so she spent an hour in the bathroom sitting on the edge of the bathtub, propping one foot at a time on the commode lid as she redid her toenails. Melissa shouldn't be able to walk in this house, demand whatever she wanted, and walk out with it. She heard her outside the door once, too proud to ask to come in. Her baby was bound to be giving her bladder hell. This, Melissa dear, is how it is around here at bathroom time. She wondered if Melissa was daring to walk through this house naked. She washed her face slowly and then decided to paint her fingernails . . . in here where the light was better. If Melissa wanted some money, let her get it the hard way like everybody else. Otto would probably really enjoy her.

She took pity on Melissa and vacated the bathroom around ten-thirty. Merle and Craig weren't home yet, but that was no surprise. She had decided she was not willing to give up her sixty dollars. But if Otto gave her more money tomorrow, she would share part of it with Melissa. Enough to send her home. She was going to go see him herself.

13

MERLE

Merle hated the bus station, hated the urine smell twenty feet either side of the bathrooms, hated the long seat without any dividers like pews in a church so that you could never be sure who was going to sit beside you. Hated the whole idea of buses and bus stations because they made him feel like a cow, and they stank from the sidewalk outside to the seat behind the driver where he usually sat to avoid the more overpowering smell at the rear.

He walked through the door marked TO BUSES even though he knew he would be breathing an exhaust smell almost as nauseating. Outside he leaned against the red brick wall of the building, propping one foot behind him and lighting a cigarette. He sucked deeply, hoping the smoke might push out the carbon monoxide in his lungs. Two buses vibrated side by side in their stalls. They had brought passengers from New York City and Spartanburg, South Carolina, and stood awaiting a new assignment. No drivers were in sight, only a young Negro boy pacing the cement.

He could smoke easily with his hand now, squeeze the fingers just tight enough to hold the cigarette between them. He couldn't reach out his index finger to pump the ash off the end, but it could fall off and that was easier anyway. His hand was stiff but at least he could do a little something. He'd begun to think of it not as something injured but as something old, a part of him that had aged ahead of time. He could almost think that it hadn't been his fault. In a couple of weeks, he would see a doctor, find out if anything could be done. He did not dislike having such a conversation piece on the end of his arm.

He'd realized on the road down the mountains that he would not see Jenny again. That whatever Melissa told him was made up and whatever was true didn't matter anyway since it was in the grave with Jay. He smiled, thinking of Melissa, that lush Garden of Eden, and the Negro boy grinned back. Merle looked the other way. When the hell was this bus going to arrive? He leaned to find the solemn round clock high up on the wall inside the waiting room and saw that it was still a few minutes before nine. He hated to wait. God, he hated to wait worse than anybody in this whole world. Especially when he had things to *do*. He had planned on taking Craig home, but now he thought he would take him along to Chunny's.

A bus labeled Atlanta pulled into the third slot. Merle stood erect and then leaned back against the wall to light another cigarette. Through the smoked brown glass he saw Craig alone in the seat behind the driver and was reminded of watching him fourteen years ago through the glass wall of the hospital nursery. No one had been allowed to touch him, not even Audrey, for the first two months after he was born prematurely.

Craig had seen him and was waving foolishly. He stroked his chin to show he noticed the new beard. Merle flushed. The Negro boy was watching. Craig was ten feet away, the bus was stopped, he waved again, and Merle looked around like it wasn't at him. Finally he threw up his hand in one short gesture and dropped it back to his side. The door wheezed open and Craig vaulted down the steps.

"Where'd you get the beard?"

Merle tried to smile, and motioned his head in the direction of the car. "I bought it," he said. The Negro boy watched them all the way, clicking his tongue, and Merle wanted to jump him and knock his head against the brick wall a few times. In the parking lot he relaxed. Craig had caught up to his stride and wasn't badgering him with questions. Merle unlocked his side of the car, got in, and started the motor. Craig peered through the window, his hand waiting on the door handle. In the dark his face shone white and anxious, but he didn't call out and there was no begging look in his eyes. Merle leaned to unlock the door, and Craig jumped in, a bit too eagerly, but that was understandable.

"I guess you're pretty mad," Craig said, settling in.

"Nope."

"Is Mom?" He draped his arm on the back of the seat.

"How should I know?" Merle turned the car toward Chunny's. Craig looked around, trying to figure out where they were going.

"You traveled light," Merle said.

Craig's cheeks puffed up under his blue eyes. "Yep." They were leaving town, and he grew more intent on their direction. He scratched the top of his head.

"Head itch?" Merle asked.

Craig nodded.

"Mine did too."

Craig turned curiously.

"On my trip," Merle added.

Craig nodded as if he understood.

"I didn't take a shower the whole time I was gone." Merle broke out laughing, a fine artificial laugh that he had perfected over the years.

"Me either," Craig said, joining him. Then they laughed again, more intensely, because it was funny and a coincidence and it did show a kind of kinship that they hadn't often found. The atmosphere in the car was as sweet as if they'd driven by a bakery.

"Did I tell you where I thought we'd go?"

"Not home?"

"Not home," Merle echoed. Conversation was a game that he was glad to see Craig learning to play. He waited, but Craig waited too, the way he should have. "I thought I'd take you to Chunny's. It's a bar that I used to take Jay to. You can't have a drink, but I thought I'd buy you a beer *if*." He felt Craig's eyes upon his face.

"If I don't tell Mom?"

"If you don't tell your mother."

Their eyes met then and locked, and for once Craig did not grin that foolish-ass grin of his.

"I won't tell," Craig said. "I won't." He wouldn't ever again, Merle knew.

They reached Chunny's and Merle noticed that the aged sign advertising the menu had collapsed in the dirt. Chunny hadn't bothered to pick it up, which Merle thought was a good indicator. Maybe he was as tired of this restaurant business as Merle was. The Budweiser sign was lighted, as well as the thin cheap clock over the bathroom door. Merle drove around back through potholes and over big bumps where a shift in the earth's crust had broken up the pavement. There were two cars here, Chunny's and another Merle didn't recognize. He'd considered fixing up the parking lot, painting a new sign, but now he realized that these outdoor inconveniences were good camouflage. When customers came inside, they would be surprised by the luxurious surroundings. In the back room where they'd play roulette and craps, there would be velvet curtains hiding the cinderblock walls and shag carpet so thick that if you dropped a piece of change you'd never be able to find it. Which would encourage people to spend dollars. He would install the carpet himself and find some sweetheart to make curtains for him. For the room that was currently the garage, he planned a bar with sweet Melissa dealing blackjack at a high table draped like a throne. The present front room, the grill, would be "out-of-business" for outward appearances. He threw the gears into park, jerking the car to a halt. Chunny would go wild over his idea. He needed something like this.

"Here?" Craig asked.

"What'd you expect?" Merle was irritated that his first customer would dare be picky before he'd even been inside. Maybe they would have to fix up the outside a little. "Stop bitching or walk home," he said viciously.

"Take it easy, Dad. I just wanted to know if this was it."

"You ain't too good to be here."

"I know that." Craig opened his door to shut off the conversation which Merle thought was a smart move. Reaching the entrance first, Craig waited. His eyes, less eager, more patient, seemed to have lost some of their boyishness. Only for today perhaps, but Merle definitely noticed. For once he wasn't sure what Craig was thinking. With his hands resting on his hips, he looked cocky. "After you," he said. Merle raised his eyebrows and went ahead.

It was dark outside, but it was positively cavelike in here. Chunny stood behind the bar lighting a cigarette for a customer. He raised his hand in a sort of salute. "Who's your friend?" he asked, his face beaming a smile at Craig. He was a little tight, otherwise he would have noticed how young Craig was.

"My son," Merle said. Chunny's eyes came unfocused, wandering back in time. "My second son," he added.

"Oh, yeah."

"He ain't old enough for a drink, but I thought I'd give him a beer if you got any." Merle noticed how his speech pattern tended to change when he talked to Chunny.

"Looks old enough to me," Chunny said. "Anyway, I don't have no beer."

The man sitting at the bar turned to stare at them. He was dressed in an ill-fitting suit, and his tie draped around his neck like a skinny muffler. He faced the bar again and lifted his glass to drain it. He stood up, still drinking.

"You don't need to leave, Harry," Chunny said. A hint of pleading, which disgusted Merle, colored his voice. He looked closely at Chunny. The skin around his eyes sagged and his voice wavered as he talked. Maybe he wasn't over being sick.

Harry said: "I don't drink with twelve-year-olds." He turned to speak directly to Craig. "You'd better get out of here, kid, before you get Chunny in worse trouble." Craig let his eyes drop to the floor. If he hadn't let Harry bully him, Merle could have let this pass.

"Leave my kid alone," he said, grabbing Harry by the elbow. He let go of the man's arm as quickly as he had seized it. He could not defend himself. He could fucking not defend himself, and he had forgotten. "Sorry," he said quickly. Craig had stepped up to intervene if necessary, and Chunny was coming from around the bar. The two men moved away from each other.

"Why did you do that?" Chunny asked after the door shut behind Harry.

"I didn't do nothing," Merle said blackly. Why was Chunny giving him so much hell? "Let's sit down and have a drink," he said, conciliatorily. "Come on, Chunny." Craig climbed a barstool, and Chunny studied him again as if trying to determine his age in light of what Harry had said. Merle sensed that he was about to ask the pertinent question. "Let me fix the drinks," he said, gliding behind the bar.

While he mixed two bourbons and water and a light bourbon and ginger ale, he asked what kind of trouble Harry was talking about. Craig watched the mixing with interest. Before answering, Chunny lifted his hands, one at a time, holding them level in front of his eyes. They trembled, and Chunny winced as if they disappointed him. Merle poured out half of his drink and filled the glass with water, but Chunny didn't even notice.

"How do you like bourbon?" he asked Craig who was sipping carefully.

"Okay. Not bad."

Merle would make the next one stronger.

He had to feed Chunny three more watered-down drinks before he began to shape up. The trouble was real. Somebody had reported Chunny's operation to an honest deputy, and the sheriff had had to put him in jail for a few days. A lot of people thought the squealer was Merle, but Chunny knew it hadn't been. He spoke with such conviction that Merle didn't even have to confirm his innocence. His heart swelled in his chest like a beach ball in the sun. Anyway, the real trouble was not being found out or going to jail. It was that now the sheriff wanted more money to protect Chunny's cover and that hardly any of his customers had been here since he was busted and that he didn't have the money to pay and that Merle had just run off one of his best customers and he didn't know what he was going to do and. . . . Chunny wasn't exactly crying, but his eyes were wet all around as if they had sprung leaks. He pushed his empty glass toward Merle.

"I rode by your house but your car wasn't ever there, and I left word at Muzzie's for you to call me. . . ." He tightened his mouth into a thin frown, fighting back a real rush of tears.

Merle looked over his head and imagined red velvet decorating the cinderblock walls. Black shag carpet that wouldn't show spills. An inexpensive roulette table that as the years went by would be replaced by a fine leather one.

"I've got an idea," Merle said. Chunny's eyebrows raised slightly, but he was still too drunk for it all to sink in. Merle decided to drop a few hints, pique his interest. Then talk about something else and let him wonder. He looked around the room, thinking about this oak board Chunny'd been using as his bar. The grain was pretty and the board was in good shape. He planned to refinish it, make it into something handsome. Craig's hands rested on it, the glass empty between them. He bent to dig into the plastic bag of Party Ice sitting in a bucket on the floor. They'd have an ice-maker—none of this cheap stuff. He gave Craig a stronger snort.

"I need to talk to you about this one," Merle said, pointing his finger at Craig who straightened unconsciously. "This boy took off thumbing last week and made it all the way to Columbus, Georgia."

Chunny gave Craig a congratulatory nod. "Did you now?" he asked. "And how old are you?"

Merle sent him a quick approving glance. "Fourteen," Craig said.

Chunny considered carefully this bit of information. He took a swallow from his glass and crunched a piece of ice. "This drink isn't very strong," he suddenly complained. "What did you want to go to Columbus for?" he asked, remembering his manners and his current customers.

Craig grinned. "Chasing after him." He nodded toward Merle.

His words were slurred without reason; he'd scarcely had a thimbleful of whiskey. Chunny didn't seem to be sobering up. Or maybe *he* was getting a little high himself and Chunny just looked that way. Give him a little booze, a fresh customer. . . . Merle wondered if Chunny was keeping track of the number of drinks they'd had. He himself knew precisely, but now he forced the number out of his mind. They might agree on three or four for him and count all of Craig's as one. Chunny was too easy to fool, which was another reason he needed a smart partner.

Chunny asked him something, but he didn't hear what. His eyes were sharper than they'd been all evening, and there was a caution in his words that floated in the air between them. Craig was drowning his sorrows.

"You ain't as curious as I thought you'd be," Merle said,

looking around at the empty bar as if that were reason enough for Chunny to be interested.

"Sure I am." Chunny leaned forward confidingly on the counter. He set his chin in his palm and gazed deep into Merle's eyes. "What you got to sell, Merle?" He looked like he was trying to be foxy, half-closing his eyes and turning his head from side to side. "Merle's got something to sell," he announced to the empty room. Craig smiled, finding someone drunker than himself. But neither one of them could be that far gone. Merle had been fixing the drinks, and he knew.

"I don't have *nothing* to sell," he said, hoping the severity of his tone might bring Chunny around. "I got an idea that'll make us *rich*." Maybe not the tone, but the word snapped both listeners to attention. "Rich," Merle repeated meaningfully.

"Oh yeah?" Chunny's thin white hair seemed to take on fullness. The wrinkles around his eyes and chin grew smoother.

Craig riveted toward him too, a hungry expression on his face. "How, Dad?"

"Not you," Merle said. Craig rolled his eyes like he couldn't care less.

"Maybe you can mix drinks," Merle said gruffly.

"Where?" Chunny asked. Merle looked at him like he was crazy. "You haven't told us your idea yet," he said patiently.

"My idea . . ."—he let his eyes open wide with excitement—". . . is to open a casino." He let the word reverberate around the cinderblock walls. Those scabby walls that soon would be adorned with the smoothest of velvets, hanging as if they covered a picture window or at least a nice painting. Craig grinned like a puppy. Chunny's eyes glistened with excitement. He nodded. He kept nodding. Without any explanation, any embellishment, it was already the right idea. He kept on, to catch them in the feverish excitement that had carried him for days. Things had been coming together in his mind for that long.

"This isn't going to be any old dump," he said. "Take for instance this board." His words soared with his thoughts until he felt like he was almost crowing. "They don't make boards like this anymore. They don't grow trees that big, so they can't," he added, thinking he might need to explain. "This is a foot-and-a-half wide, two-inch thick piece of oak board that I'm going to make beautiful. You can call it our cornerstone, but if we ever have to move we can take it with us." He laughed uproariously, and they both joined in. The thought that he might have trouble refinishing the wood with only one working hand skirted his mind, but he ignored it. He came from behind the counter, feeling like an actor. "We're going to carpet this floor." He swooped his arm in an expansive gesture. "We're going to cover all these walls with red velvet." He pirouetted. "We'll find an old roulette wheel and a couple of crap tables. . . .

"Come with me," he said suddenly. He led like the Pied Piper and they stumbled after. He dragged open the metal door that led to the grill area, noticing happily how substantial it was. "*This* room is our decoy. Craig's responsibility." Craig scuffed his fingers through his hair. Merle picked up a wooden chair and, without giving Chunny a chance to object, slung it against the counter. Chunny bellowed to wait a minute, but the chair lay in pieces. "Son, you got to make this room a wreck. Bring in a lot of junk, some dirt." Chunny maintained his scowl. "You don't make money in here, do you?" Chunny shook his head.

"Next," Merle shouted, heady with his imminent success. He went through the broken wooden door into the garage, pointing at it as he passed. "You need to fix that, Chunny." He felt a bit like an interior decorator, surveying this room. "Now here we have a problem," he said. "If we set up our blackjack tables in here, people—"

"I love blackjack," Chunny interrupted.

"Good."

"Blackjack is a great game."

"I know. Chunny, listen to me." Chunny nodded obediently. "If we set up our tables in here, people can see what we're doing."

"Blackjack—"

"*Sheriffs* can see what we're doing," he said forcefully, so that finally Chunny listened. "We paint these glass windows. I've thought of decorating them like stained glass." He had only just thought of the idea but wanted them to think he had figured out each detail in advance. "Not like in churches. We don't want any Mary-and-Jesus scenes. Maybe scenes of forests and fields."

"What about a painting of us going hunting?" Craig asked, short of breath from the excitement.

"No," Merle yelled angrily. Why did everyone have to put in his two cents' worth? Why was Craig even here? If there would be a hunting scene with anybody, it would be with Jay. "Wait a minute," he said harshly. He grew solemn. "The idea's not such a bad one. I think we should have a hunting scene." Craig swallowed rapidly a couple of times. Merle looked him straight in the eye. "It should be of Jay," he said. He noticed tears of pity filling Chunny's eyes. "Jay and me."

Chunny squeezed the back of Craig's neck with one hand. "He can't help it. You can't help who you love."

They stood there while Merle finished explaining about the blackjack and about Melissa who would be dealing. Chunny tried to interrupt three or four times, but Merle held up a finger, saying let him tell the whole story. Tears slipped involuntarily out of Craig's eyes. He was not crying because there were no sobs, no whining, only a silent flow in a single wet line through the dirt and sweat of his trip. Merle was proud of him.

The whole story about Melissa was that she was good looking, she had great knockers and a fine face. Nice red hair and strong firm legs. He paused on the legs. In Casablanca Chunny had always talked about Priscilla's legs. These were legs like firecrackers, Merle said. Firm, hot legs. He winked.

"Sure, Merle," Chunny said, but he wanted to see them: Merle could tell.

They walked away from the garage quietly like at the end of a sermon. Merle poured fresh drinks and kept talking. This wasn't *any* woman. This was his daughter-in-law whom he had perfect control over, and, by God, she was a looker. If Chunny wanted this place to take off, he had to have a woman here. Did he think men wanted to watch his ugly puss while they were gambling?

He wrapped up his argument, sure that he had won, and Chunny said there was only one thing: no women. They were the beginning and end of trouble, and they were trouble in between. With women there would be knifings and shootings and fistfights and destroyed property . . . and cops. "It won't work," he finished. "Even if she *is* your daughter-in-law. Even if she was your *wife*."

"You'll have to trust me," Merle said, looking over his nth drink. "But it has to be my way."

Chunny gazed blearily at him, too tired to argue. He looked around the empty room, pallid beside Merle's vivid descriptions, and had dreams of his own. "We'll talk about it," he said.

"Everybody likes to have women around," Craig mustered. His eyes floated everywhere but mostly back in his head. He almost fell off his stool trying to lean against the bar, but Merle caught him. He thought Craig could be a big help around here. After he mixed one more round, he came around to their side to sit.

14

CRAIG/MERLE

Craig watched as Chunny stumbled off his barstool and crumpled to the rough cement floor in the corner of the room. He worked his chin like an old thin goat. His puffy red face glowed from the corner like a coal. He waved goodbye to them as if the cinderblock walls were the walls of his house.

"G'night, old buddy," Dad murmured fondly. "Think *rich.*"

Chunny peacefully closed his eyes. "No women," he said feebly. *The beginning and end of trouble, and trouble in between.* Craig grinned. That was one argument Dad was sure to win. The only thing that Craig hated was for Melissa to have to be a part of this. Now that Jay wasn't around, maybe they could be friends.

The two of them sat at the bar, their legs wrapped around the rungs of the stools, looking ahead. Dad didn't like for people to talk in his face. If you tried to catch his attention, he would nod that he had heard you and then rivet his eyes to the drink before him or to the strange unshaped hand beside it or to the calendar girls on the wall who watched them with teasing eyes. Besides, Craig had noticed, it was easier to say important things if you didn't have to stare somebody in the eye. You could say anything if you thought the only listener might be your own ears. Why, Dad could have stepped outside to take a leak or slipped into the grill to snitch another bag of potato chips. If you told him about the letters, he might not even hear.

"He got a rotten deal," Dad said. He had been drinking steadily but not out of control all night. With his eyebrows Craig questioned toward Chunny's corner, and Dad nodded. Craig had been drinking too, but carefully. Several times he had had to laugh louder than he felt or say something dangerous so that they would feel he was with them. When he cried that he wasn't going to be in Dad's mural, it was almost because Dad expected him to.

"Almost as bad a deal as Jay," Dad continued. In his sleep Chunny wheezed and cleared his throat several times. Craig nodded. He was not interested in Chunny's bad luck, but he was interested in Dad. A bottle of bourbon sat beside Dad's far elbow so that he wouldn't have to get up anymore. They were having their drinks warm because Chunny had expected a slow night and hadn't bought enough ice.

Dad spoke in a low sad voice: "Last time I saw *him* happy was at Camp Chicago on V-J Day. They had us almost ready to ship to the Pacific theater and all of a sudden we didn't have to go. I was disappointed, but Chunny was like nothing you've ever seen. His balls were busting to see his wife. There were plenty of women around willing to help us celebrate, but he didn't want one. I told him what was at home would wait, *if* it was still there. I doubted she would be even then; you could usually tell which men would have women to go home to. But he wouldn't listen." Dad stopped talking to aim the bottle carefully over his glass. He seemed to be drinking faster now that Chunny had gone to sleep.

"It was some party. Lots of men had kept their weapons instead of turning them in, and they were shooting up the skies. Making their own fireworks. Only some guys were so drunk, they couldn't aim too good. Bullets peppered our tent. I hid under a bunk, scared out of my mind. You don't go through a whole war and want to bite the dust the day you win. Chunny perched on the top bunk. He knew a lot about guns and every time one was fired, he yelled out what make it was. Spaced in between, he babbled about Priscilla—how much he loved her, where he was going to take her when he got home, what they were going to buy. When it got so you could see stars through the canvas ceiling, I pulled him down and held on to him. He was so worked up that I knew something was going to go wrong. Right when you think it never will, it always does." Dad stopped abruptly. He moved to leave the bar, but Craig passed him his empty glass to keep him there.

"What happened?" Dad poured him a fresh drink.

"The whore left him." Dad's face darkened as he settled back on his stool. "For Chunny's own brother. He got a letter from her the day before we were shipped home. I knew it was something bad, but he wouldn't tell me what. He walked around like a zombie. We sailed on the *Europa* to New York. He was the first man down the gangplank. I saved his life and he didn't even tell me goodbye. Maybe he wished I would have let him get shot." Dad took a rushed sloppy swallow. Bourbon dribbled down his chin. Chunny moaned from his place in the corner.

The anger suddenly left Dad's voice. "Don't ever trust a woman," he said in a sad monotone. "Even if you think she might be different. None of them are. She'll just walk out the door one day, and you'll never see her again." Tears welled in his eyes, but he blinked once and they were gone.

"It's too bad," Craig said.

"Too *bad?*" Dad jerked around as if he were going to hit him. Craig shied away. Dad threw his arms wide above the bar, knocking over both their drinks. Craig thought of moving over one stool. He was confused about what Dad was saying. In the corner Chunny muttered brokenly.

After a while Chunny's noisy sleep settled down. The

room grew silent except for a slow drip from the puddle of spilled drink on the edge of the counter. Craig allowed himself a breath, his first deep one, and felt the fear in his body easing away. He thought Dad must have fallen asleep sitting up when suddenly he heard new words, thin words from deep in Dad's throat, words so soft that he wondered if they were real.

"I miss her so much." Scarred, whispered words that a man might confess while he was dying. "She left us and he never knew. He always thought *I* was the bad guy. He thought I stopped loving her. But I didn't want him to grow up hating his mother. Hell, *I* couldn't hate her, so how could I make him?" He shrugged helplessly. Craig sat perfectly still in case Dad had forgotten he was there. "If I had told him the truth, he would have known what women are like. He would have never gotten mixed up with Melissa." Dad took a long brave draught of bourbon direct from the bottle. He hid his face in his good hand.

Craig realized that Dad was talking about Jenny. He scarcely knew who Jenny was, but in Jay's letters her name had been everywhere. He'd known that Jay hated Dad because he had left Jenny. But *she'd* left Dad. Dad sounded as if he loved her, more than he loved Mom. A thick raw fear gnawed Craig's insides.

"All I can figure is that she didn't know how much I loved her." Dad's face was pale, his eyes confused. His injured hand patted the bar, gently so it wouldn't hurt. "What else could it be? She had a beautiful baby boy and a husband who adored her. She never said a word about me going with other women. I would have stopped if she'd said anything, but she never did. Only once did she ask wasn't she enough?" Dad turned incredulous eyes on him. "Can you believe she would ask me that?" His voice grew louder. "But she never said *stop*. I would have done anything she said. But she didn't *say*." In slow motion Dad raised his injured hand, watching it as it climbed inch by inch into the air. He curled it into as close a fist as he could make.

"Don't," Craig said.

Dad brought his fist down firmly on the counter, but not as hard as he'd intended. His mouth twisted, but he made no sound. When he straightened up again, he glanced quickly at Craig as if he'd just appeared. His eyes shone strangely.

"I was reading the newspaper. The Allies had just landed in North Africa. We weren't in the war yet. Had no intentions of getting in. Your mother said she was going to the drugstore for cigarettes. She had fed you and put you to bed. Our supper was on the stove. I could smell the boiled beef." He stared deep into his empty glass. "She stood close beside my chair. I didn't even look up. She said she was going to buy some Lucky Strikes. I told her to hurry back, I was hungry. She touched my shoulder with her sweet hand, but I didn't even *notice*." Dad choked slightly. "All I wanted to know was when I was going to get to *eat*."

Dad had gotten mixed up: he thought Jay was sitting here instead of him. One part of him wanted to pretend he *was* Jay, but the other thought of his own mother. He cleared his throat and Dad glanced his way, but still there was no sign of recognition. He couldn't be himself if he wanted to. He slumped his shoulders like Jay might have done and tried to cry, but his eyes stayed dry. He touched his tongue to the burning liquid in his glass. Dad hadn't added any ginger ale. He took a deep swallow, holding back a burning cough.

Dad poured his own glass full. His injured hand came to rest lightly on Craig's shoulder. "She left us, son. I don't know what I did, but she left us." Slowly the broken hand slipped down Craig's back and came to rest at Dad's side. Dad laid his head on the crook of his good arm on the bar. Soon he began a light snore which gradually deepened, but even when Craig heard his body relaxing, the lines of misery in his face didn't go away. Air whistled in and out of him.

Craig sat stiff on his stool, knees together, hands clasped tightly to keep him awake. He was giving Dad a few more minutes to get solidly asleep. It was important that he not see him deliver the letter. That way he wouldn't have to thank him. He wanted Dad to read what Jay had said about Mom. He was worried about these feelings Dad had for Jenny. Did it mean Dad didn't love Mom anymore? Was it some kind of crazy dream? She had abandoned Dad and Jay. They hadn't seen her in twenty years. This was a big country; he'd noticed on his trip that you didn't run into many people you knew.

He selected Dad's letter from the pack inside his shirt. Tomorrow morning when Dad awakened, it would be lying by his arm as if Jay himself had dropped it from heaven. Dad might even think for a moment that Jay was back, but then he would realize. Then he would remember his other son and be grateful. With hope he placed the letter near Dad's arm. Dad had already bragged about the trip he'd made to Columbus; now he'd be even prouder.

Maybe someday, but right now he couldn't imagine being able to sleep sitting up all night. He slid to the foot of the barstool and curled up to keep warm. It would be nicer to fall asleep on this floor once Dad installed the carpet. As he drifted away, he resolved to give each person the letter he was due. He would do that for Jay.

Merle woke up tireder than before he'd fallen asleep. He felt as if he'd been in a struggle, but he had only been sleeping in the wrong position. His back ached and his arms where he'd lain his head prickled as the blood flowed back into them. His legs felt stiff; he wasn't sure they would support him if he tried to stand. He raised his head higher so that he could see in the mirror behind the bar.

His hair stood up straight, nice thick hair, not so blond that it was sissy, but blond enough to interest a few women. One side of his face was a warm red color. He looked at his arm and saw the corresponding color there. The rosy cheek made him young and healthy. But then he wasn't old, he quickly reminded himself. He straightened up completely, enjoying the slight pain of his muscles loosening themselves. His eyes fell on several pieces of paper at his elbow.

He looked around for Chunny and Craig. Chunny sat in a corner, asleep against the wall. His mouth was open to snore; his arms were drawn to his chest like a mouse's. Every once in a while his hands would play with each other and then grow still. Craig slept curled around the legs of the bar-stool he had been sitting on. Merle could see one side of his plain, untormented face. When he moved the stool slightly, Craig frowned and made grunting noises.

The folded pages waited for him. There were no windows in this room, no way of airing it out, no way of knowing if this were yesterday or tomorrow. The room reeked of alcohol, the sweaty smell of their bodies, wet cigarette stubs. Chunny stirred, lost position against one wall, fell with his forehead leading into the perpendicular one. He did not awaken. From his sleep Craig called out "Mom" in a clear, absolute voice.

He saw that it was a letter to him. He didn't have to look to the end to know who it was from; he didn't have to guess who had brought it. For a moment he wished that the letter existed only in his imagination. Then he wished that Jay's spirit had somehow dropped it before him, so that he could keep their relationship separate forever from Craig. Then a feeling of cool gratefulness filled him. He would never even have thought to search for a letter. Without anger he looked at Craig lying at his feet. *People like to have women around.* He chuckled.

He read the letter twice and then again, hoping that it

would make everything clear. Phrases flipped through his mind: hated killing squirrels, nobody's fault, I love you. Merle knew Jay loved him. When had there been any doubt? But the one person who could have explained all this to him had not. Whose fault was it if it was nobody's? He would not accept that Jay was to blame. He read the letter several more times and gradually the ideas began to hold together, to give him one picture instead of so many. That part about Alaska. Melissa must have refused to go. And Jay hadn't mentioned Marty which nearly proved that nothing had ever gone on. He had said it wasn't Melissa's fault, but he said it too loudly. She hadn't wanted to go to Alaska; she hadn't wanted to do anything but have babies, sit in a stinking four-room apartment, and bitch. Which at least was all going to change. Melissa was going to pay for what she'd done. Work it out, hour by hour.

The part about treating Craig and Audrey better did not surprise him—he probably ought to do that; the part about looking for Jenny did. Why did Jay care? His mother had walked out on him, on both of them. One of those "tragedies" that helped build Jay's manhood. He should sometime have told him the whole truth.

It was time to get on with it. He slid back his stool and jumped from it, not sure that his sleepy legs would support him, but willing to take the chance. He kicked at Craig's feet a few times and then nudged him, not gently, in the stomach. "Rise and shine, Chunny," he bellowed. "Come on, boy," he said to Craig. "You two, get your asses in gear."

Craig couldn't tell whether or not it was day, and that was good, he guessed, when you were trying to get customers at a casino to stay longer. The artificial warmth of the liquor he'd drunk was gone, and the dampness of the room felt absorbed into his bones. He looked around at floor level and saw Chunny's old red face lying unprotected against the rough cement floor. Somehow Craig thought that he'd never tried hard enough.

Dad stood over him, jiggling his barstool back and forth to wake him up. He grunted as if still asleep, and Dad kicked him in the stomach, not ungently. Dad announced that half the day was gone, that they needed to move, that he wanted to open for business in two weeks. Craig could scarcely believe it was so late. His neck ached and one whole side of his body was numb. Chunny chewed the air, coming back to consciousness. Over Craig Dad picked up the heavy board that was the bar and balanced it on his shoulder. The letter had been put away, Craig imagined, inside another shirt. He touched his own chest for the three he had left.

Dad kicked open the back door and strode manfully through. Cool air and sunlight flowed into the room. Craig dragged himself to a sitting position against one of the barrels. He would not stand up until he was ready. He was perfectly willing to help Dad, of course, perfectly willing to do his part and make the front grill a mess, to even help paint the mural although it was not going to include him. What did he care? Jay was gone; Craig would always be around. Someday Dad might look at the young painted man with the dove in the sights of his shotgun and think he was Craig.

Perfectly willing to do anything Dad asked. . . . First though, whether Dad liked it or not, he was going home for a while. He wanted to see Mom whom he'd missed more, actually, than he'd missed Dad. But then he'd thought he was chasing Dad and that Dad was ahead of him when in fact he had been somewhere behind. He owed Mom an explanation, plus he wanted to tell her about his trip. He didn't expect for her to say so, but she would be proud of him, she'd think he was brave. He would tell her how easy it was to get anywhere you wanted to go, whether you had any money or not. Stick out your thumb and you were practically there. He could have gone to Ohio if he'd wanted, although he had no idea what was there.

Dad wouldn't want him to, but he was also going to give her her letter and tell her about Jay's books being gone and about Marty and about nearly starving to death because there was no food in the apartment. He thought he might even tell her about his and Dad's conversation and his worries about Jenny, although this morning Dad seemed to have forgotten her. There was no Jenny anymore, just like there wasn't a Jay.

Dad stood again in the doorway, his legs spread, one hand on his hip and one hanging loose by his side, ready to pounce on whoever wasn't moving. Craig struggled to his feet; Chunny rubbed his eyes furiously. Dad laughed at them, a deep, true, rejuvenating laugh. He started naming the order in which he wanted things done.

When he had finished, Craig called across the room in a low challenging voice: "First I want a ride home." The words bounced back to him from the cinderblocks. Their harshness startled him. Dad studied him before answering, and Craig, not waiting for the reply, started across the room. If Dad said no, if he told him to turn his ass around and get to work, if he told him to go to hell, it didn't matter. He knew at least one thing now—how to thumb. He could get home, and he could get back here. Easy.